Had We Never Loved So Blindly

In peril on land and sea

Also by the author

Love and Music Will Endure: ISBN: 978-1-907443-58-9

No Safe Anchorage: ISBN: 978-1-78279-706-7

Had We Never Loved So Blindly

In peril on land and sea

Liz MacRae Shaw

TOP HAT BOOKS

Winchester, UK
Washington, USA

JOHN HUNT PUBLISHING

First published by Top Hat Books, 2021
Top Hat Books is an imprint of John Hunt Publishing Ltd., No. 3 East St., Alresford,
Hampshire SO24 9EE, UK
office@jhpbooks.com
www.johnhuntpublishing.com
www.tophat-books.com

For distributor details and how to order please visit the 'Ordering' section on our website.

ISBN: 978 1 78904 603 8
978 1 78904 604 5 (ebook)
Library of Congress Control Number: 2020935574

Design: Stuart Davies

UK: Printed and bound by CPI Group (UK) Ltd, Croydon, CR0 4YY
Printed in North America by CPI GPS partners

We operate a distinctive and ethical publishing philosophy in
all areas of our business, from our global network of authors to
production and worldwide distribution.

Contents

Previous titles

Love and Music Will Endure: ISBN:978-1-907443-58-9

No Safe Anchorage: ISBN-978-1-78279-706-7

The title of this book comes from the song *Ae Fond Kiss* by Robert Burns, an extract of which follows:

Ae fond kiss and then we sever;
Ae fareweel, and then forever!
Deep in heart-wrung tears I'll pledge thee,
Warring sighs and groans I'll wage thee.

Had we never lov'd sae kindly,
Had we never lov'd sae blindly,
Never met – or never parted,
We had ne'er been broken-hearted

Preface

This story is a tribute to the merchant seamen of the Second World War who included members of my own family. They were the unsung heroes of the Second World War who kept Britain supplied with essential imports. Although they were civilians they suffered a higher casualty rate than members of the armed forces. Up to 185,000 seamen served in the Merchant Navy and 25 per cent of them died in enemy action, were wounded or taken prisoner. Incredibly, until May 1941 surviving merchant seamen on British vessels destroyed by enemy action received no pay from the moment that their ship sunk. Time spent in open lifeboats until they were rescued was considered 'non-working time' by the shipping companies that employed them.

Also vital to the war effort were those people, many of them women, who worked at Bletchley Park and listening stations where they intercepted and deciphered enemy communications. Their contribution to the eventual Allied victory is incalculable.

I should like to dedicate this book to all the people who have encouraged me and shared their knowledge, in particular the staff of the Portree Archive Centre and the oral history project 'The Crofters and the War' compiled by Mary Carmichael. My special thanks go to Linda Henderson for her painstaking editing of my manuscript and to my husband, Steve, for his encouragement and patience in helping me bring this book to fruition. I am also appreciative of the support I have received from John Hunt Publishing.

Part 1

John Norman's Story

Chapter 1

Isle of Skye, 1937

He heaved himself up on the pedals of the heavy bike, his arms trembling as he tried to steer.

'Are you sure you can manage, John Norman?' Mr Gillies frowned as he looked at the laden basket.

'Aye, Sir, I help Pappa haul in the nets and the rest.' He pushed his glasses back up his nose.

'Well, see how you do, lad.'

John Norman decided to get rid of the biggest order first. It meant he had to strain uphill to Kilvecken House, out of the village. But no matter how hard he pressed down on the pedals he couldn't get any speed up. He looked behind him and as there was no one to notice he dismounted and pushed the bike. Wiping his sweaty brow on the sleeve of his jacket he plodded on until he reached the long drive. The sentry pines lining the path protected him from the north-westerly wind as he crunched along the gravel. Mr Gillies had been very firm about him taking his delivery around the back so he wheeled his bike away from the shiny black front door and around the side. A new section had been built onto the house, making the short part of a letter L. It looked dingier than the rest of the house he thought as he knocked on the scuffed door. A flustered looking middle-aged woman in a white apron appeared.

John Norman touched his cap. 'I've brought the delivery from Liptons, Ma'am.'

'Oh, aye. Bring it in then.' She half-turned and called out, 'I'll be with you in a moment, Miss. The lad from Liptons has just arrived.' She waved an impatient hand at him, pointing at a big table in the middle of the kitchen. He set down the box before handing her the list of items. He could see the slender back of a girl, standing in front of the oven. 'I'm going to open it to see how it's going,' she said in a loud English voice that sounded like a crow calling.

'No, Miss. You'll make the cake sink.'

'Oh, very well.' The girl sounded peevish.

They both ignored John Norman who felt foolish holding out his list. He cleared his throat and put the bill down on the table before turning to leave. After all, he had loads more to deliver. At that moment the inner door opened. 'What's going on here? Something smells good.' A tall man with a booming voice came in.

'Mrs Patterson was helping me make a sponge cake but this boy interrupted us.' She flicked her head in John Norman's direction making her long dark red hair ripple. He could feel his face reddening. It wasn't him who had upset the cook. Surely she knew you spoilt a cake if you opened the oven door early?

The man waved the papers in his hand. 'I thought it was time for a cup of tea. I've been busy checking the latest tea prices.'

'There's no need to check them Sir, Mr Gillies has written all the prices down for you here.'

All three turned to stare at him. Mrs Patterson frowned and the girl curled her lip. The man widened his eyes before throwing his head back and roaring with laughter. 'I don't mean the tea from Liptons, young man. I was talking about the tea prices from our estate in India.'

The girl started giggling and John Norman could feel his face heating up like a furnace. If only he'd kept his mouth shut. He looked down at his boots. The laughter seemed to go on for ever but finally the man quietened down. 'Well, no harm done and you've cheered me up. It's a tedious job looking at rows of figures. You must be tired after cycling out from Portree. Give him a glass of milk, Mrs Patterson. What's your name, young man?'

John Norman told him while the cook sniffed and went off

to fetch his drink. 'MacPherson, you say? There's quite a few of you in this neck of the woods. I'm a MacDougall myself and this fine young filly is my daughter Felicity. We've been out in India but we're home now. Got a place down in London of course as well as here. We're up for the summer before Felicity goes to Switzerland to be finished.'

John Norman nodded. He sensed Felicity was staring at him, ready to pounce. He wouldn't be made a fool of a second time. He had no idea what being 'finished' meant and he didn't care. Still he was all in favour of it if it meant she would be finished off in some way. All he wanted to do was to down the glass of milk that had been thrust into his hand and escape as soon as he could.

Chapter 2

Isle of Skye, 1937

John Norman opened the back door to find most of his family already sitting at the table. 'You're late. Your herring's in the pan.' Margaret pointed at the oven with a frown.

'How did you get on?' Mamma's face screwed up into an anxious smile.

'Fine.'

'There you are. It's still warm.' She spooned a heap of potatoes beside the fish.

'Where's Pappa?' he asked.

'Off with the tide. He couldn't wait any longer for you. And Jeannie bolted her tea down so she could get back to her books.' His mother squeezed his shoulder. 'Anyway, you must be tired after riding that heavy old bike.'

'Tell us who you saw, then.' His youngest sister, Lexie, grinned, her ginger pigtail swinging as she dug him in the ribs.

'Och, no one exciting. Just the folk who can afford to get their messages delivered. Oh, but I nearly forgot. I did happen on Lord MacDonald himself. He was about to offer me a dram but...'

'He never did. You're a liar.' Lexie reached over to thump her brother's arm.

'Stop that or you'll be out the door,' Mamma pointed a finger at her.

'Well, I did meet the MacDougalls.'

'The family who bought the old manse at Kilvecken?'

'That's them, Mamma. He was posh but nice enough. His daughter Felicity was very stuck up.'

'I've heard she's your age.'

He shrugged. 'Maybe. She's off *to be finished*, whatever that means. She needs something doing to her, that's for sure.'

'I hope you weren't rude.'

'No. I was the perfect Highland gentleman, even though she looked down her witch's nose at me.'

'You can talk, with your own nose like a beak. Mamma wants you to be nice to her. If she's got lots of money, what does it matter about her nose?' Lexie giggled.

'Away with you. You've homework to do?'

'Aye, Mamma. I'll do it at once.' She dipped her head in a bow and skipped away.

'She's getting too big for her boots,' Margaret said as she carried the plates to the sink.

'Och, she doesn't mean any harm. It's just fun,' her mother answered.

Margaret let the crockery clatter into the sink as John Norman stood up, pressed his wages into his mother's hand and slipped out. He picked up his *caman* from the shed and sauntered off, resting it like a rifle on his shoulder. When he reached the playing field the others were already starting their practice game.

'You'd better go in goal. Put your glasses on so's you can see the ball.' Angus grinned and slapped him on the back. John Norman laughed to disguise how much he hated the joshing. Why did he have such bad eyesight when no one else in the family did? He delved into his trouser pocket for the despised spectacles, blowing on the lenses and rubbing them on his shirt tails. He couldn't seem to see much better with them on. Where had those scratches come from? Why him? It wouldn't matter to Jeannie if she was the one who was short-sighted. She had her head in a book all the time anyway. But for a lad like himself who hadn't cared for school and worked as a fisherman? And he knew the thick, round lenses made him look owlish, his nose sticking out like a beak.

'Look out Rookie!' Angus shouted. John Norman peered ahead, feeling rather than seeing the ball hurtling towards him.

He got his *caman* up so that the ball grazed against the wood but it wasn't enough to take the force out of it. Crack! Straight at the bridge of his nose. He groaned.

'Are you alright?' Murdo rushed up to him.

'Right enough.' He could hear the shake in his voice. 'The spectacles took the brunt of it or I would have a black eye.'

'Aye, better than losing your front teeth. You can always get new spectacles.' Angus said.

Easy for you when your pa's a butcher and can afford it, John Norman thought but aloud he said, 'Maybe I should get a helmet like those old knights used to wear.'

The worst part was skulking back home and telling Mamma. 'Not again. When will you learn not to play rough games? We can't pay for new ones, not if Jeannie wins the scholarship.'

John Norman hung his head and waited for her to stop tutting. Mamma was never as hard on him as she was on his sisters. That was with being the only boy. Lexie was a favourite too, being the youngest and because she had nearly died as a baby from double pneumonia.

Finally, Mamma sighed and ruffled his hair. He endured it without squirming. 'It's a good job that you're doing the messages on a Saturday for Liptons. Keep in with the well-off ones like yon MacDougalls. Earn a few tips. Now take those apologies for spectacles to your pappa and see if he can patch them up for now.'

Feeling relieved he went out to find his father. He was bent over his bench in the shed, cobbling new soles on Jeannie's shoes.

'For a lassie who sits down studying, your sister's awful heavy on shoe leather,' he said, taking his pipe out of his mouth. 'And you're awful heavy on your spectacles. You've snapped the nose piece. Buckled one of the legs too. It might break off when I try to straighten it out. What a clumsy family I'm blessed with. Margaret's the only one of you who doesn't smash or trample things.'

She's the saint and martyr alright, John Norman thought.

'I'm sure I've got some wire I can wind round the frame.' He scrabbled among the heaps of nails, scraps of leather and curls of string on the shelf behind him. Turning back to gaze at his son he said, 'I know you want to be the same as the other lads and play sports. But you're handy on the boat. Got a good nose for finding the fish too. It'll get easier when you're a wee bit older, you'll see.'

The gentle voice made John Norman's eyes water. He blinked and nodded, not trusting himself to speak.

Chapter 3

Isle of Skye, 1937

When he was out on the boat with Pappa and Uncle Rob John Norman forgot all about the MacDougalls. He felt in his element at sea. He knew he was a good fisherman with an instinct about where the shoals might be. Maybe his sure sense of smell made up for his weak eyesight.

But as Saturday drew nearer he dreaded the thought of going back to the MacDougalls. They seemed to speak a different language. If he tried to join in he would be made a fool of again. His feet dragged as he propped the bicycle outside the back door. But this time when Mrs Patterson answered his knock he was relieved to see that no one else was in the kitchen. She nodded at him and took the box from his hands in silence. There was no offer of a glass of milk this time. He didn't know if she was just preoccupied or always grumpy but he was thankful to escape outside again. He leapt onto the bike and pedalled towards the road as fast as he could.

'Coo-ee.' He was half-way down the long drive when he heard the call. He turned and his heart dropped like a stone down a well. It was her again, Felicity. He dismounted and stood with his fingers clenched on the handlebars. He forced his lips to stretch into a smile while he waited for her to run up to him. 'What's your name again?'

'John Norman.' He didn't remember her bothering to ask before.

'Can you fish?'

'Aye, of course, at the salmon and the herring with Pappa.'

'No silly.' Her loose red hair flicked like a pony's tail as she shook her head. 'Not that sort of fishing. I mean with a rod and line.'

He bridled at the sneer in her voice and took a deep breath before replying, 'Aye, I fish for mackerel off the rocks.' Why was she asking? Lassies didn't usually take an interest in fishing. Was she trying to catch him out? He must guard his tongue and not mention the odd salmon caught at the river mouth before it could swim upstream. He waited.

She tossed her head again. 'You'll show me how to fish then?'

'Why do you want to fish? You're a girl.'

'As if I didn't know! But I want to learn. Anyway, ladies do fish. My grandma used to go salmon fishing on the Tay.' She glared at him, with her chin up. 'And she was good.'

John Norman looked down at his boots. He was remembering what Mamma said about getting on with the gentry. He didn't want to argue with this fierce young woman.

She tapped her foot. 'Wait here a moment.' She was already running back to the house, leaving him with no choice. Who did she think she was, ordering him around? Well, he wasn't having it, even if it meant no tips from her father. He had done his job of delivering the messages. He swung his leg up over the bike and started pedalling.

'Hey, wait for me.' She loped up to him and pulled on the back mudguard, making him stop.

'This is one of Daddy's rods. I found it in the gun room.' She thrust it at him and he took it reluctantly from her large, freckled hands. The rod was supple and well balanced – expensive, no doubt. 'Aye, it's a good one, right enough but I have to go. I'm working, in case you hadn't noticed.' He set his foot ready on the pedal.

'What I notice is that your basket's nearly empty. You've got time to show me.' She stared at him, or rather down at him because she was several inches taller. Her eyes gleamed as she tilted her head on one side. He hadn't looked at her closely before. He had noticed her hair because it was so long and wavy and a striking colour, a real chestnut dark red, not gingery like

13

Lexie's hair. Now he looked at her properly he could see that her long nose and wide mouth seemed to have outgrown the rest of her features. She was awkward in her tall frame, with clumsy feet and those mannish hands.

His voice hardened, 'I have to go now.'

The spark in her eyes was doused. 'Please. Just stay for a few minutes.' Her fingers brushed his sleeve.

He recoiled. He didn't know what to make of her. Was it another trick, pretending to be coy? But something about this strange girl touched him, like one of those sudden shivers down the spine that come from nowhere. 'Alright, just a wee while then.'

She smiled. 'We can get to the sea over there,' she said, striding over to a track that sloped down through rough pasture. She held the rod in front of her like a bayonet. He dropped the bike on the ground, leaving the back wheel spinning and followed her to a platform of rock. 'Will this do?' He nodded. She dug into the pocket of her coat and handed him a package.

'What have you got there? Fishing flies? Wasted on mackerel.' He took off his shoes and socks before treading down to the wet sand at the water's edge. He dug down with his penknife and flipped up a winkle. He gouged the soft body out of its shell. 'Mackerel are greedy. They'll eat anything.'

Felicity watched him open mouthed as he impaled the soft body on the hook but at least she didn't shriek. 'I'll show you how to cast,' he said, drawing the line back over his head before swinging it forward. He reeled the line in and gave her the rod. 'You have a go.'

She stood holding it. Her head poked forward as she hunched like a cormorant on a rock. Then she splayed her feet and swung her arm back as if she was holding a lasso. The line swerved wide, forcing John Norman to duck. The hook snagged among some rocks behind them. He ran back to release it.

'What do you think you're doing? Are you blind?' he shouted.

Her shoulders slumped. 'Yes, actually. I am nearly. It's all a blur.' She fumbled in her pocket and thrust a pair of spectacles onto her face, smart tortoise shell ones. He touched his own battered spectacles. 'Snap!' he said, laughing.

She didn't laugh. Her glance shied away and he felt a prickle of sadness. The spectacles distorted her mismatched features even more, making her nose jut out like a ship's prow. The lenses were so thick that her eyes shrank and wobbled in their depths.

She looked up and shouted, 'It's not funny. It's alright for a boy like you. No one cares what you look like. It's a disaster for a girl.'

His pity shrivelled in a flare of anger. 'No it's not alright for me. I have to work on a boat. What do you think it's like in lashing rain when you can't see anything? Or what about lads picking fights with you because you're easy prey? Or breaking the damn things playing shinty?' He touched the repaired bridge on his nose.

'Stop swearing! It's rude. Wearing glasses isn't half as bad for you. You don't have to worry about being a wallflower. Wanting the floor to swallow you up. No one asking you to dance. Knowing no one will ever want to marry you. Knowing you'll die an old maid.' Her voice rose to a wail before she clapped her hand over her mouth. John Norman was lost for words. She started sobbing and swallowing great mouthfuls of air. He was stunned. When Lexie turned all dramatic he could joke her out of her tantrum. Not this one though. If someone from the Big House appeared they would think he had hurt her. But he had to say something.

'You're too young to think about getting married. How old are you?'

She stared at him as if he were a horse who had suddenly started to speak. 'Sixteen.'

'Same as me. Try casting again. You'll do better now that you can see properly.'

She nodded, sniffed loudly and picked up the rod. She was still awkward in her movements but she stopped talking and concentrated. After a few tries she called out, 'There's something there.'

He helped her land the squirming, silver grey fish. 'Take the hook out,' he said. She frowned but did as he asked. The fish lay thrashing and gasping on the ground.

'Put it out of its misery,' he told her, handing over a stone. She smashed it down on the fish's head. No girlish wincing but he wasn't going to praise her.

'Collect some more winkles,' he said, throwing her his penknife. She grinned as she ran down to the shore. They stood side by side on the rocks for the next hour, not talking much, except about the fishing. They caught six mackerel between them. 'Three each?' Felicity said as they packed up. John Norman was surprised to realise that he had enjoyed himself, so when she · said, 'Will you come fishing with me again before I have to go back to London?', he found himself agreeing. 'I'll ask Daddy if we can try for trout or salmon in our stretch of river.'

She laughed as she saw how the idea lured him. The next week found him wearing her father's waders, legs braced in the shallows of the river and watching for movement. She kept still and silent as he told her to and they were rewarded by a catch of two decent-sized salmon.

They walked through the back door, glowing with windburn and pride.

'Look, Mrs Patterson,' Felicity said, brandishing one of the fish, 'We can have this for dinner tonight.'

'More like tomorrow. I'll need to poach it and let it cool.'

At that moment Mr MacDougall appeared and Felicity held out the fish to him.

'Well done, dear. It's a healthy specimen,' he said as he prodded its flesh. 'Well, at least it was healthy when it was alive,' he snorted. 'Put it down on the sink. Well done to you too, young man. You two did better than I managed last time I fished in the river.' He slapped John Norman between the shoulder blades, making him stumble.

'Pappa always says I've a good nose for the fish,' he said.

'We can eat the fish for our last dinner before we head back for town,' Mr MacDougall said, ignoring John Norman and turning to his daughter.

'So soon?' All the joy flushed away from her face.

'You'll not want a delivery next week, then?' John Norman said.

'No, Mrs Patterson will let the manager know when we come back.'

'I'll wish you a safe journey,' he said. Mr MacDougall nodded and Felicity silently watched her feet while Mrs Patterson draped a cloth over the salmon and carried it to the pantry.

John Norman carried his own salmon out and wrapped it in some old newspaper he found in the bottom of the basket. That was the gentry for you. Friendly one minute and then sending you on your way, with barely a second look. He wondered what Mrs MacDougall was like. She was never there and never mentioned. Never mind, Mamma would be pleased with the salmon. But he would have to explain how he got it and face questions about the MacDougalls.

'Mr MacDougall let me have a try on his river,' he told her as he slapped the newspaper clad fish on the draining board. Mamma turned to look but Lexie rushed in at that moment, with her darting eyes and ferreting nose.

'Did you go out fishing with your posh girlfriend? Do you call her "Your Ladyship" or are you allowed to call her by her Christian name?' she asked.

'It was her father who said I could fish there.'

'But I bet she was there. Did you kiss each other?' She started to giggle.

'Shush Lexie with your nonsense. See, son. I told you it was a good idea to get well in with the gentry.'

'Sucking up, you mean,' Lexie flounced out, making kissing noises. John Norman pretended to be deaf.

Chapter 4

Isle of Skye, 3 September 1939

It was a bright morning, holding the promise of a sunny day to come. John Norman met his oldest friend, Murdo, at the end of the road and together they strolled along the track leading down to the Scorrybreac shore. They had known each other all their lives. Mamma said how they used to toddle out to play together in the garden from when they were barely able to walk. Murdo wasn't just a friend, more like a brother. He was small and wiry, quiet and easy to overlook. But if there was any trouble he would be there beside you. The others, Angus and Donnie, the friends from schooldays, were there already, perched on the wall near the bottom of the slope, their legs dangling. The wall marked the boundary of the croft belonging to Donnie's family and the gang had always used it as their meeting place. When he saw them John Norman broke into a run. He felt as frisky as a spring colt after escaping from home.

'I'm not having you gadding about on the Sabbath,' Mamma had said frowning as she stirred the breakfast porridge.

'Och, why not let him go and have a wee cèilidh with his friends before the service?' Pappa put in his penny h'penny and John Norman had rushed out of the kitchen door before Mamma could object.

'It's going to happen, you know and when it does I'm for joining the army – or the Air Force,' Angus said, his foot jiggling as he spoke.

'What's wrong with the Navy, then?' Donnie asked.

'I don't want to be the same as everyone else, that's why. I might even go to be a pilot.'

'Listen to you, big man.' Donnie laughed, spiking Angus hard in the ribs with his elbow.

'They'll call up the reservists first. Not lads like us yet awhile,' Donnie said, scratching his thatch of curly dark hair. 'The Navy's better, anyway. We all know about boats.'

'Aw, you've no spirit of adventure.' Angus jumped to his feet, pushing Donnie backwards so that he lost his balance and toppled head over heels into the field behind.

'You bloody devil! I've landed in a cowpat.'

John Norman leaned over the wall and reached out an arm to help him back up. 'At least it's a dry one.'

'Aye. They look like berets, don't they? For boy scouts maybe?' As he spoke Donnie jumped back down again and scooped up a flattened pancake before vaulting back over the wall. 'Or soldiers,' he said, pressing the crusted, flaking round cowpat down onto Angus' head.

That set off a free for all. Angus grabbed Donnie in a bear hug and soon they were all piled up together in the field, barging and wrestling.

'What a way to behave, and on the Sabbath too. What would your poor mothers say?' They hadn't seen Mrs MacArthur, bundled up in her good tweed coat, Bible clamped in her hand, charging uphill towards them, an avenging Prophet. She glowered at them, balanced on spindly legs, her puffed up bosom straining forward. Shamefaced the young men peeled apart. They muttered apologies, brushed down their trousers and straightened their caps.

After she had stormed ahead up the hill, Angus tossed his head. 'Is all that cow shit out of my hair now?'

'Here, take my comb. We can't have you smelling like a byre,' Murdo grinned.

They cantered up to the church, slowing their pace as they drew near and pulled off their caps before creeping into the back pew. John Norman smoothed down his hair and squinted to see where his family were seated. Although in a pew near the front, Mamma's pricked ears had detected their shuffling steps. She turned round to glare at them for being late. It didn't matter though because the minister hadn't yet arrived. It was unheard of for him not to be on time and soon people were looking at watches and whispering to each other. One or two of the men were getting to their feet, only to be pulled down again by their wives.

Finally, half an hour late, in he bustled, his face pale and startled. He stopped for a moment beside John Norman's pew to tweak his clerical collar before walking to the front and facing the congregation.

'I regret my unusual tardiness,' he began, his voice sounding squeaky and his Adam's apple wobbling. He gulped a breath and slowed his speech down. 'I've just been listening to the wireless. The Prime Minister has announced that we are now at war with Germany.'

His words lit a fuse in the quiet space. The congregation held a collective breath while they waited for the words to detonate in their minds. They sat stunned. How could this be happening when light was still streaming through the windows, birds still twittering on the roof and all the world outside the same as always? The world had shuddered and shifted. Would it shake itself back to its old shape again?

'Let us bow our heads in prayer for our King and his government in these dark times, for our fighting men and for our families.' His voice had firmed again, calmed by the familiar intonation. The restive listeners allowed the words to settle them back to silence. John Norman watched the sun flaring through the glass and felt he was one of the dust motes, strung across suspended time.

A shriek ripped the taut silence. A terrible throat-tearing sound, from near the front. He could see Mamma stand up. Surely not? But she was hurrying to the row behind and leaning over a bent, trembling figure. A clammy mist of fear swirled along the pews but the minister kept talking and his flock settled again. Later, long after the war had claimed its sacrifices, the congregation would remember this service like one of those flickering dreams that sweep past you so that you wake remembering nothing but a sense of dread. Dazed folk stepped outside blinking in the sunshine, shaking their heads and shuffling away. The lads looked at each other and waited until the crowd thinned out.

Angus made the first move. Rushing forward he tripped over his feet in his eagerness to get through the door. The others scooped him up as they hurried back down to the sea. Once there he lit a cigarette and his smouldering excitement caught fire.

'The war's really here! And the minister gave the shortest sermon of his life.'

'Hoping to be up in your 'plane, eh? But it could all be over before you can join up,' Donnie said.

'That's what they said about the Great War,' added Murdo, 'but it went on for years.'

'But it won't be fighting in the trenches again. It'll all be down to the Navy, this time.'

'Aye, John Norman, and the Air Force, like I said.' Angus grinned in triumph.

'There's no shutting you up,' Murdo groaned, 'Well, I'm away for my dinner. Are you coming?' he asked John Norman. The friends walked back in silence. How odd it was to still be doing the same everyday things, John Norman thought. Everything had changed but they were still carrying on in the same way.

He found his family standing in the kitchen as if they didn't know what to do next and were waiting for some sort of sign to tell them.

'I hoped I would never see war in my lifetime again,' Pappa said. 'Too many good men died the last time.'

'Will the Germans come here?' Lexie's face was pale under

her freckles and she was gnawing her lip.

'Of course not. They could never get here.' Margaret told her. 'I suppose the young men will get called up, like the last time, maybe the women too.'

'Surely not,' Jeannie gasped. She dropped the book she was holding. 'Will I still be able to go to university?'

Margaret rolled her eyes. 'It takes a war to get your nose out of a book. The world is turning upside down and all you can think about is the wretched university? Anyway, all the men going to war should make it easier for you to get in.'

Although he had no idea what they should be doing, he felt certain that it wasn't arguing. John Norman turned to his mother. 'What was all that upset about in church?'

'Poor Mrs MacPhee. The news struck her down. She had four boys, all called up in the last war. Three died. Only Sandy came back. He was never right again and died young. His son Alasdair's all she has left and he's of an age to be called up.'

She looked at them all in turn. 'The Great War was terrible. Me with a babe in arms and worrying all the time about my brothers off fighting. Thank the Lord your father was a fisherman and out of it. You're too old, John, to be called up now,' she said reaching over to squeeze his hand.' You girls should be safe.' Her gaze settled on John Norman. 'And your bad eyesight is a blessing. You won't have to fight either.' She reached out to stroke his arm but he flinched away as if her touch was a naked flame. He grabbed the door handle and hurtled out, slamming it behind him.

As he marched down the road he heard footsteps behind him. Lexie caught him up and grabbed his hand. 'Don't be upset. I'm glad you won't have to go and get killed.'

He patted her head. 'Och, you don't understand.'

'Can I ask you something? Could you loan me half a crown?'

'Maybe. Why?'

'Well with the war on there won't be sweeties in the shops. I need to buy lots tomorrow and save them.'

He laughed. 'That'll be the day. But I'll lend you if you give me a sweetie or two.'

Chapter 5

Isle of Skye, June 1940

It seemed strange and lonely to be sitting on the wall, just him and Murdo, without the other two. It was silly too still meeting outside Donnie's croft when he had already left home. Old habits made them head here, looking for an anchor in the swirling tides of change.

John Norman thought about Donnie leaving. He was the first to go two weeks earlier, off to join the 51st Highlanders. He remembered the conversation, almost word for word.

'But you were all for the Navy before,' Angus had said.

Donnie shrugged. 'I changed my mind. It was hearing about getting the soldiers out of Dunkirk.'

'If it had to be the army, why not the Camerons? That's the regiment for Skye men,' Angus had continued.

'Well, the Seaforths are recruiting.'

'Maybe that's because they didn't all get back. My pa heard a story from one of his customers that they had to stay in France to let the rest get away.'

'I don't know about that. I just want to go and fight.'

First Donnie, then Angus himself, soon after. His uncle down in Glasgow had pulled strings for him to join the Air Force.

'You'll be slaving in the cookhouse. It's only posh English fellows who get to be pilots,' Murdo taunted him. John Norman stood between them to stop a fight.

'Come on now. Neither of you wants to hit a man who's wearing spectacles.'

'But as usual, you've not got them on,' Murdo said.

'Well, I'll put them on if it stops you scrapping.' They all laughed and the danger passed.

John Norman sighed as he remembered what they had all

said. Two gone and two left behind.

'You're looking down in the mouth,' Murdo said as they sat together but apart, as if leaving room for the two who were away.

'I'm wondering what Donnie and Angus are up to,' John Norman replied.

'Aye. Training still, I expect. Marching, polishing, getting yelled at.' Murdo stood up and started scuffing a stone with his toes. He seemed far away and John Norman suddenly felt a chill on the back of his neck.

'You're joining up, aren't you?'

Murdo finally looked up and sat down again on the wall. 'Well, I'm turned eighteen. It's time. I'd rather join the Navy now than hang around waiting for my call up papers.' He groped for the cigarette packet in his pocket. 'Do you want one or have you got your dirty old pipe?' He laughed uneasily. 'You've not had your birthday yet?'

'I'll have one of yours. I don't think they'd bother about me being a few weeks short of eighteen. They didn't care last time round. They took lads of sixteen.'

Murdo concentrated on inhaling his cigarette. It was John Norman who broke the silence. 'We both know what the matter is. They won't take me because of my eyesight.'

They sat, smoking together and swinging their legs in unison but John Norman felt alone, cast off, as if his friend had already left.

'It's rotten luck. Apart from your eyes you'd be OK. You used to win the sprints at the Games. Remember that time you carried on running past the finish post because you couldn't see it properly?'

'That's rubbish. I knew fine when to stop.' John Norman grinned despite himself.

'I've an idea.' Murdo gripped his arm, making him jump. 'We'll go to the Drill Hall together, tomorrow. You wait while I go in first and have my medical. I'll memorise the letters on the sight chart and tell you them when I come out.'

'You're a miracle worker! But will you be able to remember the letters in the right order?'

'Oh ye of little faith! Have you forgotten how I got that prize at school for reciting poetry from memory? "The Rime of the Ancient Mariner" it was. The title was the best part of it.'

'Aye I do. Jeannie sulked for a week because she was sure she would win. She was practising "Tam O' Shanter" for ever. But her nerves got the better of her and she dried up half-way through.'

'I can still remember it. Shall I recite it for you?'

John Norman groaned. 'No, just learn that old chart for me.'

'I will. Let's shake on it.' Murdo clasped John Norman's hand and patted him on the shoulder. They threw their cigarette stubs over the wall, smoothed down their trousers and strode up the hill to the road.

John Norman was whistling as he came in the back door. The others were sitting down and he realised they had all gone quiet. Mamma smiled at him. 'Were you talking about me, then?' he asked. His parents looked at each other. Jeannie's face flushed pink. Lexie just grinned and piped up.

'You've found another lassie, haven't you? Deserted her Ladyship MacDougall? What's her name, then?' He smiled and tapped his nose, happy to go along with a make-believe lassie to put them off the scent.

The next day he met Murdo down in the village and the two of them strolled over to join the queue of young men waiting outside the Drill Hall. John Norman knew most of them and they greeted the lads in front of them in a solemn Sunday kind of way. We're all trying to look like proper fighting men already, he thought. Then he felt a hand on his arm.

'Didn't you see me, John Norman? Where's your spectacles?' It was Dougie, a cousin on Pappa's side of the family, a small cheerful lad who lived in the north of the island, up in Kilmuir.

John Norman glared down at him, standing as straight as he could manage.

'What makes you think they're taking midgets?' he said and turned away, not wanting to see the shocked look on Dougie's face. Murdo frowned and pulled him forward, closing the space with the men in front of them.

'Don't draw attention to yourself, you idiot.'

John Norman nodded and stood close behind his friend so that no one could get between them. 'You're treading on the back of my shoes,' Murdo complained as they shuffled along behind the others.

Soon they were standing inside the Drill Hall itself, with its stuffy atmosphere and smell of polish. A bearded petty officer with a smug look on his face jabbed his forefinger at Murdo and led him away. John Norman walked up to an officer who was sitting at a table and shuffling through papers.

'I need the lavatory,' he said. The officer nodded, without looking up. Murdo tried to look relaxed as he walked away. Once he was in the toilets John Norman waited in one of the stalls and leant against the door while he listened out for Murdo and shivered.

After what seemed an eternity John Norman heard footsteps. He opened the door a crack to check it was Murdo and then rushed out.

'Wait,' Murdo whispered before disappearing into the other stall. He yanked the cistern pull before emerging, looking all around and finally pulling out a piece of crumpled paper from his trouser pocket.

John Norman gasped with relief. 'Why all the drama? You're carrying on like a spy.'

Murdo puffed out his cheeks. 'You can't be too careful. There could have been someone else listening.' He smoothed out the paper. 'Learn these, especially the row two up from the bottom. I'll wait for you outside.'

'Should I eat the paper once I've learnt them?' John Norman grinned but Murdo was already on his way out. Maybe his friend was right, he thought. Retreating into a cubicle, he stared hard at the letters, mouthing their names, willing them into his brain. Then he flushed the paper away, flattened down his hair and strode back into the hall.

'What kept you?' The officer looked annoyed. 'Hurry up. We can't keep the doctor waiting.'

'Sorry, Sir.' John Norman panicked. Where was the doctor? The officer looked down his nose and pointed towards a screen at the bottom of the hall. It was made of rough wooden battens with cloth stretched between them, like sails straining in a wind. The doctor was sitting behind the screen, with a stethoscope drooping around his neck. There was a man in front, busy buttoning up his shirt. John Norman dreaded him looking up and greeting him but instead the man picked up his boots and marched off. His confident strides suggested that he must have passed his medical. The doctor gestured to John Norman to remove his clothes. He did as he was asked, putting them carefully down on the chair and forcing himself to breathe deeply. He was weighed and measured, his chest sounded and his teeth examined. Like a beast at the mart, he thought. The doctor grunted. He seemed to be satisfied. John Norman put his clothes back on, eager fingers stumbling as he tightened his belt. It would soon all be done. Good old Murdo. He was a canny lad.

'Look at the chart over there. Read the letters two rows up from the bottom.'

Just like Murdo said, he thought, as he rattled them off. He could feel sweat oozing down from his armpits but all the while hope rising in his heart. The doctor, a heavy man with a stoop, looked at him directly for the first time. John Norman risked a half-smile but the doctor's face stayed stiff. 'Go back and wait by the table outside.'

What did this mean? He clenched his fists to stop his hands

from trembling as he walked away from the screen. The officer glanced up, rose to his feet and straightened his jacket before going behind the screen. John Norman could see his outline through the fabric as he bent down to speak to the doctor. They were talking too softly for him to hear. He wondered whether to shuffle closer and eavesdrop but while he dithered the officer came back. He glared at John Norman and barked, 'Go back in.'

John Norman felt uneasy but not too worried. He knew that he had got the letters right. Maybe the doctor had forgotten something, like tapping his knees with a wee hammer. The doctor was seated at a table with a sheet of papers heaped in front of him. 'Read the chart, starting from the top,' he ordered without looking up.

Was it a trick? John Norman could remember the order of the letters. 'A, L, P,' he said. But the doctor was staring at him and John Norman felt his heart lurch. Was it a different chart? He screwed up his eyes but the letters kept wriggling. 'T, um H, er X.' He could hear the stutter in his voice.

'That'll do.' The doctor strode up to the chart, pulled it down and thrust it under his nose.

'Now read it, from the top.'

'D, P, V.' He stopped as his voice started to shake.

'Not the one you memorised, eh?' The doctor's voice dripped contempt. 'Did you think you could fool me? With those dents in the sides of your nose? What a give-away. Get out of my sight. It's cheats like you put their comrades in danger.'

John Norman tried to walk steadily out of the room. He could feel bile rising into his throat. Once he reached the toilets the pent-up tears started to flow. He splashed water on his face and smoothed down his hair. He went outside to find Murdo leaning against the wall with a cigarette dangling from his mouth, the picture of contentment. He must have passed. John Norman felt the acid drip of envy. He struggled to smile.

'You're in? Good for you.'

Murdo wasn't fooled. The pity in his kind grey eyes was hard to bear. 'But what happened? We had it sewn up.'

John Norman told him, trying not to choke on the bitter words.

'Why did that doctor speak to you like that? Anyone would think you were a coward. Or a spy. Not just a lad wanting to serve his country.' Murdo, usually so easy going, was furious. 'I hoped we could join up together – like we started school together.'

John Norman nodded, not trusting himself to speak. He watched his friend sucking hard on his cigarette and fumbling for the right words. Then he felt Murdo's punch on his arm.

'Well, I won't get my papers straightaway. We'll go to a few dances, have a drink or two. You'll have the pick of the lassies with so many lads going away. You'll be the only cockerel in the yard.' But his laugh faltered. John Norman felt his friend's words splitting the wound open further. There was an ocean stretching between them. He was rooted on the shore while Murdo was sailing out of sight.

Chapter 6

Isle of Skye, July 1940

In the early evening John Norman could hear the murmur of Pappa's wireless as he walked up to the kitchen door. The sound meant that Mamma was out at a meeting of the Rural. She couldn't bear the broadcasts about the war. If she didn't hear the news she could ban the conflict from her mind. The only way she admitted it was happening was by knitting socks and scarves for soldiers. But then she had always knitted so she could still pretend that nothing was different. Life wasn't changed much up here, away from the big cities. And even there the expected bombing hadn't happened and the evacuated children had gone back home. The 'Phoney War' they had called it until France was invaded but even after Dunkirk it all seemed far away. He too could pretend that nothing had changed when he was out on the boat with Pappa and Uncle Rob. But even out at sea he could see the new buildings at the naval base at Kyle, extra trains too bringing in mines for the Minelaying Squadron. Once ashore he couldn't ignore the gaping holes, his life a torn net. Not only his friends had left but so many of the boys he had been to school with. And it wasn't only the lads. Margaret had breezed back home the week before to announce in her bossy way, 'I'm part of the war effort now, working for the Royal Navy,' with a heavy stress on the 'Royal'. He bit his tongue back from saying something sarcastic. She wasn't going anywhere new, would still be working as a receptionist at the Kyle Hotel. It was just that the holidaying guests had been replaced by naval officers. Jeannie would soon be gone too. She fidgeted at the window every day waiting for Alec, the postie, expecting but dreading the letter about the scholarship. He couldn't understand her fears. She was bound to have got it after all those years poring over her books and the headmaster always heaping praise on her. He couldn't say that he would exactly miss either of them but it would feel empty at home, left behind. Everyone's life changing except his. Lexie would still be there. She was the best of his sisters but she was only a schoolgirl.

He sighed and put his hand on the door handle. 'John Norman. It's yourself. Come and have a dram with me.'

He turned round to see Archie from over the road. He was a few years older and John Norman didn't know him well. He hesitated but then he thought, why not? Anything was better than sitting inside, feeling fed up.

Archie was grinning.

'Where to?' John Norman asked him as he crossed the road.

'The Royal, to start with? Have you money?'

John Norman rattled his pocket. 'Aye.'

Archie walked fast and although John Norman had longer legs he found himself almost running to keep up. Archie shouldered open the door into the smoky bar and John Norman got their drinks. They settled with their beers and a chaser each in a dark corner. 'You've not joined up yet?' John Norman said.

'That's all everyone talks about.' Archie took a slug of beer. 'Not bloody likely. I'm needed on the boat. Too important, me. Indispensable, in fact.'

John Norman widened his eyes in surprise.

'Why are all these lads rushing off to war? Rushing to meet a bullet. Haven't they seen all the names on the War Memorial from the last time? If the war goes on, there'll be conscription soon enough. But I'm keeping out of it if I can. I'm damned if I'll volunteer to be shot at.'

'But we have to stop Hitler before he invades all of Europe.'

'Do we? You can if you like.'

'I can't join up. They won't have me.'

'Because of your eyesight? It's a stroke of luck, isn't it?'

'Not for me.'

Archie frowned. 'Are you wise enough? You should be thanking your lucky stars. Never mind. I won't hold it against you, you daftie.' His laugh took the sting out of his words. 'Another one?' Punching John Norman on the arm he stood up, swallowed the last of his beer and wiped the froth from his mouth. 'I'll drink to celebrate being free and you drink to drown your sorrows.'

He strolled up to the bar and returned with new drinks. They talked about other things, or rather Archie did most of the talking, turning and twisting like an otter from one tale or snatch of gossip to another. He told the story of how he had been poaching salmon with a net when the gamekeeper and his dog appeared. The animal was sniffing the air suspiciously. So there was nothing for it but to sneak into the river up to his neck until they had gone by. 'And I had to clasp that wriggling salmon to my chest all that time, like a frisky lassie it was.'

Archie nudged him in the ribs and John Norman had to stop himself from flinching. He hoped that the gloomy lighting hid the red glow of his face. 'Still, it tasted all the better for the tussle I had with it.'

John Norman listened and drank steadily. He let the currents sway him along. It was too much effort to think or protest, even when Archie returned to talking about the war. 'I'm damned if I'll be ordered around by beardless sons of the gentry. Scots who sound like Englishmen when they open their mouths.' He moved closer so that his lips brushed John Norman's ear. 'If I get called up I can always slip away over to family in Ireland.'

He must have dozed off and awoke to find Archie shaking his shoulder. He lifted his head from the table and wiped the beer that had somehow smeared itself across his forehead. Pulling a handkerchief from his pocket he tried to clean his spectacles but his hands shook. He had to give up, leaving the lenses cloudy.

'Come on laddie, time to get you home.' Archie dragged him to his feet. They staggered up the hill with Archie propping him upright. John Norman felt like an untethered balloon that would drift away if Archie released his grip. 'I'll take you up to your door. There's no lights on so you can slip in with no one knowing.'

But as John Norman groped for the handle the backdoor suddenly gave way so that he lurched inside. A small hand clamped itself over his mouth. 'Shhs!' hissed Lexie. She pulled out a chair from the kitchen table and pushed him into it. 'Don't make a sound. Mamma and Pappa have long gone to bed but she'll be listening out for you. I'll make you a cup of tea. They say coffee's better to sober you up but we don't have any.'

'What do you know about sobering up?' he asked, his tongue tripping over the words.

'I know there'll be a right royal row if you don't.' Her green eyes flashed. If she had a tail it would be swishing in rage he thought, smiling.

He drank the tea and ate two pieces of bread before clambering up the stairs in the dark, with Lexie hovering behind him. 'Can you get yourself undressed alright?' she asked as she opened his bedroom door and pushed him inside.

'Of course.' He shut the door in her face, horrified at the idea that she might decide to help him.

Chapter 7

The next day

His churning stomach left him tossing all night so it was a relief when Lexie tapped on his door early the next morning. It was still dark outside. She handed him a cup and a bowl of porridge. 'I found some coffee at the back of the cupboard, a bottle of Camp Coffee. Get it down you.'

'It smells disgusting. And I feel too sick to eat anything.' Seeing her disappointed expression he smiled. 'I'll try to swallow something.'

'Well, hurry up. Pappa's nearly ready to go.' She darted off downstairs. He could hear the murmur of his parents' voices. Lexie had done a good job in covering for him. He must thank her properly later when his head was clearer and give her some money for sweeties. Reaching out for his spectacles he groaned at the hammering in his head. At least he wouldn't have the bother of getting dressed as he had fallen into his bed with his clothes on. A quick splash of water on his face, a flick around his mouth with the toothbrush and a daub of Brylcreem. He ran a finger over his chin. His face would do. With his fair hair he could get away without having to shave every day.

He couldn't quite escape unscathed though. 'Did I see you speaking with that tinker, Archie Stewart?' Mamma asked as he put his dishes in the sink.

'Och, he's not a tinker. His family live in a house.'

'They do now but they still have tinker ways,' she sniffed. 'He's a bad one.'

'We must be off to catch the tide,' Pappa said, winking at John Norman behind Mamma's back.

There was a strong swell as the boat set off from the harbour. It was John Norman's job to winch up the sail. He managed to, despite his grinding headache. But as he tilted his head back to check the rigging at the top of the mast he was swamped by a wave of nausea. Rushing to the side of the boat he emptied his breakfast into the sea. Pappa was busy steering but Uncle Rob saw him. 'What's wrong with you? It's a good job you're not a lassie or I would be wondering what you'd been up to.'

John Norman felt too wretched to be embarrassed. 'Go and get a hot drink,' his uncle said. 'We need you right so that you can sniff out where the shoals are.' John Norman went into the cabin, trying not to look at the mucky stove, barnacled with grease. The whole place reeked of engine oil, rancid sweat and salt saturated clothes. And fish of course, as did the whole boat. His stomach was starting to heave again. He tried to distract himself, by thinking about how Mamma would never come aboard. Just as well. She would be disgusted by the grime and mess. Wouldn't be able to stop herself cleaning it up. That would lead to ructions because although Pappa was a mild man he couldn't stand anyone interfering with his boat. That was why he always joked with her that a woman on board courted bad luck.

He drank the tarry tea and felt a little better for it. He could cope with the lurch of the boat but his knack for tracking down fish seemed to have deserted him. They only had a small catch, the nets sagging rather than bulging. As they were tying up at the pier Uncle Rob said, 'Come back and have a bite with us? We're expecting Iain on the late steamer.'

John Norman grinned. Since boyhood his cousin, five years older than him, had been his hero, the nearest he had to an older brother. He used to be always at Iain's heels. Looking back, John Norman could see how good-natured Iain was about his puppyish adoration, teasing him but letting him tag along. Except for one time.

'Can we go out to catch some mackerel tomorrow?' John Norman had pleaded one day.

'Hmm. It'll have to be early.'

'Why so early?' he had asked, but Iain just grunted. Nonetheless they were lucky with their lines and headed back after less than an hour. Usually Iain would let John Norman row some of the way but this time he had grabbed the oars and pulled as fast as he could.

'Off you go home now with those,' Iain had said and waited while John Norman trotted off, swinging his fish by a string threaded through their gills. When he looked back he was puzzled to see Iain haring off, in the opposite direction to his house. Something was up and John Norman was determined not to be left out.

'Won't you wait for a *strupag*?' Mamma had asked him when he handed her the fish.

'No, I'm in a hurry.' And off he had rushed down to the shore again. Whatever Iain was plotting, he suspected that boats would be involved. He decided to wait, crouching down on the far side of the bigger rowing boat, the one that belonged to Uncle Rob. It wasn't long before he heard footsteps crunching on the shingle. He peeped out and saw Iain, gobbling a bannock as he ran towards him. Behind him was Iain's friend, Peter, a boy who scowled every time he saw John Norman. He was laughing and wiping away a milk moustache from his face. John Norman hesitated for a moment as they raced down and started to push the boat out. But there was no way he could stay hidden now.

'Can I come too?' he called out. The boys looked startled as he popped his head up.

'Ah, it's yourself,' Iain said.

'I ran home like the wind with the fish and came back again.'

Peter groaned and rolled his eyes. 'It's a pity the wind didn't whisk you out to sea.'

Iain looked from one to the other. 'Well, we better let the wee lad come too as he's been so smart, spying on us,' he said, laughing.

Maybe that was when John Norman grew up a little and realised that he sought out Iain's company more than Iain wanted his. That five-year gap between them never narrowed. Iain was always older, stronger, smarter, always mastering the next stage. After leaving school he had gone straight into the Merchant Navy. Away for months at a time. The only messages from him were postcards from ports around the world: Singapore, Cape Town, Montreal, Bombay. These were propped up on his parents' mantelpiece until they dried and curled up at the edges like autumn leaves. John Norman always flipped over the latest card but they only had a few words in his cousin's sprawling hand – 'Glad to be ashore after 2 months at sea,' or 'Very hot, here. Reminds me of Skye weather!'

Back at school John Norman would rifle through the atlas when the classroom was empty, stroking the coastline with his forefinger as he tried to visualise the teeming, exotic ports, booming with the voices of sailors from all over the world.

One time he was so absorbed in his task that he hadn't heard the tip-tapping steps through the doorway.

'What a miracle! John Norman MacPherson with his nose in a book,' Miss Fraser had said. 'Even if it's only one full of pictures.' Her gaggle of teacher's pets at her heels sniggered. He longed to retort that he would go to those vivid places one day. Leave behind the schoolroom with its scuffed walls and broken-backed books. But, of course, he'd stayed dumb; the small and scrawny Miss Fraser was a demon with the strap.

All that was in the past. John Norman would see his cousin for the first time since they were both grown up. The cousin he admired and envied for his adventures, his easy way of talking and now especially for his bravery. A few months ago, Uncle Robert had announced that Iain was going to be awarded a special medal for saving a drowning man from the Thames. Unlike most of the local lads Iain had braved the chilly sea and taught himself to swim.

'You've grown, wee man!' were Iain's first words when they met. 'Turn around and let's measure you.' They stood back to back.

'Who's taller, Auntie Marian?'

'Well, I do believe it's you, John Norman. But only by a whisker, mind.' She laughed at Iain's indignant face.

'Well, he's grown up stringy. I'm still broader than him.'

They sat down to eat salt mackerel, tatties and rice pudding afterwards. John Norman loved it here at Bayfield, the inlet of Portree Bay where so many of his ancestors had lived as fishermen. It was so close to the sea that they could see the approaching weather from the front window and almost leap into a boat straight through the door. His own family had moved up Stormy Hill to one of the new council houses. 'I'm tired of the smell of salt always on my washing,' Mamma had said. But Uncle Robert didn't want to leave the row of fishermen's houses where everything was to hand: the green for hanging out the nets, mooring on the shore for smaller boats, the stepping stones over to the crofts at Fisherfield opposite and, above all, the guardian Cuillin Hills behind Pennifiler. Uncle Robert had once told him that when he was a boy he used to think he was held in the centre of a separate, magic world, a net of land, mountain and sea all bound together.

Afterwards the cousins strolled along the shore, turning up their jacket collars against the wind. It was still light, the sky was clear and the moonlight flickered over the waves.

'What's up? You seem down in the mouth, John Norman.'

'Everyone's going away to fight except me. I feel useless.'

Iain wasn't like most people. He didn't rush into reassuring him or telling him how lucky he was. He paused to light up a cigarette before replying, 'I'm not in the Forces either. But I'm not useless. I'm doing one of the most important and dangerous jobs there is. It's the sailors who will stop the country being starved of supplies.'

'That's the Navy's job, I know that.'

'Aye. But which Navy? It's the merchant seamen who man the ships. Far more of us than the fellows in uniform.'

'And I could sign up? Although I was turned away by the Navy?'

Iain turned to face John Norman and seized him by the shoulders. 'Of course you can. The government's crying out for sailors to man the boats, even ones that are half-blind.' He said this with a grin and a playful punch to the chest. 'Your eyesight's not stopped you being a good fisherman, has it?'

John Norman stared back at him, not daring to let hope open its wings. But this was Iain who knew what he was talking about and had never let him down.

'What do I do then? I don't want Mamma to know until it's all settled.'

Iain nodded. 'I go back to Greenock in a few days to find my next ship. I'll put in a word for you.'

'Would we be on the same boat?' John Norman could hear his voice squeaking with excitement.

'Maybe but you'll need to be trained up so we might not get a berth together. Good if we did. Like the old days when I took you out as my crew.'

John Norman grinned. He had caught up with his hero cousin. Hope beat its wings and flew up.

'I'll find out what's going on and send you a letter.'

'I'll have to look out for the postie and get it before Mamma. Write a bit more than you did on those old postcards. It's not much use putting, "Good weather here in Greenock."'

Iain cuffed him on the ear. 'It's good that you're a wee bit older than I was when I got my first berth.'

'Why's that?'

'Well. You likely know how some old sailors take a fancy to a fresh, young face.'

John Norman's mouth hung open. 'What, they go after a lad?'

'Aye, use them like they would a lassie. You can shut your mouth, John Norman. You're older and no one could say you've got a pretty face. Let's go back.' They sauntered back to Iain's home, hands in pockets, men of the world.

Chapter 8

Two weeks later

John Norman's head was filled with thoughts of the letter, like a net stretched to bursting, thrashing fears and hopes trapped inside. He longed to slash the net to release them but he didn't dare speak to anyone in case it all came to nothing. Who could he talk to anyway without the worry of it getting back to Mamma? It was harsh weather, lashing rain and whipping winds, so he went for long walks, not caring if he got soaked. One day he tramped along the road south, covering the ten or so miles to Sligachan. He stood for a moment on the high point of the old humped bridge. It was too narrow to carry modern cars. Like him, it wasn't considered up to the job. Yet it was well-made, its stones shaped into a perfect curve. He looked up towards the valley to where the Cuillin would be if the mountains hadn't been spirited away behind a curtain of cloud and mist. The heavy rain meant that the river was surging under the bridge. The bridge still had a purpose, after all, providing a dry path for walkers to cross over.

He ran his fingers along the parapet. Thinking about how the bridge had endured cheered him up. He strode into the hotel for a dram to banish the bone chill before he started trudging back towards Portree. The road was empty and everywhere was awash, torrents of water spawning new waterfalls down the rocks beside the road. No one was about, all the young ones away and the older folk tucked up in front of the peats. The warmth of the drink in his belly was wearing off. He felt shivery and depressed.

He didn't hear the engine, coming up behind him. It was the braying horn that made him jump. He turned round but couldn't recognise the driver through his streaming glasses. The vehicle

43

stopped, the windscreen wipers struggling against the rain and the headlights only giving a faint torch beam. Was it a visitor who had lost his way? But folk were no longer coming up to Skye for their holidays. The car door opened and a rain-coated figure leant out. 'Is that you, John Norman?'

He would know that ringing voice anywhere. He moved closer to peer at the driver's face beneath the dripping hood. 'Felicity? Is that yourself? Driving a car?'

'Of course it's me. Now get in if you want a lift. I'm getting drenched holding this door open.'

He did as he was told. As she put the car into gear he noticed the water from his sodden turn-ups pooling on the floor. She followed his gaze. 'Don't worry about the drips. But did I detect a note of surprise that I, a mere woman, was driving a car?'

As so often with Felicity he felt he was being tested. 'I was surprised to see any car on the road in this dreadful weather.'

'Well, I was surprised to see anyone out walking in it. I'll have you know that I passed my driving test and I've driven up all the way from London.'

'How long did that take you?'

'Three days. I broke my journey in Edinburgh. Anyway, you'll have to get used to women drivers now there's a war. Women drove ambulances in the last war, didn't they?'

'Do you hope to drive an ambulance, then?'

'Maybe. I want to do something. I could be in the ATS I suppose. Pa has some sort of hush-hush Ministry job so he might find me something in an office.'

'So how come you're up here?'

'I'm collecting some papers for Pa before we close the house down for the duration.'

'You've finished with getting finished, then?' He hoped that a joke might give him some hold over the conversation.

'Oh, that. What a waste of time. Silly girls scheming to find a rich husband by learning about deportment, flower arranging and table settings. I can't see me needing all that sort of stuff when we're fighting a war.'

'Mamma had to learn about laying tables for grand dinners when she was in service in Glasgow. She's still particular about having the table look nice.' He regretted the words the moment they were out of his mouth.

Felicity looked down her nose. 'Not quite the same thing.'

He decided it was best to stay quiet. Felicity was leaning forward, peering ahead through the gloom and didn't seem to notice his silence. Portree appeared through a tear in the mist, its buildings tucked tight into the bay.

'Can you drive?' she asked him.

'I've not had the chance yet but I've had plenty of practice steering a boat. So I'm sure I could soon learn.'

'You're still fishing?'

He was stung by her dismissive tone. 'Aye but I'm going to join the Merchant Navy. My cousin's seeing to it for me. He's been all over the world. Won a medal for saving a man's life. You can drop me here, at the bottom of the hill.'

He climbed out and turned to thank her. She reached out and shook his hand, squeezing his fingers in a tight grip. 'I probably won't see you again, at least not for a long time. But I'm sure you'll serve your country well, John Norman.' Her voice was solemn. He watched her speeding off. How strange she was. Superior one minute and then speaking to him like an equal.

* * *

The next morning he was on the alert again for the letter, waiting in the hall to hear the postie's footsteps and get to the door first. He seized the envelope as it slipped through the letter box, ran upstairs with it to the bathroom and locked the door. He ripped it open with fumbling fingers. It was type written. How odd. But maybe it was an official letter Iain had got for him. But why was there a picture of a coat of arms? He had better slow down and read the whole thing.

Dear Miss MacPherson,
We are pleased to inform you...

Oh No! It was Jeannie's letter about the scholarship. She would be so vexed he'd opened it. He scanned the first paragraph. Yes, she had won it right enough. Thank goodness. She would be excited, too excited to be cross with him. He breathed more easily until a second thought hit him like a bow wave. He would have to tell her why he was expecting a letter. He never got any at all. Not like Margaret and Jeannie who were for ever writing to school friends who had moved away. It was so hard to keep anything to yourself in this house of women. They stalked secrets like a collie working sheep.

He crept downstairs in his stockinged feet. He was in luck! There was Jeannie in her school uniform, lifting the letter box. She let it spring back with a sigh. He felt for her. It was agony waiting to know about something that would change your life.

'No news yet?'

'No. I'm so weary of all this waiting.' He could see her eyes were gleaming with unshed tears.

'It's hard for you.' She nodded, looking surprised at his concern. 'You're off to school? Wait a moment until I put my shoes on. I'm going out too.'

As he opened the front gate he put his hand on her arm. 'Wait a second.' He fished the ripped envelope out of his jacket pocket and held it out. 'Your letter did come. I opened it by mistake.'

'By mistake?' She gawped at him before turning her attention to the envelope. She frowned. Her usually ruddy complexion had turned white. She lifted out the piece of paper with shaky fingers. Her eyes flickered down the page. 'I've got it,' she gasped.

'Of course you have. Congratulations. You deserve it.'

She was dazed for a moment before staring at him. 'You read it. Why?'

'I told you it was by accident.'

'But why would you think...'

'Wait a moment!' a voice shouted. John Norman turned, relieved to see Alec the postie, scurrying towards them on his bandy legs. 'This one hid itself away in the bottom of the bag.' He grinned as he presented the letter to John Norman. 'I hope it's good news.' He waved and beetled off down the road.

'That's what you were waiting for. I should open it, like you opened mine.' Jeannie lunged for it but he dangled it high above her head.

'I'm not playing games with you or I'll be late for school.' She marched off, her nose in the air.

He stood still to read it and then ran to catch her up.

'Hold on a second. I've good news too.'

'Tell me then.'

'You must promise not to tell anyone.'

'What's the big secret?' She snatched the letter from his hand.

'I'm not joking, Jeannie.'

'Alright, I promise. Cross my heart and hope to die.'

'It's from Iain. He said he would get me a berth on a boat.'

'And has he?'

'Aye. I've to report to the shipping office at Greenock in a week.'

'So you'll be in the Navy?'

'No, I'm still a civvie, not in the Forces.'

'But still dangerous? Mamma won't like it.'

'That's why you must keep quiet. Until I find the right moment to tell her.'

Chapter 9

Later that day

Mamma put the teapot down on its stand on the table and then she sprang.

'What was all that nonsense outside the house, this morning?'

Her dark eyes probed their faces. 'I was excited about getting my letter,' Jeannie blurted.

'Aye. You did well. Showed the high-ups what a Skye lassie can do.' Jeannie smiled and John Norman breathed again.

'But what was all that carry on with Alec?'

'He found the letter stuck to the bottom of his bag,' Jeannie said.

'But you had another letter in your hand, John Norman. What was that?'

Jeannie looked startled and he bit his lip.

'It's a secret. A secret love letter, from that posh Felicity.' Lexie clapped her hands.

John Norman glared at her. 'What rubbish.' They were all looking at him. He sighed. 'I was going to tell you all later. I've got a berth on a boat.'

'You've joined the Navy?' Mamma whispered.

'No, a merchant ship.'

'What will he be doing, John?' Mamma's words sounded strangled as she turned to Pappa. She leapt to her feet, scraping the chair legs across the linoleum. Pappa swallowed the mouthful he was eating, lowered his fork and turned to look at his son, before he replied. 'He'll be helping the war effort, getting supplies through.'

Mamma's lips were wobbling as she gasped for air. Everyone was frozen, holding their breath. Mamma's voice shuddered, 'Just steaming across the oceans, an ordinary sailor?'

No one met her gaze. 'Just like Iain's been doing all these years?' She stared at each of them in turn but no one responded. Until John Norman pushed his spectacles up his nose and looked her in the eye. He felt as scared as he did when he was eight years old and Mamma had found out about him skiving from school. 'You're already helping the war effort.' Her voice was dangerously quiet. But he kept looking at her, willing himself not to blink. She stood up and slapped her hand down hard on the table, making the plates rattle, gathering her voice into a shout, 'You must think me a fool. Are you telling me the Germans don't have submarines anymore? You'll be a sitting target. More dangerous than being on a proper naval ship with guns.' She shut her eyes and swayed. Pappa jumped up to catch her.

'Go and get a dram,' he told John Norman as he eased her back into her seat.

John Norman did as he was told although his legs were twitching with his urge to run out of the house and over the hills. Her eyes were closed and her eyelids flickering. As he pressed a glass into her hands her eyes snapped open. 'How could you cause me all this torment? Was it Iain who put you up to it?'

'Stop making it hard for the lad. He only wants to serve his country.' Pappa's usually soft voice had hardened. 'We're blessed in our children, all of them. Now, we need more glasses to toast both John Norman and Jeannie.'

'I'll get them,' Lexie said.

'Remember you're only having lemonade,' Mamma called after her.

* * *

That wasn't the end of it, of course. Mamma said nothing more about John Norman going but her refusal to speak about it was in itself a reproach. A hard frost of disapproval clung to her but John Norman gained strength each passing day. He was reaching away from her, away into the world of men. When he was out on the boat he had felt free but now he could see that he hadn't really escaped. The net had opened out and the mesh spread wider so that he couldn't see the fine threads that still dragged him home. It was only now that the drawstring was loosened that he could swim free.

And he had done it through his own skill, with some help from Iain. At last he had finally caught up with his big cousin. He was glad now that he hadn't done it through cheating. Even if he had got through the eye test how would he have managed afterwards, always straining to see properly and terrified of his weakness being discovered?

He could sense the difference in how his family saw him now. Pappa hadn't said anything more about him going but he had done enough already. He had never before seen his father stand up to Mamma. The shock of it seemed to have silenced her on the subject. Margaret paid attention to what he said rather than looking down her sharp nose at him. Jeannie, who used to ignore him, now treated him like a fellow adventurer. 'We'll both be off on our travels, soon.' Lexie, though, was the only one who said that she would miss him. 'I'll be left behind, with no one to talk to,' she complained. He forbore to say that she only talked to him when she wanted something. 'You'll enjoy getting all the attention,' he laughed.

Neighbours and relatives usually visited for a *cèilidh* on Friday evenings but this Friday would be special, the last one before he left. Usually he was bored with the same old stories and Uncle Duncan's wheezy, sentimental singing but this time was different. He could look the older men in the eye, all those who had fought in the last war, stand shoulder to shoulder with them. He overheard their neighbour, Mr MacLeod, talking to Mamma in the kitchen doorway.

'Well, your lad's off to do his bit in the war. You must be very proud of him.'

'Indeed I am. I know he'll do his best.'

John Norman nearly dropped his glass with shock. Who would have guessed from the warmth of her words how furious she had been with him? Was it all pretence or was she coming round? At that moment she turned to look at him, or rather stare at the glass he was holding. She frowned. Well, he better not tempt his luck and have another whisky. Suddenly he wanted to escape them all. He would go into the garden for a smoke. Uncle Donald was already out there.

'Did you want a bit of peace from the womenfolk?' he said as he teased tobacco out of his pouch and tamped it down into the bowl with a stubby thumb.

John Norman smiled and lit up.

'Looking forward to going off to war, are you?'

'Aye. I don't want to be left behind.'

'I can understand that. But I'll be bound your mother's not happy about it, with you being her only son.'

John Norman sighed. 'No but I've made my mind up.'

'Aye. I did the same thing in the last war. Volunteered as soon as I could, wanted to go with my pals. A big adventure, it seemed – going to France. Looking back I wish I'd waited until I had been called up. I wouldn't have been stuck in the trenches for so long. Might not have got wounded.'

John Norman stared at him. 'You've never said that before.'

His uncle shrugged.

'But all those stories everyone tells about you – mentioned in dispatches for going back into No Man's Land for your comrades who'd been shot. And that time you were brought back on a stretcher out cold and left for dead in a heap of bodies under a tarpaulin...'

'And saved by my love of tobacco. Woken up by a soldier smoking nearby.' He drew on his pipe. 'The stories were true enough as far as they went. Everyone likes a good tale with a happy ending. No one wanted to hear what it was really like and we wanted to forget. Bad enough waking in a sweat every night from the nightmares without talking about it in the daytime. No one thought our sons would have to face another war. It was meant to be the war that ended all wars.' He rubbed his calloused fingers over his face.

'But this war's different. There won't be men rotting in trenches, this time. And I'll be at sea anyway.'

'What's worse? Drowning in water or drowning in mud?' Uncle Donald spoke so softly that John Norman had to lean towards him to hear.

'I'll say no more. You're a brave lad and I wish you well. Just one piece of advice. It's the only thing I ever heeded. Steer clear of the prostitutes. Like rats, full of diseases.' He patted him on the shoulder and strolled away to join the others in the front room. John Norman stood still, his mouth hanging open in amazement. Fancy Uncle Donald, an elder in the church, saying such a thing.

Part 2

Felicity's Story

Chapter 10

Isle of Skye, July 1940

She pushed the back door open. Mrs Patterson had left it unlocked. Of course she would, here on the island. 'We don't need keys. We all trust each other here, Miss. I dare say it's different in the big city,' was what she said the first time Felicity came to the house.

There was a musty, neglected smell. It was odd how you could tell at once when a house had stood empty. Was it the same when someone died? Could you tell at once when life ended? She shuddered and thrust a Kirby grip back into a hank of hair that had flopped forward over her ear. Now that she was released from the strain of the journey she felt deflated. All her energy had gone into escaping in the car. She had been so furious at what Pa had said when she asked him about war work.

'Wait until we know what's happening. Surely you don't want to wear one of those ridiculous uniforms?'

'What do you mean?'

'An unflattering khaki battledress top and skirt just to sit in front of a typewriter,' Pa had scoffed.

And it wasn't as if she could even type. She had been raised to be decorative, preening herself in a cage until she was claimed, absorbed into some man's life. On an angry impulse she had left the next morning. She had scrawled a terse note to leave on the kitchen table and crammed a few clothes into an old grip. Now she stood at the kitchen window watching the plummeting rain, her mood as bleak as the weather. Even when she managed to flutter free she felt too feeble to survive in the wild. Why had she rushed up to Skye? For the freedom she remembered – the freedom to leave her hair loose, to tramp through wet grass in battered boots and eat doorsteps of bread and cheese. But those were summer freedoms, not part of real life.

Well, she had better see what things needed taking back to London. She could bring back business papers as a peace offering. Walking up the mangy strip of burgundy carpet on the stairs she sniffed as the damp smell grew stronger. Was water getting in through the roof? Pa's makeshift office was in a small bedroom with a sloping roof at the back of the house. A maid's room originally. His desk was pushed into the eaves where the metal bed had once stood and left rusty footprints on the lino. She reached up to the shelf for the boxes where he stowed the papers about the Indian property. Flicking through sheets clamped together with bulldog clips she scanned wage bills, receipts from shipping companies and records of tea yields. Boring stuff but he might need to pass it on to the accountant so she stuffed it back into the boxes and forced the lids into place. The desk itself was clear apart from a splattered blotter, last year's diary and a dented shell case that served for storing pencils. Maybe there was something left in the desk drawers. The top drawer was stuck. After cursing it she went to the kitchen, returning with a knife to prise it open. A leather letter case had got jammed. She worked it free, unfolded it and peeked inside. There was a sheaf of letters. Pulling them out onto the desk she selected one from the manager of the estate, asking Pa for money to send the clever son of an estate worker off to school. She wondered what his reply had been. Did the boy get his chance? She realised with a jolt that she really couldn't predict his response to the request. Pa never talked to her about anything serious and certainly not about business matters. 'Be thankful you don't need to worry about tedious things like money,' he would joke. She put the letter case on top of the boxes and was about to shut the drawer when she felt resistance. Something else had become wedged at the back. Kneeling down she lifted the whole drawer off its runners and pulled out a thin manila folder that had curled round the back. More business correspondence, probably.

Barely glancing she leafed through the contents. Something secured with a rubber band dropped out. Photographs, stacked like a deck of cards. She dealt them out in front of her. Groups of adults holding glasses in front of a bungalow, shimmering in a white heat. A man with a dense black beard wearing a white turban. He was holding a tray and a child peeped out behind him. It took her a few moments to recognise her young self. She didn't remember seeing these before. There used to be the formal wedding portrait on the mantelpiece in London but even that had disappeared years ago before…when it happened. Even now she found her mind slammed shut when she tried to form the words, 'When Mummy died.' Maybe she couldn't say the words, even to herself because for so long she hadn't believed them. She had been at that horrible boarding school down in Sussex when Pa had suddenly appeared in the middle of the winter term.

'You've come back! Is Mummy here too?' She'd run up to him where he stood rigid as a lead soldier in the headmistress's study. He unclasped her arms from around his waist. 'Come out to the car.'

How had he told her? Had he muttered something about Mummy being in Heaven now? Something that he imagined would soothe an eight-year-old child? All her memories were muffled, like standing on a bridge when a train comes underneath, smothering everything in smoke. And every morning she would wake up in a tangle of sopping sheets, telling herself that it wasn't true. Mummy was in India, sipping tea with the memsahibs beneath the mango tree in the garden.

Pa never spoke about Mummy again. Never returned to India. She had longed to leave the hated school and stay in the London house with him but that wasn't allowed, except for a week or two in the summer. When she'd burst into tears he'd said, 'Now come on, old thing. Stop the waterworks.' Terrified that he might banish her for ever she had blown her nose in her crumpled hanky and bit her inside lip until it bled. She stayed with the great aunts, Constance and Emily, for the holidays. Their gloomy house in Dorking was stuffed with massive furniture. She especially hated the footstools made from elephant's feet, with the stiff leathery skin and the polished nails.

'Did the elephants die from old age or were they killed?' she'd asked meekly.

'What a strange child you are! I've no idea. Our pappa bought them from a native a long time ago.' Aunt Emily frowned as she'd peered over her lorgnette. Her lips were always pinched and disapproving of the modern world, especially of Felicity.

Auntie Constance was different. She would keep hugging her, pressing Felicity's face into her jutting bosom that smelt of moth balls. Or try to console her with food, kedgeree and mulligatawny soup. 'To remind you of home, my dear,' but the smell of curry powder made her retch. She preferred the school meals of gristly meat and congealing tapioca pudding. They didn't have the bitter taste of loss. Auntie Constance's fluttering was harder to bear than Aunt Emily's ignoring her. 'O you poor motherless lamb,' she would sob as her face crumpled into creases. All that she had left of Mummy were tatters of memories – a rustle of silk, a waft of perfume, a parasol twirling in the sun.

Now, her streaming tears were blotting the photographs. . She rubbed the back of her hand over her eyes and stood up, staggering as the blood flowed back into her numb legs. Snapping the rubber hand round the photographs she thrust them into her coat pocket. This wouldn't do. She would light a fire and make herself a meal from whatever Mrs Patterson had left in the cupboards. And there was the half-eaten ham sandwich she had left on the dashboard. She could bed down on the sofa for the night and set to in the morning.

Chapter 11

The next day

Felicity surprised herself by sleeping late and waking feeling ravenous. The night before she had found a rust-speckled tin of condensed milk in the back of the pantry. She used it to make a sickly bowl of porridge. As she ate, she decided that she would finish sorting out Pa's papers and leave as soon as possible. She had the boxes piled into the back of her car by lunchtime. After driving into Portree she ate an overdone lamb chop and stiff mashed potatoes in the echoing dining room of The Royal Hotel.

Suddenly she made up her mind. She left her car parked in the Square near the parish church and set out on foot. She didn't want to draw attention to herself. As she climbed Stormy Hill she felt oddly nervous. Why was that? After all, she was on a goodwill errand, an act of kindness. True, she hadn't introduced herself to the family. But she did know something about them. She had quizzed Mrs Patterson for information.

'I was in school with Mary MacPherson. A decent woman. Her husband, John, has his own boat, with his brother.'

Not much to go on. Mrs Patterson was not one for gossip but John Norman himself had told her the name of the road where he lived. She found it. Stopped to gather her breath and her wits together. Was it the corner house he had said? She hadn't paid much attention at the time. As she hesitated, the back door of the corner house opened and a girl of about fourteen appeared. Felicity almost laughed. She was so obviously John Norman's sister. She had the same nimble, slight frame and the same long face with a prominent nose.

'Excuse me. I'm looking for John Norman MacPherson.'

The girl came closer and Felicity could see that she had alert, green eyes. 'I'm his sister, Lexie. He's not back home yet.'

'Do you know when he's expected?'

The girl looked hard at her with those glinting feline eyes. She shrugged. 'I just came home to put on my Guide uniform.'

Felicity could see a flash of a blue blouse and a metal belt clasp under her open coat. The girl watched her, waiting.

'I used to be a Guide myself. I even helped to organise the Brownies.' Felicity wanted to engage the girl in conversation while she decided what to do next. It hadn't occurred to her that John Norman wouldn't be at home.

Lexie nodded. 'Aye. We have an Honourable lady leading our company.'

'Oh, I don't have a title, at all.' Felicity knew that her laugh sounded forced.

'You haven't a moustache either, like our lady leader has.'

The girl had a deadpan expression and Felicity didn't know how to respond. There was a pause while Lexie stared at her in that appraising way that was so disconcerting. Felicity cleared her throat and decided that she must take charge.

'I would like your brother to have my address in London so that he has a pen friend to write to when he's away at sea. If I give it to you will you make sure that he gets it when he comes home?'

'A pen friend?' Her slanting eyes widened.

'Yes, of course.' This exasperating child made her feel like Alice talking to the Cheshire Cat. Felicity scrabbled in her handbag and smoothed out a crumpled envelope to write on. The wretched girl was still staring at her. Never mind, money always oiled these sorts of things.

'Make sure you give it to him,' she said as she handed the paper over and drew out a ten shilling note.

'I'm relying on you,' she added waving the money under the girl's nose. That caught her attention.

She took it, turned it over and put it in her coat pocket. Felicity felt exasperated at the way Lexie did everything with a sort of casual insolence. 'I'll make sure he gets it, Miss,' she said with a solemn expression. Then her face broke open into a grin. 'And I won't tell anyone else.'

What a cheeky minx, Felicity thought as she walked down the hill. She hoped that the large bribe would be enough to ensure the girl's co-operation. The next task was to return home and sort out her own future. If John Norman with his bad eyesight and lack of education could find a role in this war, so could she. He had a home and family too, not just faded photographs, but she drowned that unwanted thought at birth.

* * *

The long drive back to London crystallised her thoughts. She didn't want some tedious office job found for her by someone Pa knew. She wanted to set her own compass. She had despised the Swiss finishing school but maybe she could get some ideas from the girls who had been there. What about Charlotte Ponsonby? She pretended to be feather-brained but Felicity had noticed how quickly she became fluent in French and German. She seemed to know everyone and if she wasn't already engaged to be married would have wriggled her way into an interesting job.

Pa was pleased with his boxes of papers. 'Well done. If this war carries on there might not be another chance to get up to Skye. Now you're back I'll put out some feelers for a job, shall I?'

Felicity wondered whether to mention the photographs but feared that shuttered look appearing in her father's eyes, the expression that used to be there all the time. No, she wanted him to stay cheerful so that he would go to his club for a drink and she would have a chance to use the telephone. She could have taken the tube to see Charlotte but walking up the wide steps to that tall, stuccoed town house in Kensington was too daunting. If the telephone conversation became too much she could always put the receiver down and let them think a bad connection was to blame.

Luckily, it was Charlotte herself who answered. 'Felicity MacDougall?' There was a pause while Felicity imagined her mentally flicking through her address book. 'Of course, Switzerland.' Another pause. 'What a lovely surprise. I haven't heard from you since we left Verdienne.'

'I hope it's not an incon...er...venient time to speak.'

'No...not at all.'

'I'll come straight to the point. May I ask you a favour? The thing is, I'm looking for war work. Something worthwhile and not boring. I thought you would be the one to ask. You know so many people and...' Felicity could feel her words bolting away from her so she gulped a breath.

'I believe I can help.' Charlotte's voice became warmer. With relief? What had she imagined Felicity was going to ask of her? An invitation to a party? Borrowing a ball gown or a fur wrap like the other girls used to do?

'Well, I'm just starting myself at something new in...To do with the Foreign Office. No, I can't say where of course. It's frightfully hush-hush.' She giggled. 'Out of town. We have to stay in digs. Would that be alright for you? I know they're keen to recruit more girls, ones they know are from the right sort of family.'

Felicity's spirits rose. 'What a piece of luck. That would suit me down to the ground. Do I need to write an application?'

'Wait until I put in a word for you. You'll need to have an interview but that's only a formality, really. It's all by word of mouth. And we do get time off. You can get to Claridges to meet the chaps when they're on leave.' She giggled again.

Felicity grimaced at the end of the line.

Charlotte broke the silence. 'Well, what have you been doing with yourself? Your family still has that bolt hole up in Scotland? We've the villa in France but I don't know what will happen about it now.'

'Thank you so much for your help. I'll wait to hear about the interview.' Felicity put the receiver down with relief. Making small talk was such a strain.

Chapter 12

A month later

Time sagged while Felicity waited for a summons, but the knock on the door pulled it taut again. The shy boy waiting on the doorstep made her think of John Norman in his baggy Fair Isle pullover and lopsided glasses. But this was a different boy, in Post Office uniform and handing her a telegram. She hung between fear and excitement until she read it.

'Report to Bletchley Park Bucks STOP In 3 days STOP.'

'You think this'll be better than the Ministry post I was arranging for you?' Pa said in a tight voice when she showed it to him.

'No, probably just as lowly.'

'And you'll have to stay in digs?'

She noticed a flicker of regret in his pale eyes and surprised herself by hugging him. 'I'll be allowed out now and then. It's not a prison.'

He stiffened. 'You'll be fine. All those years at boarding school were good training.' She held back the groan that crawled up her throat. 'I'd better think about packing.'

'I'll fetch the suitcases down from the loft. You'll need to get the train from Euston.'

* * *

Felicity arrived in the afternoon after two hours of travelling. Euston station had been crammed full of people, many of them in uniform but the grubby local train to Bletchley was only half full. Pa insisted on getting on with her to stow her suitcase and bag up on the rack. He hovered as she settled herself in a corner seat. 'Have you everything you need?'

'Yes, thank you Pa. Listen – there's the whistle. You'd better go. I'll write in a day or two.'

He had thrust a copy of *The Lady* into her hand as she got on the train. She discarded it on the empty seat beside her and took out *The Thirty-Nine Steps* from her bag. An adventure set in the Highlands was much more her cup of tea. If this new job was for the Foreign Office who knew what it might lead to? She must be ready for anything and the genteel pages of 'The Lady' wouldn't be much use.

She had got off the train at a nondescript station in the countryside. There didn't seem to be any porters around but the ticket collector told her it wasn't too far to the Park. 'That's the edge of the estate,' he said pointing to a high fence, alongside the railway track. 'I don't know if the barbed wire's to keep the workers in or everyone else out.'

Felicity had slung the strap of her bag across her body and struggled with her suitcase along the narrow path, shifting it from hand to hand. The trees planted alongside the fence scratched the overcast sky. They led her towards a driveway. After announcing herself to the sentry she caught her first glimpse of the house. It brooded behind a lake, big but not beautiful, an expanse of gables, arches and turrets. It was impressive in its way, the sort of sprawling country house that girls like Charlotte would feel at home in but much grander than either of Felicity's homes or the rundown manor house where she had gone to school. As she peered more closely she realised that it was less impressive than it had seemed at first. The drive and paving around the house were pocked with potholes and small wooden huts were camped on the lawns, like the quarters of a besieging beggar army.

As she stepped inside the house she stumbled in the abrupt darkness, confused by the distorted light from stained glass windows. A middle-aged woman with a stern expression loomed in front of her. Felicity started and the woman frowned. 'Follow me,' she ordered as she turned and her high heels click-clacked up a scuffed oak staircase. She pointed to a room off the first landing where an unsmiling man in naval uniform handed Felicity a sheet of paper and told her to sit down at a rickety desk. She was to write a translation of a German passage. Feeling nervous but not too anxious she settled down but when she scanned the writing she was swamped by panic. It might as well be in Russian for all the sense she could make of it. She forced herself to breathe deeply while she tried again. It seemed to be a technical piece of writing, full of words she had never encountered before. After a flustered half hour of writing, crossing out and sucking the pencil she heard the naval officer return.

He snatched her untidy sheet and held it at arm's length, scowling before dropping it back on the desk. 'Useless. You don't have a clue about the German language. I should have known. You didn't even gain your School Certificate.'

Felicity could feel her face staining red.

'Just another silly debutante,' he muttered.

She got to her feet, scraping the chair legs on the floor. 'I'm not a debutante. And I explained in my application that I learnt French and German in Switzerland.'

She was surprised at how her voice boomed out. His patronising words had fanned her rage. 'That translation was much too difficult. I know it was about a submarine but how could I be expected to know all those technical terms? If you had asked me to translate anything reasonable, about history or literature, I could have done it.'

'Wait here.' His voice was cold. When he left the room she let the scalding tears squeeze out of her eyes. She had blown it now. She would be sent home in disgrace and Pa would put on that long-suffering face of his.

She heard the door open behind her, quickly rubbed her wet cheeks and stood up. He stared at her before saying, 'You can stay.'

Felicity realised that her mouth was gaping open in shock. She sat down again while he stood on the landing and shouted for Miss Brooks. The click-clacking shoes trotted up the stairs again.

'Here you are, Commander Harrison,' she said handing over a folder. Neither of them glanced at Felicity. He walked across and leant over her. His breath reeked of tobacco and his jacket smelt fusty. She held her breath to stop herself from gagging.

'Read this all the way through and then sign it.' He jabbed a nicotine stained finger on the papers. 'If you disclose anything at all that could benefit the enemies of our country you will be guilty of treason.' He paused. Images of a hooded executioner with a blood-stained axe splattered her thoughts. 'The penalties for treason are severe and rightly so,' he continued.

Afterwards Felicity couldn't remember what she had read but relief, excitement and the habit of obedience meant that she did as she was asked. Then she had to listen while he lectured her, his blood shot eyes burrowing into hers so that she didn't dare look away.

'Careless talk costs lives. Signing the Official Secrets Act is only the beginning. You must tell no one outside here, not even your family, what you do. "Clerical work for the Foreign Office" is all you may say. You mustn't even say anything to other people who work here. Not even what hut you are based in. You will never visit another hut unless ordered to do so. Is that clear?'

Felicity nodded, listing between fear and hope as she wondered what on earth her new job might demand of her.

Chapter 13

The first few weeks at Bletchley

They stopped at a small terraced house with a tiny front garden. Felicity put down her case and stretched her numb fingers while Miss Brooks strode up to the front door. The woman who responded to her sharp knock had a wrinkled face and sparse grey hair dragged back into a bun. A faded, floral overall was bunched around her thin body.

'Good evening, Mrs Boulton. I've brought this young lady, Felicity MacDougall, to lodge with you.'

Mrs Boulton wiped her hand on her overall before extending it warily. 'Pleased to meet you, I'm sure. That's a Scottish name, isn't it? Like the flour?'

'Yes, it is,' Felicity replied. Miss Brooks waved her hand impatiently, her long curved nails flashing like talons. She looked down her nose at Felicity as if she was a wrongly filed document. 'I'll leave you to get settled,' she called as she stalked off. Mrs Boulton smiled at Felicity and rolled her eyes. Felicity had to put her hand up to her mouth to keep her laughter in. It's going to be alright, she thought.

And so it was. The house itself was cramped, every flat surface capped with crochet work. Felicity's room had space only for a narrow bed and a chest with drawers that stuck when she opened them. The toilet was a freezing shed in the yard. But she didn't care. This pokey house felt safe, a proper home.

Over a cup of tea Mrs Boulton explained that she was a widow. Her husband had been killed in the Great War, soon after their marriage.

'We only had a week or two together before Tom was called up. But they were wonderful, you know. Well, you don't, of course, you not being married yet.' She giggled and Felicity found herself joining in, feeling happy and embarrassed at the same time. That was what was so unusual about Mrs Boulton, or rather Winnie as she preferred to be called. She spoke like someone much younger and didn't talk down to her like older people usually did.

'When I first saw you I thought you'd be a snooty madam, wanting to be waited on hand, foot and finger. But when you laughed I knew we would get on fine.'

Felicity went to bed, exhausted but content. After a dreamless sleep she was lured by the smell wafting up from below. She ran down the stairs, ducking at a tight half landing and rushed into the kitchen. Winnie presented her with a sizzling plate of bacon and eggs.

'Living here in the countryside we're never short of good food. And you look as if you need building up.'

The next morning Felicity walked to the Park, striding out and swinging her arms. The row of houses led to a lane with a scattering of older farm cottages. She caught herself skipping with happiness and looked round to make sure that no one was watching. There was no human life to be seen but she had startled some hens that clucked and skittered away under the hedge. A hunched ginger cat glared at her from a gateway. What a shame that people didn't skip any longer once they were grown up, only when they were dancing. She stopped to fill her lungs with the country air. This was comfortable countryside, softer than Skye but so much better than the dismal city streets. She glanced at her watch and realised that she would need to rush to arrive for her 8am start in Hut 10. The sentry grinned at her as she hurried past.

'Hello Miss. You'd better get a move on.'

She laughed and waved at him. There were plenty of people finishing their shift and heading towards the gates, older men in uniform and gaggles of girls, some in Wren uniforms and others in civilian clothes. Inside the hut the grim Commander Harrison was waiting for her.

'We're breaking German codes,' he told her. She nodded and tried to look serious. She didn't want to risk her tongue running away with her again. But her mind was swarming with pictures of invisible ink, crossword clues and hidden treasure maps. Maybe she would become a spy? How would she endure the danger? She didn't have much time to speculate as she was set to the task of translating and sorting endless messages. She had no idea where they came from or what they were used for. She sensed that her work was one tiny fragment in an enormous jigsaw but she had no idea what the finished picture would be when the pieces were all assembled. That didn't matter though. She didn't care that she was stuck in a bleak hut or that she would have to work night shifts. She was doing something useful, earning money and serving her country. She no longer felt like a freak of nature who couldn't fit in anywhere.

'There aren't any good-looking men here. All the young ones are off fighting,' Susan told her later that day. They were hurrying towards the canteen, shivering as the wind nipped through the gaps between the huts. The canteen stank of overcooked cabbage but it was a relief to escape for a break. Felicity's stomach had been proved by years of boarding school meals and she had learnt to shovel in whatever food was on offer.

'There are some clubs you can join,' Susan continued as they sat down with their plates of greyish stew, slick with grease. A rounded, jolly girl, she had worked at the Park for three months and had appointed herself as Felicity's instructor. 'Scottish Country dancing, drama groups, listening to gramophone records.'

Felicity chewed on a stringy piece of beef while she weighed the options. Dancing seemed the safest choice. At least she knew the steps for the Gay Gordons and the Dashing White Sergeant so two evenings later they were standing in the hall of the mansion itself, waiting for the dancing to begin. 'It's a good long hall.

Plenty of room for a few sets,' Felicity observed.

'Just look at them. You would think they're naked underneath,' Susan whispered as they watched some of the men arriving, their stockinged legs poking out under their coats.

'I suspect you'll find that they're wearing kilts,' Felicity replied, laughing. She had always enjoyed Scottish country dancing. She could forget her usual awkwardness and let the beat lift her. Flitting from one partner to the next she didn't have to make conversation or even look the dancer in the eye. Susan was panting and red-faced after a few dances.

'You really know how to do this dancing lark,' she gasped, a tinge of indignation in her voice.

'It's all those years of going to cèilidhs when we were up in Skye.'

'What? Oh, never mind. I can't hear you above the racket of that piper. Do they always play so loudly? Let's go and get a glass of squash.'

Everything had fallen into place well, at work and in her digs.

'I'll give you some wool to make comforts for the troops,' Winnie said to Felicity the next evening. She rummaged in her patchwork bag and took out a half-made sock.

'But I can't knit, I'm afraid.'

Winnie raised her eyebrows. 'Never mind, I'll soon learn you.'

'Will I knit one of those?' Felicity asked doubtfully as she looked at the sock, bristling with needles.

'Good Lord, no. I'll start you off with a scarf. I remember doing lots of knitting in the last war for those poor lads stuck in frozen trenches.' She closed her eyes for a moment. 'It's different this time round but I'm sure they still need to keep warm.'

Felicity struggled with her needles, her tongue sticking out as she concentrated on getting her tension even. In a funny way her knitting seemed to be a symbol of her life now. Thanks to Winnie's kindness she was learning how to pick up all the dropped stitches, all the hard things that had happened to her after Ma's dying.

Her landlady was determined to make her learn new skills, it seemed. The next week she presented her with a bicycle, painted a glossy black and with a basket on the handlebars. A picture of John Norman flashed into Felicity's mind. She could see him straining to get his heavy machine moving with its load of groceries while she had watched, smirking. What would he say if he could see her now? He would stand with his arms folded and a smile tweaking the corners of his mouth.

'Your turn now,' he would say.

She felt a twinge of home sickness and realised with a start that she hadn't thought about him since she had come down to Bletchley. Now she was a proper grown up working person all her past life had drifted away on the tide.

'You have such long shifts at the Park. This'll get you home faster.' Winnie looked at her expectantly.

'Er…thank you. How kind. Lots of the girls have bicycles. But I'm afraid that I don't know how to ride it. I would be sure to fall off.'

'Rubbish. You'll learn in a flash. Come on then. I'll hold it for you while you get your balance.'

After a few wobbly turns up and down the road she felt brave enough to pick up speed. 'How do I stop?' she shrieked as she turned back towards Winnie.

'Squeeze the brakes. But not too hard.' The warning came too late. Felicity would have catapulted over the handlebars if Winnie hadn't scurried up to her, surprisingly fast on her skinny legs and caught her as she lunged forwards.

'Oh dear, I've hurt you,' Felicity cried out as they landed in a tangle of wheels and limbs. 'Speak to me Winnie, do.'

'I'm quite alright my dear, just winded for a moment. A nice cup of tea will put me right.'

Felicity found that she loved cycling. It was much better than skipping. She was on a daytime shift that week and could just manage to ride home in the light. She felt confident enough now to freewheel down the hills, with the wind ruffling her hair and her feet lifting off the pedals as if she was becoming airborne. If she saw John Norman again she would have to tell him how much fun she had cycling. She was sure that she could out-race him any day.

The second week she was on from 4pm until midnight and had to travel home in the dark. The blackout cast a thick blanket over everything but there were pinpricks of stars and a smear of light from a half-moon to guide her. She was peering ahead, trying to pick out the way when she became aware of the crunch of wheels behind her. It wasn't the sound of car tyres but definitely someone cycling. She told herself not to worry but found her legs were pumping faster. The bicycle behind her speeded up too. Too scared to look round she bent over the handlebars and pounded as fast as she could.

'Stop Missie,' a man's voice called out but she kept going, her heart leaping into her throat. Thank goodness – there was the end of Winnie's road. She skidded up to the gate, scarcely braking so that she had to scrape her feet along the path to slow down. She flung the cycle down, its pedals still spinning and threw herself against the front door. Behind her she could hear creaking brakes.

'Well Missie, I know who you are now. Surely they told you at the Park that you girls are allowed to use lights on your bicycles? You were tearing along like a bat out of hell. That's dangerous, you know, in the pitch black.'

Felicity turned and saw the outline of his policeman's helmet. 'Of course. I'll put my lights on next time. Thank you, officer.' Her voice came out as a wheezy laugh. An arrow slit of light appeared as Winnie opened the front door, a cup of cocoa ready for Felicity in her hand.

'Hello Constable Bruce. Isn't it good that Felicity here has a bicycle now? She goes like the wind on it.'

'She certainly does. I'll say goodnight to you two ladies. Hurry up and put that light off.'

Chapter 14

November 1940

'Cycle going alright?'

Felicity was walking out of the Methodist Chapel at the end of the morning service. She turned when she heard the unfamiliar voice. It came from a tall, thin young man with a prominent Adam's Apple.

'Didn't Mrs Boulton tell you that I repaired it? A hard job getting all the rust off it, I can tell you.'

'Yes, of course. She told me your name. So kind of you, thank you very much. It's handy when I come off shift, especially when it's dark. Ted, isn't it? You've been working away, I believe. This is the first chance I've had to thank you.'

'That's right. But I'm back now for good, working with my dad. Edward Thornton and Son, Electricians.'

'You've not been called up yet?'

'No. I'm in a reserved occupation, being an electrician.'

'Ah, there you are, Ted. I was just talking to your mother,' said Winnie, hurrying up to them. 'I'm glad that you two young people have met at last. I've already asked Madge to come for tea next Saturday. If you come as well, Ted, Felicity can show you what a demon she is on that bike.'

Felicity laughed but she could feel her face reddening. 'Nearly got arrested by Constable Bruce for speeding, didn't you?'

'No, Winnie, it wasn't that at all. Only a misunderstanding about using the lights.'

After they said goodbye to the Thorntons, Winnie squeezed Felicity's hand. 'You know I tease you because you always fall for it.'

'I hope you're not trying to match make. He's older than me

for a start and a bit serious.'

Winnie opened her eyes wide. 'Good Heavens, no. Never occurred to me. You've got a suspicious mind, my girl. It comes of working at the Park.'

Madge didn't come after all on Saturday. 'She's feeling under the weather,' Ted said, in his solemn way.

'Ahh, I understand,' Winnie replied, in a serious voice.

Were they talking in some sort of code? Felicity wondered. 'She's going through "The Change",' Winnie mouthed while Ted went to hang up his coat in the porch. Was that some wartime regulation, like blackout curtains? There wasn't time to ask Winnie as Ted had joined them in the parlour. He didn't say much and Felicity felt ill at ease. It would have been a strained tea party if Winnie hadn't darned over the silences with her chatter. She talked about how expensive everything was, whose sons had got their call-up papers and how busy it was in the town with all the people from the Park.

'You work there, don't you? What's it you do?' Felicity tensed. She felt as if she had signed that Official Secrets paper with her blood and she was terrified of revealing anything.

'Just routine clerical work,' she said, with a bored shrug. It was her stock answer and usually people didn't pursue the matter. They only asked out of politeness. But Ted was persistent. 'Who for?'

'Just a branch of the Foreign Office that's moved out of London.'

'A lot of people work there. Some of them in uniform. Why's that?'

She squirmed in embarrassment but Winnie rescued her. 'The lady who does the billeting said it's all a bit hush-hush.'

'Well, it's mainly young girls there. It can't be that important.'

Felicity felt herself bridling at his words. If only you knew how important it is, she thought, but she looked down at her plate and stayed silent.

Over the next few weeks she saw more of Ted. They always spoke after Chapel on Sunday morning. Felicity didn't much like the Methodist services. The building was modest, drab even, no sense of occasion. The minister had a dreary nasal voice. She found herself hankering after the good old Church of England services she used to take for granted – the cheerful organ, the whiff of incense and the priest's lush robes. Come to think of it, Ted himself was rather like the chapel, well-intentioned but a little dull. But he was company and someone to talk too, a change from the grind of working at the Park. Even more important she felt the weight of Winnie's kindness. She didn't want to hurt her feelings by insisting on attending the parish church instead.

Soon she was invited for tea to Ted's house, a semi-detached villa a little larger than Winnie's terrace. It had a proper front garden, with a barbered privet hedge. The inside was drilled to precision and ready for inspection. The brass coal scuttle and candlesticks blazed from polishing and the covers of the settee were pulled taut. Felicity lowered herself into an armchair, trying not to disturb its parade-ground perfection.

Mrs Thornton, who didn't invite Felicity to call her Madge, looked very similar to her son. They were both narrow and stork-like, their most striking feature being their bulging hazel eyes, the prominent whites like unpeeled hardboiled eggs. Mr Thornton was absent. 'He's exhausting himself with all his war work. He's an ARP warden, you know, and on all sorts of special committees. He's keeping the town going single-handed.'

Felicity listened and nodded, relieved that Mrs Thornton showed no curiosity about her work. 'Ted's like his father of course. He drives himself hard. Does lots of electrical work for the government.' Suddenly, though, she turned her sergeant major's glare on Felicity. 'Ted tells me that your father has a shooting estate in Scotland.'

'Nothing as grand as that. Just a house with a few acres

of moorland attached. It used to be a manse, you know like a vicarage. We've a good fishing river, though.' She felt a sudden tug of homesickness.

'And you went to boarding school?'

'Yes. My parents lived in India, you see, so I had to. And then when Mamma died, I carried on as it was easier all round.'

Mrs Thornton nodded. 'Mr Thornton's done some wiring up at the Park.' Felicity braced herself for a cross-examination about her job.

'They seem very forward, some of those young ladies who work there. Two of them came swanning into our shop the other day, demanding to inspect every wireless we stocked.'

Felicity finished her dusty mouthful of Victoria sponge. 'What a delicious cake. I don't know how you manage with all the rationing.' Mrs Thornton smirked and the danger passed. She returned to her hymn of praise about her husband and son.

Afterwards Ted walked her home, holding her hand rather too tightly. He stood awkwardly at Winnie's gate before saying goodbye. As she walked inside she thought how she wasn't sure about him. In a way she felt grown up, to have a young man to walk out with, if that was what they were doing. He had taken her on a few strolls on Sunday afternoons, all very proper. What if he tried to kiss her? What would it be like? She didn't feel excited at the idea, only a slight disgust, but maybe when the moment came she would be keen. She had overheard some of the debutante types squealing and whispering about their young men. She wasn't one of them. There was no one she could talk to about how you were meant to feel. She wasn't brought up with boys. They were a different race. They could choose to roam free. They weren't tied up, like girls were. She remembered that argument with John Norman about wearing spectacles. His silly claim about suffering as much as she did. What was John Norman to her? She hardly knew him but looking back she had felt at ease with him in a way she didn't with Ted. Anyway that was all over. He hadn't written to her. Maybe it was just a question of time before she got used to Ted. After all she had never imagined she would have a boyfriend at all. It was something that a man, any man, was interested in her, especially when she didn't get to meet many. She could feel one up on Susan when she got bossy, scatter snippets of information about their outings. That's what all girls wanted from life wasn't it, to get married? Everything that went before, like getting a job, was just waiting in the wings? Felicity decided to stop worrying. She had never felt so alive before. So why waste time looking for storm clouds? Live for the moment.

But the past came calling. 'You've got a letter,' Winnie told her when she came in a few days later.

'Thanks, Winnie. I'll read it when I've had a cup of tea. Cycling always makes me thirsty.'

It would be from Pa. No one else wrote to her. His letters came once a week and left her feeling guilty that she didn't miss him more. He never said anything about himself but instead vented his opinions about the progress of the war. Last week he had written about the increase in bombing raids. He explained that it was mainly the East End that was suffering. He had no intention of panicking and moving out. He could always make it to the nearby Underground station if necessary. He believed that the German tactics would only strengthen our resolve. 'We're at our best when our backs are against the wall.' Rations being cut was a nuisance. How could you manage with only two ounces of tea a week? He was eating at the club as much as possible.

Should she be worrying about him? Reading his words each week Felicity thought how the war seemed as distant as Pa himself. If the wind was in the right direction she could hear anti-aircraft guns but the war seemed far away. The Park was cut off from the outside world, like school had been. There were no concerns about getting enough to eat. Winnie got eggs, butter and rabbits from local farmers. Writing to Pa was such a chore. What was there to talk about? She couldn't say anything about her work, even if he would be interested and she wouldn't dream of mentioning Ted.

When she finally picked up the letter she was surprised at how heavy it was. Maybe he had put in a newspaper article for her to read? He was always complaining about her ignorance of what was going on in the war. But no. There were two letters inside. Pa's two sheets were folded around an envelope with her London address written in an unfamiliar hand. She ran her eye down Pa's letter.

I opened the enclosed in error. As I didn't expect you to be receiving any communication I naturally thought that the letter must be for me. I was puzzled by the childish hand on the envelope but all was explained when I saw the letter within. I don't know if he wrote on his own initiative but I can't believe that you would invite him to correspond. I'm sure you will discourage him, in a polite way of course.

Felicity screwed up the paper and threw it across the room without reading any more. Opened it by mistake, indeed! More like snooping. She read the single sheet, written in pencil, the marks pressed down hard on the paper.

Dear Felicity,
My wee sister Lexie said she saw you. I didn't believe her at first as shes a real actress always making up stories. I signed up on a boat like I said and were docking safely now. Theres men here from all over on the boat but none from the highlands. i've learnt something new, would you believe? An old sailor taught me to knit. Even socks with 4 needles and all. Mamma will be amazed.
Have you found war work yet? Skye and the fishing seem a long way away. I never thought I would miss home so much I was so keen

to get away and see the world.
   Are you well? I'm in my usual.
   Yours sincerely,
   John Norman

Felicity's eyes were damp but she wasn't sure why. Maybe it was something about the effort he'd made when writing didn't come naturally to him.

Chapter 15

The next day

John Norman's words burrowed into Felicity's brain. His work sounded dangerous and she wished that she had paid more attention to the news so that she would understand what he was doing. She couldn't ask Pa of course. It would just make him suspicious. She would have to find out at the Park, look at the papers they kept in the library there.

The next day she arrived early for her shift. She didn't want to go during the lunch break and have Susan asking her about her sudden interest in war news. What she discovered in the newspapers alarmed her. She read that the convoys of merchant ships were protected by naval vessels and holding their own against the packs of German U-boats. This conjured up pictures from fairy tales of dark forests full of wolves pouncing on flocks of sheep with nothing to protect them except a shepherd boy, his sling and a dog. Then she remembered one of Ted's favourite sayings. 'You can't trust the papers. They're not going to tell us the bad stuff, are they?'

She kept her worries buried. There was no one she could trust with the weight of them. Susan would say something like, 'Well, it's dangerous everywhere. Stop brooding.'

Winnie would be kind as always but Felicity felt uncomfortable at the idea of telling her. She couldn't properly explain about John Norman. It would seem odd when she had never mentioned him before.

'Come to the pictures with me,' Ted said on Sunday after chapel. 'They're showing *Gone with the Wind* this week, in Technicolor.'

Her first instinct was to refuse but she wanted a rest from worrying, the sharp rodent teeth gnawing away at the edges of her mind. Maybe an outing would help.

'Oh yes, please. Clark Gable and Vivien Leigh!'

As she concentrated on the film she decided that the change in routine was a good idea. The story transported her away from the cinema that stank of sweat and smoke-saturated coats. She was so absorbed that she forgot completely about Ted's presence until she felt his heavy arm land on her shoulders. The dark must have made him feel bold but she was captivated by the screen and pretended to take no notice. She was focused on the terrible scene where the hundreds of wounded soldiers were lined up in the square of Atlanta. She gasped as the view widened to show row upon row of them, laid out on stretchers. She gasped again as a moment later she felt Ted's fingers creep spider like and grab her left breast. Horror and surprise made her leap up from her seat.

'Sit down! You're blocking the picture,' someone called out. What should she do? She supposed that a lady would storm out in a flurry but she was furious that Ted's groping would stop her from seeing the rest of the film. She crouched down and looked around her. Ted was sitting there, staring stiffly ahead as if nothing had happened. The seats around them were all full except for one empty one just ahead in the row in front. She hitched her skirt up so that she could straddle the back of the seat and haul herself into the empty space. She sat rigid, her eyes glued to the screen until the film ended but the magic had leaked away.

She was still angry. She pushed her way out into the foyer and into the street, blinking as she adjusted to the light before striding out for home. She was not going to speak to him. She knew now that he disgusted her.

'Wait a moment, Felicity, please!' Ted had caught up with her and was trying to take her arm. She shook him off. 'Leave me alone.'

'I just want to walk you home.'

She walked faster, looking straight ahead.

'I know I shouldn't have done that but...'

'No, you shouldn't. You ruined the film for me,' she hissed.

'You didn't need to make a spectacle of yourself.'

'What do you mean? You were the one with the wandering hands.'

'Shhs. Someone might hear.'

'Is that all you care about?'

'Of course not. I know you're not that sort of girl.'

'But you still tried it on.'

'But the thing is, I couldn't help it. There's an answer – we should get married.'

'Married?' she croaked.

'Why not? We get on and my mother approves of you.'

Felicity's tongue felt paralysed. 'You want to marry me?'

'Why not? As soon as possible. A long courtship's a terrible strain on a man.'

'But you haven't asked me properly.' Amazement made her stop dead and stare at him.

'All that romantic guff of going down on one knee? Would you do me the honour? I'm asking you now.' His words hurtled on, 'We're suited well enough. We can live with my mother. You can leave that silly job of yours.'

'You've got the future all settled, haven't you? Isn't there something you've forgotten?'

He looked at her blankly while she felt her anger rising. 'You've not asked me what I want? Not said anything about love.' To her annoyance she could hear the catch in her voice.

He shrugged. 'But you want to marry me? I've got good prospects. You could do much worse.'

'No, I don't want to marry you.' The voice seemed to come from outside her and she had to stop herself from turning round to see who was there. She paused and then heard herself repeat, 'No, No, No.'

'Shut it. You're getting hysterical.'

'I'm too young to get married. I'm barely twenty.'

'Plenty old enough. Lots of girls are mothers at your age. I can afford to keep you.'

'But I don't want to be kept. Or to have children.' She tossed her head and hurried down the path, half running and half stumbling. She called over her shoulder, 'And I don't love you.'

'Come back. I'm not going to run after you.' She started to speed up.

'Don't be so hasty. You might not get another offer. You're no oil painting.'

Half turning she shouted over her shoulder. 'I've a sweetheart already. He's worth ten of you.'

'You're a hussy, then, leading me on like that.' His words rang in her ears as she sprinted towards Winnie's door, her refuge. She stopped dead. What would Winnie say? Ted and his family were her friends. She would have to sneak in and slip up to her room while she decided what to do. The wireless was on, thank goodness. She took off her shoes in the hall and crept barefoot up the stairs. She lay down on her bed, shivering in the cold room. Pulling up the eiderdown she lay tucked up in a ball. Her numb toes bumped into a hot water bottle. She clutched it gratefully to her stomach but gratitude to Winnie for her kindness made tears trickle down her cheeks. She wouldn't be so kind when she heard about her row with Ted.

There was a cough followed by a soft tap on the door. 'Are you alright Felicity? I've made us some cocoa.'

Felicity swept the dampness from her cheeks and opened the door a crack, trying to make her wobbling lips form a smile.

'Oh, my dear. What's wrong? Can you manage to come downstairs? I've got a good fire going.'

She shuffled down and settled in the armchair, blowing on the hot drink. Winnie sat opposite, silent but tense as Felicity poured out the tale of the evening.

'Well I never. You poor lamb.' Winnie leant forward to pat her hand.

'Are you angry with me?' Felicity whispered.

'Angry? When you're all upset? Of course not.'

'But Ted and his family are your friends. And you got him to repair the bicycle for me. I suppose I should be grateful he wanted to marry me.'

Winnie let out a great whoop of laughter. 'Grateful, my foot! He's got an opinion of himself. There's plenty more fish in the sea. You've no need to hurry with your rod and line.' She gazed into the flames. 'It's not wise to marry in wartime.' For a minute her eyes were desolate but then she shook her head. 'And I don't think you should marry a man because he pushes you. Or you feel sorry for him.' She paused. 'I had an offer after the war. Everyone told me how lucky I was. He was honest, had a steady job, a good catch.'

'But you turned him down?'

'I did. I didn't love him, not like I loved Harry. I couldn't settle for second best. Now you go up to bed. Things are always clearer after a night's rest.'

To her surprise Felicity fell into a deep well of sleep. The next morning, though, as she walked downstairs the doubts pounced again.

'I can't face him, him and his mother on Sunday morning.' She pushed a bite of bacon around her mouth, unable to swallow it.

'Yes, you can. Hold your head high, smile and say, "Good Morning". The first time will be the hardest. It'll get easier.'

Felicity pricked her fried egg with her fork and smeared it across her plate. 'I'm not brave enough to face them yet. I'm owed a few days of leave. I might go up to town and stay with Pa.'

Winnie was standing at the sink, scrubbing the draining board. Her hands stilled. 'You must do what you think best, my dear.'

Chapter 16

The following day

Felicity raced to work, hunching over the handlebars on the downhill stretch in an effort to go faster. She ran to Commander Harrison's hut and knocked on the door, feeling her courage leak away. It was true that she had leave owing but you were supposed to wait to be told when you could take it. She had barely spoken to him since her interview. She usually scurried away if she saw him in the distance.

'Ah, Miss MacDougall.' He raised his eyebrows as he came out, shutting the door behind him.

'Hello, Sir. I know I shouldn't come to another hut but I have some l...l...leave due and I wondered...'

'And why do you need to take it now?'

'I want to see my father in London.'

He waited.

'He's not been well. He lives on his own and I've been worried about him, with all the bombing and everything.'

She wondered where that lie had sprung from, ready formed and leaping from her lips.

The harsh lines around his mouth eased a little. 'Very well. You may take three days' leave.'

Felicity remained on the step, nonplussed. 'Off you go, now.' He half smiled.

Back at her desk, she scribbled a note to Pa and that evening told Winnie she was going for the first London train the next morning.

The carriage was stuffed full of people but Felicity wriggled through the crush to find herself a window seat. She looked out of the bleary window, expecting the countryside to be scarred by bombing but the fields were freshly harvested and the trees still had some leaves. As she neared the city she could see some signs of damage. Houses stripped of an outside wall, their interiors exposed as if a giant had just opened them up to play with the furnishings inside. She remembered the pleasure of moving the small, stiff figures inside their miniature rooms. But these weren't like the well-appointed dolls house she had once enjoyed. As the train came closer she could make out the shredded wallpaper, the sagging ceilings and the gaping doors. She felt nosey peering at these inside-out private spaces. How many people had escaped when their homes had been torn open? She shuddered and looked away.

When she reached their road in Knightsbridge she was relieved to see that it looked much as before, just shabbier. She let herself into the echoing house and prowled through the neglected rooms. Pa had left a scrawled note propped up by the clock on the mantelpiece.

Back about 7 o'clock.

She swallowed her disappointment that he wouldn't break his routine to return earlier and welcome her home. Why had she expected anything different? Sighing, she dumped her case on the bed of her old room and raised a flurry of dust. Gnawing on a corner of a loaf and a wizened apple from the larder she wondered what to do. She couldn't bear to stay in the cheerless house. But where to go? She had no friends or family to visit. When they had time off, the debutante types at the Park would emerge from Mr Wesley's salon in Hut 23, damp towel in hand, hair shampooed and set, trilling about going up to Claridges. 'Get your pearls out girls. Alasdair should be on leave, maybe Algy too. Anyway, Gibbs on the door will tell us. He knows everyone.'

Well, she had the pearls to wear but no boyfriend, titled or otherwise, to meet. But thinking about pearls and parties reminded her of Charlotte Ponsonby. When Felicity had first arrived at the Park she had tried to find her to thank her for her help. She had not dared venture to other huts after all the warnings about secrecy but she had looked out for her in the canteen and the recreation room. She had even braced herself to approach some of the debs. Most of them peered down their aristocratic noses or stared at her blankly. But one girl had nodded and drawled, 'Old Charlotte? Didn't she get transferred somewhere? Too clever by half to work with duffers like us.'

Charlotte would probably not be at home but at least she could leave a message. It would be better than kicking her heels and feeling miserable. Felicity found herself standing in front of the grand front steps of the tall house in Kensington, gazing up at the four floors above the pillared porch. She was surprised to see that the smooth complexion of the walls was peeling and pitted. The other houses in the row were equally neglected but the steps of Charlotte's house were grubbier than their neighbours' and the railings above the basement were rusty. Felicity lifted the heavy knocker and released it with a thump. There was no response and she was turning away when the wide black door inched open. A pale face, belonging to a very young maid, peered out. Her frail neck sprouted from a black dress that swamped her. Too young to be called up for war duty yet. Felicity stepped inside. Footsteps plodding down the wide staircase made her look up.

'Mrs Ponsonby? I hope I'm not disturbing you. I'm enquiring after Charlotte. She was kind enough to...to...'

Her voice failed her as she locked eyes with the woman in a trailing dressing gown, her grey hair springing above staring eyes. 'Who are you?' she boomed.

'Felicity MacDougall. I...I was at finishing school with Charlotte. I wanted to thank her for putting in a word for me over a job.'

Mrs Ponsonby tottered towards her and Felicity had to steel

herself not to flinch away from her wide-eyed stare. 'She's gone.' Her mouth clamped shut.

'Ah, of course. I thought she must have been posted somewhere.'

'Posted!' She jabbed a finger at Felicity's chest. 'Posted to where? Heaven? "Gave her life for her country," the letter said. They sent her abroad to be killed. Because her French was so fluent.'

'It was. What was she doing abroad? Some sort of agent?'

Mrs Ponsonby lurched forward. 'My beautiful girl dead, sacrificed,' she wailed.

'I'm so sorry. I had no idea.'

'And you're still here and not beautiful at all. Is it only the beautiful who die?' She glowered, her face so close that Felicity could see the spittle foaming against her teeth. She froze until Mrs Ponsonby pushed her. 'Go away. Coming here to mock.'

'Not...not at all. I had no idea.' The blazing hatred in the other woman's eyes was terrifying. Felicity backed away towards the front door. Mrs Ponsonby stayed still. Her shoulders slumped and she lowered her head. She began to howl in a terrible inhuman voice and clawed at her dressing gown. The young girl was cowering at the foot of the stairs, her face an ashen blur. She fumbled with the door handle and reached out to touch Felicity's arm. 'Best go Miss.'

Felicity nodded, stumbled down the steps and stood shivering at the bottom. Three days ago her life had been safe, a little boring maybe, but now it had smashed and splintered around her. She clasped the railings and rested her forehead on the cold metal until her heart stopped hurling itself against her ribs. Breaking into a wobbly run she headed back the way she had come, slowing down as she noticed people staring at her. She wanted to get as far away as she could from the Ponsonby house but where should she go? A park where she could walk and settle herself down?

She strode along and soon began to get hot. She shrugged off her jacket. But the sweat trickling down the back of her neck and her ragged breathing made her feel alive. Not like poor Charlotte. It was hard to believe someone so lively could be dead. Surely she was sitting in a French café somewhere, a beret tilted on her head, her shapely legs crossed while she sipped coffee and eavesdropped on the conversations swirling about her? Had she been some sort of spy? Betrayed, tortured, shot? No wonder her mother was out of her mind. Perhaps Pa would know about these secret missions. How long ago had she died? Should she send a letter of condolence to her parents? But then what could she say that wouldn't make things worse? What use was etiquette? She felt a surge of rage at the finishing school. Learning how to be a lady was a waste of time when war was turning their world inside out.

Her thoughts whirled and swooped. She bent forward and covered her ears to stop their silent screams. That was when the noise erupted. She looked around her and saw people running but her own legs had become rubbery. A man in a white helmet rushed up and shook her arm. 'Air raid,' he shouted. 'Get down the Underground.' He pointed across the road and shoved her in the back so that she stumbled and almost fell to her knees. Bodies were jostling past her. She righted herself and followed the stampede across the road and towards the steps. She hesitated and looked back, fearing she would be lifted off her feet by the press of people. She squeezed into the edge of the first step to make way for a woman holding hands with two small children. The boy had a mangy teddy bear clasped to his chest while the girl was dangling a doll by its arm. A man hurried past them, startling the girl so that her grip slackened. The doll fell down on the next step. The girl cried out.

'Oh dear! I'll get your dolly.' Felicity lunged forward but before she could pick up the doll someone's foot caught it. It plummeted down two more steps with its limbs flung out before landing, its head smashed into pieces. The little girl's blue eyes widened and her mouth opened into a howl of pain.

'It's only a bloody doll,' someone said, laughing. Other people joined in. The child stood rigid. Her mother tugged her arm.

'Shut the racket, Annie. You're doing my head in.'

Felicity reached out to the child. 'Let me give you money for another doll.'

The mother stared at her before brushing past. The girl's jagged howls continued. Felicity could feel tears streaking down her face as she let the surge of bodies carry her down to the platform. A sour stench made her gag. People were squirming and shifting like maggots in a tin. She felt she would never rise again if she sank into this swamp of bodies. So she backed against the wall, jammed between a cigarette machine and one for chocolates. Both of them had been forced open, the metal sides stoved in and the glass broken. She held herself still, scarcely breathing, more scared of her fellow beings than she was of any bomb. She closed her eyes and imagined herself at the landing window of the house in Skye. Gazing out at the hills, softened in summer green, the mournful call of gulls in her ears.

Part 3

John Norman's Story

Chapter 17

July 1940

John Norman enjoyed the motion of the train clattering along the coast from Kyle. At Inverness he changed trains, elbowing his way past men in uniform, speaking in a jangle of different accents. He strode along, trying to look confident. He had never travelled this far south before and he scanned the crowds, hoping to meet up with other merchant sailors he could follow. He boarded the crammed Glasgow train, not certain what he was looking for. Maybe a particular kitbag over the shoulder, a weathered face or a rolling gait would give him a clue. But it was impossible to tell a man's occupation from his clothes and he didn't want to look foolish approaching a stranger. What a pity that Iain had gone down earlier. John Norman had never felt so alone before. Maybe he should turn back now? Would anyone think the worse of him if he did? Pappa would be glad of his help on the boat and Mamma would have a smile on her face like a crescent moon. He dug his nails in the palms of his hands as he hesitated in the corridor but then the guard blew his whistle and it was too late.

He followed Iain's instructions, taking the train on to Greenock before making his way to the docks. This was more what he was used to. Harbours were the same everywhere but the size and noise left him open mouthed. Ships and warehouses stretched as far as he could see, smothered in a pall of smoke. Everyone seemed too busy to be asked for help. Where was the shipping office Iain had told him about? John Norman groped in his jacket pocket to find his spectacles. He spat on the smeary lenses, wiped them on a crumpled handkerchief and shoved them onto his nose. Now he could see a queue snaking towards a dingy shed. He quickened his pace and called out to a man in overalls coming towards him. 'Where do you sign on for a berth?'

'O'er there, laddie.' You're nae frae here? Frae the islands, aye? Ye'll be after an office job, nae doubt?'

John Norman smiled his thanks but grimaced and thrust his spectacles back in his pocket when the man walked away. He joined the back of the line and peered at the men in front of him, old hands, bearded and sure of themselves. He jumped as one of the group in front turned round and spoke. 'It's yourself, John Norman. Didn't you see me?' a familiar voice asked in Gaelic.

'Archie! What are you doing here?' John Norman replied in English, not wanting to draw the attention of strangers.

'What do you think, you idiot? Same as yourself, looking for a berth.'

'But you said you'd never join up.'

He shrugged. 'I'm not joining up, just getting away for a while.'

'Who's after you?' John Norman prodded him in the ribs but his friend stayed silent. 'Never mind. Maybe we'll be on the same boat. That would be grand.'

The queue shuffled forward and John Norman fumbled for his spectacles as they reached the doorway. A man looked up from the scratched desk inside. John Norman hung back.

'You were here before me,' he said but to his surprise Archie pushed him forward. 'You go first.'

'What experience do you have of seafaring?' The man's voice was brisk as he fished out a new form from the pile in front of him.

'Er, I've been a hand on my father's and uncle's fishing boat for years. I wanted to join the Royal Navy but...'

The man waved an impatient hand. 'We'll sign you up for a boat to Canada, *The Corsair*. You'll stay there to join a ship from the Montreal Pool when it's ready. Take this sheet and fill it in at the table over there.'

John Norman didn't budge. 'What's the matter? Can't you write?'

A red tide flooded his neck and face but he stood his ground. 'Of course I can but I was wondering if my friend could get a berth on the same boat.'

'We'll see. Now get a move on.' The man stared at Archie who was leaning on the doorframe.

John Norman did as he was told and after filling in the form he hovered outside until Archie appeared. 'Are you off to Canada too?'

'No. They're saving me for something special. I've to come back tomorrow.' The angry glint in his eye stopped John Norman from probing.

'I'll see you later at the Mission, then?'

Archie shrugged and walked away. 'I'm off for a drink.'

John Norman felt relieved to be settled. It had been easier than he had imagined. He found his way to the Seamen's Mission and lay down on his bed, scratching his head as he thought about all that had happened that day. He fished in his pocket for a cigarette and felt the edge of the postcard he had bought as he left the docks. It was a daft thing with a picture of a Scottie and 'Welcome to Glasgow' written on it. He had picked it up without looking at it properly. Who should he send it to? Mamma? She was still furious with him. The storms of words had abated, replaced by an Arctic chill. She refused to look at him, let alone speak. Even at the last moment she wouldn't thaw, turning her face away when he tried to kiss her cheek. But yet…despite his own still smouldering anger he couldn't bring himself to go across the Atlantic without sending word. The answer came to him and he quickly wrote,

'Hope you are all well at home i'm in my usual signed up for a ship and sailing tomorrow.'

That would do. He couldn't say where he was going. That was secret. He addressed the card to Margaret at the hotel in Kyle.

She would let Mamma know. He couldn't be accused of leaving without a word. Maybe Mamma would come round by the time he was home on leave. He worried about Pappa, though, doing all the heavy lifting on the boat without him there to help.

Getting to his feet, he ran his fingers through his hair, pushed the postcard into his pocket and strolled out into the street. In spite of everything he was glad he had cast off and set his sails. Who knew what adventures were to come? The first one was to track down Archie.

Chapter 18

Later the same day

John Norman spent the next hour trailing through bars. Who would have believed there were so many so close together? All full to bursting and so fogged with smoke that he could scarcely make out any faces, whether he wore his spectacles or not. At least no one paid him any heed as he peered through doorways, muttering apologies as he squeezed his way inside. Fed up and footsore, he was on the point of giving up when he saw three figures sprawling across the path towards him. He stepped into the road to let them past. The man on the outside was burly and fair, his head flung back as he bawled out a song in some strange language. The man on the inside was joining in noisily and jammed between them was Archie, laughing and nodding his head in time to the tune. John Norman was ready to slink away but Archie jerked his head up. 'Look, it's the wee Canadian himself.'

'Shhs. It's secret.'

'Oh, aye. Well there's no room for me on the fancy trip to Canada. I'm off on some old puffer, God knows where to.'

'That's a pity. You should have kept your place in the queue.'

'Oh, aye. Well, you go and get your beauty sleep. I'm off with my Viking friends here for another dram or two.'

The sailor on the outside lurched towards John Norman who side stepped him. 'Skol!' he bellowed, his mouth stretched wide to reveal horse-sized teeth. John Norman watched the three men stumbling their way down the street, bumping against each other like trees in a storm. A sudden tug of wind made him shiver. It wasn't good to part like that but what could he do? He turned up his jacket collar and went back to the Mission.

The groans and snores of the other men sharing his room

woke him early but he was keen to get up at first light to see what the day would bring. He avoided the greasy bacon and nibbled on a piece of dry toast. He didn't want to embarrass himself by bringing up his breakfast in a rough sea. He had never felt ill on a fishing boat but Iain had warned him, 'Some of those boats wallow like a barrel and turn your belly inside out.'

The *Corsair* was a solid ship, workmanlike and recently painted. She looked big enough to carry passengers as well as freight. A bored looking lad jerked his thumb towards the fo'c'sle head when he spotted John Norman. He led him to a long thin cabin with rows of bunks on each side, enough to sleep eight men. Some already had bags flung on them but there was an unclaimed upper bunk at the far end. John Norman prodded the rough straw mattress. No sheets, only a horse blanket. Mamma would be horrified but at least there was no stink of fish, only of men.

He sauntered along the deck, trying to look like an old hand. As he leant over to peer into the oily Clyde a man not much older than himself but wearing a uniform jacket shouted out in an accent so odd that it sounded like a foreign language. John Norman turned and frowned. The man sighed before speaking very slowly. 'Are you a deckhand? Go aft and help. We're off.'

John Norman bit his lip, angry at the man's mockery and his own reddening face. He hurried to join a group of six others who nodded at him before they all got down to casting off. He always enjoyed the adventure of setting off, each departure feeling like his first trip when he was only seven years old, the boat slicing through the waves, as eager as he was himself. And this time there was the excitement of a new horizon as the river spread its fingers wide to the ocean beyond.

The other men were mostly young, except for Duncan, a grizzled sailor in his forties, nicknamed, of course, 'Grandad'. 'Don't fret about Johnson. He's a wee third officer, a dour Aberdonian, who gets above himself,' Duncan told John Norman while they were waiting for their dinner. It was brought in by a lad who looked far too young to be at sea. He staggered under the weight of two pails that slopped as he tried to tip the food out onto the plates. John Norman steadied them for him. He was hungry enough not to care about the toughness of the beef stew. He gobbled it down and smacked his lips.

'Don't imagine it's always like this. We'll soon be on the salted stuff,' Duncan said as he gouged out a piece of gristle from between his teeth with a forefinger. As he did so John Norman noticed that his middle finger was missing its top joint.

'Surely that lad who brought it in is too young to be at sea?' John Norman said.

'Sam? He's the Peggy.' John Norman looked blank.

'It used to be the peg-leg sailor who helped the cook in the galley. These days it's the youngest one of the crew. He's not as young as he looks, just wee. The story goes that when he was on the train coming to Glasgow it was so full that the other sailors stowed him up on the luggage rack for the journey.'

John Norman laughed with the rest. He felt sorry for Sam who had looked miserable but it was all so new for him that he let the boy slip out of his memory. The other sailors were all from the Clyde and had been to sea before. John Norman was disappointed that there was no one else from the islands. He felt on the edge of things when they talked about places in Glasgow he had never been to, boats they had been on before or especially the football.

'You follow Rangers?' Rab, asked him as they were sweeping the deck. He was a sailor about John Norman's age, with crow black hair and sharp blue eyes. 'Or Celtic? Had a lad on the last boat, came from Barra. Papist and Celtic, he was. Good lad, though.'

'It's shinty that's our game,' John Norman replied.

'Like the Irish? Isn't that right Sean?' Rab turned to a wiry young man with curly hair who was strolling past.

'No, you eejit. We have proper sticks for hurling, not like the shinty ones. They're like the hockey sticks posh lassies play with,' Sean told him.

'Aye but it takes more skill with a *caman*. You lot use a stick as big as a paddle.' John Norman laughed and Sean joined in.

John Norman and Rab went back to their sweeping. Rab started whistling 'The Skye Boat Song'.

'Did your folk come from the Highlands?' John Norman asked.

Rab grinned. 'No, I was just trying to make you feel at home. Well Dadda maybe did, way back when. He's a MacGregor.'

'Have you always been a sailor?'

Rab's mouth twisted. 'Aye but it's not what I chose. I wanted to build ships.'

John Norman opened his mouth but before he could speak, Rab continued, 'Before you ask – I wasn't allowed to.'

'Well, that just leads to another question, doesn't it? You know we Highlanders are a nosey lot. When we meet someone new, we like to milk them dry.'

Rab shrugged. 'My name's wrong. You wouldn't know how it works. MacGregor's fine but Mam's a Doyle. Dadda got cold shouldered for marrying a Papist. No chance of me getting an apprenticeship at a yard.'

John Norman frowned. 'That's very harsh.'

'Aye, well, like I say, you've no idea. It's easier for you. You don't have all that bigotry.'

John Norman was so astonished that he stopped sweeping and leant on his broom handle. 'I can tell you've never spent a Sunday on Skye – no music, no drink, talking in whispers, services so long that your backside goes numb with sitting.'

'But you're not kept out of a job because of your religion or who your family are.'

'Don't you believe it!' John Norman found himself thinking of Archie, condemned because his family were tinkers. 'But getting a job of any sort is the hard thing. That's why so many get forced off the land and go to Glasgow.'

Sean came strolling back towards them, grinning. 'Are we competing to see who's had the hardest time? No one can beat us Irish. My great, great, great grandad was so starved in the Potato Famine that he ate his last goat, every last bit – skin, hooves and horns. Then he boiled up his old boots and ate the soles.'

'You're making that up. You got it from that Charlie Chaplin film,' Rab said.

'*The Gold Rush* wasn't it?' John Norman added.

'What, you get to see films out in the wilds?'

'Aye Rab, we do now and then. My Pappa's fond of Charlie Chaplin.'

'Take no notice of Red Rab,' Sean said, digging John Norman in the ribs. 'He's always on about politics and getting people's backs up.'

Not so different from the banter of his friends at home, John Norman thought, with a sudden shiver of homesickness. What were they doing now? He hoped they were safe. He sighed and started sweeping again.

As the voyage went on, John Norman took the teasing in his stride, kept his head down and learnt the ropes. He was a sailor who took his share of the work, not a shirker. That's what mattered on a boat. But he hadn't realised what a long trip would be like, weeks rather than a day or two, with no shoals to chase and catch. The cargo needed no attention because they were sailing in ballast. Instead there was a timetable of watches and a lot of cleaning and polishing that seemed a waste of time. Then nothing to do when he was off duty except sleep in the stifling, sweat soaked air of his quarters.

'Make the most of it,' Grandad had told him. 'Better bored than shitting your breeks with fear. It's on the way back that the subs will be about.' He brandished his strip of knitting. 'Get the pins out. Stops you fretting.'

John Norman recoiled. 'Knitting! It's what Mamma and my sisters do.'

'Women's work you mean? You don't mend nets, then?'

'Aye, but that's different.'

The older man shrugged but John Norman came back later, brandishing a sock with a gaping hole at the toe. 'I need new socks. So maybe I'll give it a go.'

'Socks is hard but you could maybe darn that one. I'll start you off with a scarf.'

Knitting was calming, right enough. The rhythm took him back home, to Mamma sitting by the tilly lamp, her fingers jigging over the needles at a speed he could never match. The only time he was involved was when she'd asked him to hold his arms out so that she could wind the yarn round them.

'Here comes the Hieland Granny with her knitting,' Rab mocked but John Norman had his answer ready. 'At least I'm doing something useful with my fingers. Not like you, groaning and rocking every night while you work away at yourself.'

'Well said, laddie. He keeps me awake too,' said Sean, laughing.

Chapter 19

August 1940

'You two, go and clean up for the officers. I won't have those Royal Navy fellows aboard turning their noses up at our Mess.'

'Bloody cheek,' Rab said as he threw his cigarette stub over the side. 'That damn Johnson. Drunk on his wee bit o' power. We're no skivvies.'

John Norman laughed in agreement but secretly he was pleased to be busy. The third officer came back after an hour to check on their work. He ran his finger over the brass rail around the table and bar. 'Not bad.' They kept their faces frozen while he looked them up and down. 'The cook needs help. Serving food and clearing up.' John Norman saw Rab was about to protest so he nudged his friend and spoke first.

'Aye, Sir. We're willing.'

'What you sucking up to him for?' Rab asked when Johnson had marched off.

'You're not after wanting a taste of their food? I bet they get better than us.'

John Norman was right. As well as their own officers there were three from the Royal Navy on their way to Canada. They all sat down to hotel meals. Fresh white rolls, a choice of thick or thin soups, sardines and smoked fish, just to start with. Followed by roast meats, fruit pies and cheese. And no stint on the beer and spirits. Bert the cook was a dour man but they did his bidding. In return they filled their bellies with high class leftovers.

'I told you it was worth our while,' John Norman said as they downed fresh sole.

'Not a patch on fish and chips back home. Sole Moonie, my arse.'

'Not as tough and stringy as your arse. Just enjoy it.'

'How come they get this stuff? Not salt beef and hard tack like us? Aren't we all meant to be fighting this bloody war together?'

Bert wanted their help again the next day.

'Were you chaps stewards before the war?' John Norman started in surprise. It was one of the Royal Navy officers who spoke, a slight man who was growing a wispy beard.

'No Sir, I was a fisherman.'

'This work suits you?'

'Aye, well enough.'

'We didnae get food like this though.' Rab was thrusting the menu under the officer's nose.

'You idiot. He was only being friendly,' John Norman hissed once they were back in the galley.

'I'll not kowtow like you do.'

Johnson got to hear of it and Rab was sent down to join the stokers for the rest of the voyage.

'Who does he think he is?' Bert said. 'Officers is different. On land and sea. It wouldn't be right to give them the same as the crew.'

John Norman didn't have time to think about it. He was too busy doing Rab's work as well as his own. He hid some of the leftovers in his pockets for him. 'All squashed, like a bloody dog's dinner,' Rab had complained as he'd gobbled it up.

'The boy will help you serve up now that gobby one's cleared off,' Bert said.

John Norman had forgotten about the sickly-looking Peggy who was never around the boat. He seemed to spend all his time in the galley. Sam looked even more pale and scrawny than he remembered. 'How come you look half-starved when you work in the galley?' he joked.

Sam flinched as if he was expecting a blow. 'Can't keep food down.'

'Still seasick?'

He nodded. 'Bert threatened to make me eat a piece of fat

bacon on a string. It made me feel worse.'

'Aye, it would.'

'Then he made me walk around with a pail around my neck. "Saves you having to mop up your vomit," he said.'

John Norman's eyes widened. 'That's rotten.'

The boy shrugged. 'Anyway, I've got the pots to clean while Bert goes to have a fag.'

'I'll give you a hand,' John Norman said.

The boy looked surprised. 'If you want.'

'You wash and I'll dry?' John Norman said. Sam had to stand on tiptoe to reach down into the sink.

John Norman was struck again at how mouse-like the boy was, cowed almost. He tried again to get him to talk.

'Where you from? Somewhere in England?'

'London. I'm a Barnardo's brat.' John Norman looked puzzled.

'An orphan.' Sam hung his head.

'Oh, that's why you got shoved onto a boat so young. Not much fun, eh?'

John Norman heard a muffled sob. Sam's shoulders were heaving. He lifted a sopping hand from the suds to mop away tears. Then he put his hand in his mouth and bit down. What on earth could the matter be? Suddenly John Norman was reminded of Lexie. The same age, the same smooth cheeks blotched with tears, the same long eyelashes, curling with damp. The same defenceless courage, like an unfledged eagle wrenched from its nest. Well he knew how to console his sister. He could do the same here.

'Come on, I didn't mean to upset you,' he said, putting an arm around the boy's bony shoulders. The next instant John Norman found himself thrust backwards, hard little fists jabbing him in the stomach.

'You're all the bloody same,' Sam yelled as he pummelled him.

'Hey, what are you doing?' He caught Sam's fists in his own hands. 'I'm trying to help. I'm not your enemy.'

The boy wriggled and kicked. John Norman let go of him and held his hands up in the air. 'I'm not going to hurt you.'

Sam stood still, shivering.

'Look, let's sit down for a moment at the officer's table. "I'll have some steak and make it quick. And a glass of wine,"' John Norman drawled in a high-pitched voice and clicked his fingers.

Sam giggled at his imitation of the superior young officer with the wispy beard. John Norman sat down opposite him. 'So what's going on? Is it Bert?'

Sam looked up, his face full of a wordless despair.

'He works you too hard? Does he hit you?'

Sam nodded. 'That's not the worst of it.'

'So what else...?' Suddenly John Norman knew. But how to ask the question? 'Does he er...lay hands on you? Interfere with...'

Sam nodded. His eyes looked less wild but then misted over and slid away towards the door. John Norman turned.

'What the hell are you two layabouts up to?' Bert had sneaked in quietly for such a lumbering man.

'We've cleared everything away.' Sam's voice was a squeak. 'John Norman here helped me.'

'Well, you can bugger off now.' Bert padded up to them, scowling. John Norman stared back. He clenched his fists to stop them trembling and took his time getting to his feet. 'I'll be back, tomorrow,' he said, still staring. He willed himself to stride slowly through the door.

Chapter 20

The next day

John Norman went to bed, his mind coiling and twisting, like a heap of ropes. He had to do something but what? Rab came in at the end of his watch and sat down to pull off his shoes.

'I've got to talk to you,' John Norman said.

Rab scratched an armpit and groaned. 'I'm too tired. It can wait.'

'No, it can't. I'm just back from the galley.'

Rab held out his hand. 'You've brought me some tasty leftovers.'

'No. I hadn't time to think about that. It's Sam I was thinking about.'

'Fancy him do you? He's a bit skinny. And grubby.' Rab laughed.

'Cut it out. I'm not joking.'

'OK, keep your hair on. It happens. A bit of buggery. All those weeks at sea and no women. Stop looking so shocked. You Highlanders are a prim lot.'

'The lad's terrified of Bert.'

'Well, leave it for now. Wait till tomorrow.' Rab yawned, stretched out under his blanket and was soon snoring.

John Norman took a long time to drop off. When he finally did his mind was tossed with strange dreams of a boy trussed up and thrown onto a luggage rack. The train hurtled through a tunnel and he was flung down onto the floor, howling in fear. John Norman rushed to his aid and at that moment he jolted awake, his heart hammering.

'You woke me up with all your shouting and moaning in your sleep,' Rab complained in the morning. John Norman pretended he hadn't heard. He would have to sort the problem out on his own. He went to serve up the officers' breakfasts, determined to talk to Sam again. The boy avoided his eye and kept scurrying back to the galley whenever John Norman drew near. He looked even worse today, hobbling as if he was in pain. John Norman hung around after everything was cleared up. He knew Bert would be gasping for a fag out on the deck. Once he had shuffled out John Norman pounced.

'You're avoiding me,' he said trapping the boy by the sink.

'Let me go. I don't want to talk.'

'But you can't go on like this. I've been thinking. You could come and sleep with us deck hands. And I should tell the Capt...'

'No! Don't do that. You'll make things worse.'

'But you can't go on like this. It's wrong.'

'I wish I'd never told you. Stop poking your nose in.' Sam spat the words out and lunged past John Norman, leaping up the companionway to the deck before John Norman could stop him. What should he do now? He was getting pulled under by currents he knew nothing about. But how could he pretend he didn't know what was happening to Sam? He couldn't abandon the lad even if he regretted confiding in him. Grandad Duncan would know what to do. Feeling lighter, he went in search of the old sailor. He found him on watch duty. 'What's wrong lad? You look as if you lost a tenner and found sixpence.'

John Norman took a deep breath and blurted out, 'It's Sam. Bert's hitting him and bugg...buggering him too. I wanted to tell the captain but Sam won't hear of it.' He could feel his cheeks reddening.

Duncan took his time replying, 'No, best not get the Old Man involved.'

'But why not?'

'Hold on. It ain't right what Bert's doing but it won't help the lad if we set all the fire alarms off. I'll have a word with Bert. Tell him to lay off.'

'I told Sam he could bunk down with us.'

'There's not room to swing a cat as it is.' He held up his hand to stop John Norman protesting. 'You're not helping the lad if you make it awkward for everyone else. Leave it with me. Slowly, slowly catchee monkey.'

John Norman found it strange that no one else he had told seemed as dismayed as he was about what was going on. Still, he was relieved to leave things in Grandad's hands. The bosun called him to have a turn at steering the boat. John Norman was thrilled to have the chance. So the time passed quickly and Sam slipped out of his mind. On his way to bed he bumped into Duncan. 'Did you speak to...'

'Have you seen the boy?' the old sailor interrupted him.

'No, I've not been near the galley since breakfast. Why do you ask?'

'He's nowhere on the ship.'

'What do you mean?'

Duncan stayed silent, waiting for understanding to seep into John Norman's mind.

'Overboard?'

Duncan nodded.

'But how? An accident? Or jumped?' John Norman felt faint. The truth was flooding over him now, threatening to sink him. 'Is the captain turning back?'

Duncan slowly shook his head. 'It's too late. He wouldn't last more than a few minutes in these cold waters.'

John Norman staggered as he felt his legs sagging. 'He wouldn't have done it if I hadn't interfered.'

He longed to be reassured but Duncan sighed and said, 'You can do more harm sometimes by interfering.'

'How do I live with myself?' John Norman struggled not to wail but he could hear that his voice was wavering.

'You weren't the one who hurt the boy, the one who made his life hell. Maybe he tripped in the dark. We'll never know.' He seized John Norman's arms and shook them. 'Put it behind you.

"Accidents happen at sea," don't they? We'll soon be at Montreal. You'll have other things to occupy your mind.'

But how could he think about anything else? He searched the ship again, willing Sam to be lurking under the cover of a lifeboat, in the engine room, even in the officers' cabins he was not supposed to enter. He leant over the rail to stare at the sea, calm today, with its endless waves cresting and retreating. He imagined the horror of leaping in, limbs flailing and mouth spluttering for breath. Maybe Sam could swim? Then he would be struggling against the creeping chill, regretting his action and bellowing for help. Until the cold stopped his heart and he sank unnoticed to the bottom. That was the worst of it. Sam was an orphan with no one to mourn his death. No rumble of the sea, sob of the wind or scream of a gull to mark his end. Nothing left of him. No smear of oil on a rope, scuff marks on the deck or creased photo on his bed.

'Hey, come on. You're not thinking of jumping in too?'

John Norman jolted as he felt Sean's hand on his shoulder. 'No, but I keep thinking how miserable and lonely he must have been.'

Sean crossed himself. 'A poor lost soul. May he find peace.'

They stood side by side. 'Duncan told me to find you,' Sean said after a while. 'I'm to work as a steward until we get to Montreal and you're to take over my deck duties.'

'I'm grateful for that.'

'Don't thank me. The bosun was pleased. You're a better seaman than me, so he said. He told Duncan you should look to getting your papers.'

John Norman couldn't stop a spark of joy at hearing what the bosun had said. No one had ever thought him capable of passing exams before.

'We can't have a burial service but the captain's saying some words tomorrow,' Sean said before leaving him.

The captain's words were rushed and mumbled. John Norman

heard them as a drone, not as anything that made sense. But then the bosun brought out a sailcloth sack and lowered it overboard. John Norman gasped. Had someone found Sam's body after all?

'It's weighted down with fire bars,' Duncan whispered in his ear. 'It's better to have something to put over the side.'

John Norman nodded. It was better. Sam was somewhere, rather than nowhere.

Chapter 21

A week later

John Norman was leaning over the rail as they docked at Montreal. In spite of Sam's death he couldn't stop feeling excited. His heart aloft, fluttering and waving. They had passed through the open gape of the St Lawrence. It was strange how all harbours seemed familiar even though each was different. There was always shipping arriving and leaving, the dockside stacked with crates, the relief of landing safely. It was the scale that varied. This wide waterway was full of giant cargo ships. He remembered all those postcards Iain had sent home from ports around the world, bright fragments propped up on the mantelpiece. He could send them himself now, even to Iain. That would make him laugh but it would be proof that John Norman was a proper man, a hardened sailor, caught up with his cousin at last.

His conscience prodded him. He had family he could write to. He wasn't adrift like Sam. He knew that Mamma would be proud to receive his letter, to tell everyone about it and keep it folded inside her Bible. More important, though, a letter would set her mind at rest. He went below and sat on his bunk to write but found himself chewing his pencil while he pondered what to say. He couldn't write about Sam's death. How could he explain? She would never understand what the boy had suffered. It would only distress her. She would be torn between pity and her belief that taking your own life was a sin.

Dear Mamma,
I've arrived safely. i better not say where. i'm well and the food is *
good. The other lads are fine. None from the highlands though. The
bosuns pleased with me. said i should aim to get my papers.

Give my love to Pappa and the girls. Tell Lexie I hope shes still getting hold of sweeties. I bet she begs for other peoples rations.
    Your loving son,
    John Norman

Not much but they would be amazed that he had written at all. He put the letter into his pocket to wait for when he had a chance to post it ashore. His fingers bumped into a ragged scrap of paper and he fished it out. Felicity's address. For a moment he was buffeted by homesickness as he remembered Lexie in a fit of the giggles holding the paper aloft and making him jump up to reach it.

'She's very ladylike, your posh girlfriend. Very keen she was that I give you her address.'

'She's not a girlfriend. It's something girls do, isn't it, offering to write to lonely sailors and cheer them up?'

'You can't fool me. All those fishing trips together.'

He had stuffed the paper into his pocket and refused to say anything more. Should he write to her? She could be so stand-offish but she had bothered to come and find him. And dealt with his nosey wee sister. Despite her being a lady there was something lost about her, something that left her open to bullies, a little like Sam. And she was the only other person his age he knew who had to wear damned spectacles. He found another sheet and, sighing, chewed the pencil again. What on earth could he say? What did they have in common, apart from bad eyesight? Well, two important things – they both loved Skye and fishing. He scribbled quickly and was soon back on deck.

'Glad to see you, lad. You've been a lone wolf the last few days.' Grandad Duncan appeared at his shoulder.

John Norman nodded. He didn't feel up to talking.

'Time to find a job, eh?'

'How do you mean? I'll be back on this boat, once she's loaded.'

'You've not heard? She's to be refitted for the convoy. Could take weeks.'

'What will I do?'

'Don't look so worried. Happens all the time. Some lads get jobs on the docks or the slaughterhouse. But that's heavy work. You'd be better as a night watchman or in a bar.'

John Norman ran back to get his gear and ask the others what they were doing. But Rab and Sean had already left. He hurried ashore, his eyes smarting with pain and disappointment. Why had they dumped him? He could believe it more of Rab but Sean had seemed decent. Duncan stood on the quay watching him clattering down the gangplank and took his arm. 'They stick with their own, those lads, clannish. Let's get a drink and see what gives.'

If Greenock had seemed enormous the Montreal docks were never ending. If Archie had ended up here he would never find him. They stopped at a bar that seemed less noisy than the others.

'You let me buy you a drink,' John Norman said.

'Two beers, please' he asked at the bar. He was surprised to be served by a young woman, with reddish hair and a wide smile.

'I love your accent! You're Irish?'

'No, Scottish. From the Highlands – the Isle of Skye.'

'Pa, come over here. There's someone who might be a relative.'

A burly man with a ruddy face approached, wiping raw hands on a tea towel.

'This guy, what's your name? is over from Skye.'

John Norman introduced himself. 'I'm Pam Gillies and this is my Pa, David. My Great Grand Daddy came from Skye to Nova Scotia. That's right, isn't it, Pa?'

'He did. Fished first. Then worked in the mines in Sydney. My Pa moved over here – for an easier life, he thought. Married a French Canadian and ruined the breed.' He roared with laughter.

By this time Duncan had wandered over, wondering what had delayed his drink.

'Here's my shipmate, Duncan. He's shown me the ropes on my first trip.'

'He's a good sailor is John Norman. Works hard and learns fast. Needing a job ashore while our boat's refitted.'

John Norman's cheeks grew hot but he was pleased at Duncan's praise.

'No problem. You can work here, with bed and board. I'll even up your wages if we turn out to be related.' David slapped him on the shoulder.

So it was settled. John Norman slept in a storeroom behind the bar. It was bare except for a bed and a chest. But it was a proper mattress, not a lumpy thing stuffed with straw. He enjoyed not having to share. It was like being back at home where, as the only boy, he had the right to a room of his own. Not like his sisters who had to bed down together and were always squabbling. When they checked out their genealogy he discovered that he wasn't related to the Gillies' at all but they couldn't have been kinder, nonetheless. He ate all his meals with them and at first he dared to hope that Pam might be interested in him. But within a day or two he found out that she was engaged to a strapping young docker called Charlie. Canadians, John Norman decided, were friendly and talkative by nature. They spoke to everyone as if they were old friends. Any Highland reserve must have sunk in the Atlantic when they emigrated. He fell into a teasing, joking way with Pam, like with an older version of Lexie.

His days fell into a pattern. Hard work, dense and dreamless sleep and mountainous meals. He served in the bar, dragged in new barrels and swilled out glasses until late when he downed a beer or two himself. After that he fell into bed, taking off his shoes but sometimes too exhausted to remove his clothes. Now and then he wandered along the docks but he was wary of going into the city. Most sailors seemed to be the same, anchored to where they could see and smell the sea. Duncan came in for a regular drink in the early evening. He had found work as a night watchman and digs with a widow who fed him well.

'I'm like a cat. Always land on my feet,' he said with a grin. He had bumped into Rab and Sean who were working at the slaughterhouse, near the docks. John Norman's life felt full and he didn't miss their company, especially Rab with his rough tongue.

Then one night Rab and Sean strolled into his bar. They were already half cut. John Norman didn't want to banter with them. Their presence brought back memories of Sam. He greeted them and walked away to collect empty glasses from the other tables but he could still hear them.

'Aye, we have some fun with the animals. Wrestle them with their horns. Give 'em a shove or a kick to get them going.' Rab was boasting to a stranger. 'Better than being on a bloody boat.'

'Had a race, riding the sheep until one of the eejits tripped and broke its leg.' Sean spluttered over his beer.

'Talking of riding, it's time we found those lassies again. Do you think yon wee virgin, John Norman, will join us?' Rab raised his voice.

John Norman clenched his fist around a glass and slipped away out of earshot.

Chapter 22

October 1940

'You're a good worker. I'll keep you on, if you want.'

John Norman gaped at David Gillies. 'But I'm back on my boat soon.'

David shrugged. 'Think about it. The offer's open.'

John Norman swabbed the floor, his mop and his thoughts swishing and swirling. Duncan had told him stories of sailors jumping ship or making off.

'I knew a lad got left behind in California. Drank too much, overslept, ran to the docks to see the lights of his boat winking at him from out at sea. Decided he liked the life there. Travelled around, hitching lifts on trains. Got a berth back from San Francisco months later.'

'And was he put in prison?'

'Good Lord no. Good sailors are too valuable to lock up.'

He could change his mind and stay. Plenty of Highlanders had emigrated to Canada over the years. What was different for him? Shame. A stain that couldn't be wiped out. Mamma hated him being in danger at sea but she was proud too. How could he ever tell her or Pappa that he had bolted?

'You look down in the mouth, lad.' He jumped as he felt Duncan's hand on his shoulder. 'Feeling homesick? Well, I've heard we're sailing the day after tomorrow. Into London and then a wee rest. Have you bought your presents for home yet? And stuff to sell on?'

'Sell on?'

'Aye, watches, make up, lighters. You can make a bomb with those.'

John Norman shook his head. 'In Glasgow maybe. What would folk say if I tried that on at home?'

He couldn't go back empty handed though. He would have to venture into Montreal now, towards that green bump they called a hill and those spires spiking the sky. He walked through the old port alongside the St Lawrence, craning his neck at the fancy buildings but shying away from the grand churches with their Catholic showiness. He could never think of staying here, too foreign. Plenty of shops, though. He made himself saunter in and point to what he wanted when a gust of French hit him. Tins of ham, maple syrup and a hairnet for Mamma, tobacco for Pappa. For the girls, silk stockings, hair clips and brooches. Chocolate and sweeties of course for Lexie and two colourful postcards of the city, one for home and one for Iain, just to show him he was catching up. He spotted the sign for a seamen's club across the road, written in English as well as French, thank goodness. He could pop in for a quick cup of tea before he went back to the bar.

He nodded at the handful of men who were drinking and reading newspapers. He didn't speak as he didn't know if they understood English. He sat down at a corner table and took the postcards out of his pocket. Maybe the government would censor them for giving away where he was? Well, a good reason for not writing much.

'*Soon be back*' would do for Mamma and Pappa.

'*different here from Portree*' for Iain. He would see the joke.

A smiling older woman approached him, holding out a cup. 'Coffee?' she asked. He nodded, not liking to say he preferred tea.

'We've got boxes for you brave lads.' She handed over a shoe box. Socks for the troops, he thought, like Mamma knitted. He didn't expect to be getting them himself. 'Thank you.'

'You're very welcome, I'm sure. There's a bag of doughnuts too.'

He frowned in puzzlement. 'You've not eaten them before? Very good with coffee. I make them all the time for my husband.

He's American.'

When she turned away he opened the box. Socks, of course, but also a thick navy pullover, scarves and balaclavas too. He would give some of it to Iain. He nibbled the doughnut. The sweet breadiness of it hit his tongue. He gobbled down the whole lot and licked all the sandy grains of sugar from his lips. He sighed. Going home, a deep-water sailor with money heavy in his pocket. He would keep out of the way of Rab and Sean. Finish knitting those socks too. That would impress Mamma.

But Rab and Sean weren't aboard. 'Scunners. Doing the dirty on their mates.' Duncan spat when he told John Norman. 'We're better without scum like them.'

The two sailors who came in their stead were Aberdonians, capable but silent men. There were changes to the boat too. The passenger accommodation had been taken away to give more cargo room and her decks cleared to house a couple of guns. John Norman stroked one of the barrels, his eyes gleaming. Third Officer Johnson was watching. 'Leave it alone. It's for trained gunners, those who can see well enough to spot a U-boat on the horizon.'

'I hope the sub has special ammo for idiots like him,' he said to Duncan later.

'Aye, but don't jest about shelling. We don't want to wish it on us.'

They weren't travelling alone this time but as part of a herd. He counted over twenty vessels, lumbering tankers, low in the water and steamers of all sizes, some carrying iron, others like their ship, filled with grain.

'It'll be fun and games keeping this lot together. And there's our sheepdog.' Duncan pointed at a naval sloop. 'I heard the old man swearing about the commodore. "Bloody trumped up old bugger. Covered in gold braid like a frigging Christmas tree. Bloody rules – no straggling, no romping ahead, no smoking funnels. What's he know about sailing? He's our leader, God help us until we meet two more of the buggers nine days out. We'll look after ourselves, thank you bloody much."'

John Norman laughed. 'We're faster than the tankers. We can steam out of danger, can't we?'

Duncan took his time replying. 'Aye, we've a chance, laddie.'

Once they were through the fog swaddling the Canadian coast the weather stayed calm and clear. John Norman was relieved. All the hands kept telling him how terrifying Atlantic storms were.

'We need high seas on the way back to keep the U-boats away,' Duncan said, but John Norman wasn't listening. No stewarding for him this time. He was happy to be working as a deckhand as well as being on watch at all hours. He enjoyed the peace of being on deck at night when sea and sky blurred together. It was an escape from the tension on the boat, the crackle in the air like waiting for thunder. Everyone was willing the voyage to be over and their cargo safely landed.

On the fourth evening out he was on watch and struggling to keep his eyes open. He knew the U-boats liked to come to the surface and attack as night fell. Like breaching whales they were hard to see. If only he could sense their presence, smell them as he did with shoals of fish. Here he had only his fuzzy eyesight. He could see the shapes of the nearest ships, the lighter vessels that could make a good speed. The puffers would be wallowing in the rear. He screwed up his eyes as he saw a bulkier outline cloaked in smoke. One of the stragglers trying to catch up. 'The commodore won't like that smoke,' he was thinking when a flash ripped the sky, like sudden lightning. But it wasn't an arc of lightning, rather a ripening and bursting fire flower, splattering seeds of flame along the hull of the puffer. They sprouted and sprang up the masts as if they would devour the sky itself. He was mesmerised by the terrible splendour of it but he must have shouted because Duncan appeared from the other side of the vessel, stood by him and clasped his trembling hand.

'It's terrible, lad, but there's nothing anyone can do.'

His instinct was to pull away. He wasn't a child or a frightened beast but he found the contact quietened him nonetheless. More men appeared, staring and pointing open mouthed. With a final squeeze Duncan loosened his grip. They all watched the wounded vessel shudder and jerk herself upright before listing again and slipping under the waves stern first. It happened in an instant. It was as if the boat had never been there. Sucked under with no ripples, only a spreading lake of treacly oil.

At once they were speeding away, the engines straining. All the vessels were fleeing, scattering and skittering through the waves. Morning brought a guilty relief at being alive mixed with pity for the sailors who had sunk with no chance of escape.

'Why did the boat go down so fast?' John Norman asked Duncan.

'It was carrying iron. No chance of staying afloat.'

'Thank God we were spared.'

'Spared? What's God got to do with it, laddie? Blind chance, that's all. Just make sure you keep off tankers. They're sitting on explosives.'

John Norman was surprised at Duncan's anger. 'Bitter experience, lad. Some folk see the hand of God in what happens or think they'll be safe if they keep some lucky charm with them. I learnt in the Great War. Called up to the Western Front. Going over the top with my best mate Tom, side by side. A shell ripped off his head and I was untouched, except for being spattered with his blood and brains. It could have been me but it was him. Where's the meaning in that, eh?'

The storm attacked the convoy later that day. A new threat to their lives that made them scupper the memories of the stricken ship. John Norman had been at sea in bad weather but that was like churned up bathwater compared to the power of the Atlantic. The world turned upside down with waves climbing to the heavens, scraping and scouring the sky as if it was the seabed and the stars had become shells. Waves like mountains freed of their moorings, soaring up, range after range of them. A world being created and destroyed before his eyes. No one on board could eat or sleep. They couldn't turn their backs on the sea or it would swallow them whole. On the second night John Norman lay in a stupor on his bunk when he had a waking nightmare, as if the storm was pouring into his cabin. He could see a helpless ship being flung by the sea, swallowed whole and then spat out by the waves. Each time it sank lower in the water. It was bobbing blindly in a watery gulley until a final breaker swiped it up, tilted it on the crest and tossed it upside down.

John Norman's whole body was shaking and he was glad he was on his own. The vision was so clear. Was it second sight? Was he foreseeing what would happen to this boat? No. It was a different ship, helpless because its engines had failed. He remembered Grandma saying how second sight came unbidden, a curse and a burden. It warned you about what was going to happen, not to you but to someone close to you and you were powerless to stop it. He had nodded, half listening to her but now he was shaken. Who could it be? Murdo? But he would be aboard some naval ship, not a boat like the one he had seen. With a shudder he remembered Duncan talking about blind chance. The two soldiers running side by side, one killed and one saved. With his head in his hands he remembered Archie telling him to go first when they signed on their berths. What was it he had shouted when he was in his cups? 'I'm on some old puffer.' One drowned and one saved?

He tried to light a cigarette but couldn't still his fingers. He would have to keep his fears to himself or the others would laugh, even Duncan. Sailors might be superstitious but unless they were Highlanders they laughed at the idea of second sight. The storm wore itself out the next day. There was still the worry about colliding with other boats as the convoy shook itself back into order. Sailors were used to navigating on their own, not having to march in time and as they approached the port of London they were forced to huddle closer together. John Norman couldn't banish the feeling of dread, like a dead finger stroking the back of his neck but he was glad that he would soon be ashore. He would collect his money and have a day or two in the big city before catching the train home.

Chapter 23

November 1940

John Norman was horrified by what he saw when he came ashore. Craters where buildings had been bombed to kingdom come, leaving no trace, like that poor ship. Buildings that seemed whole until you came closer and saw the eyeless, glass-blown windows or missing roof. Headless like Duncan's friend. After a night in the Mission he knew he had to escape from the destruction.

'Where's Trafalgar Square?' he asked a man. It was the only place in London he could think of. He replied in a strange accent, saying something that sounded like *Est hand.*' John Norman walked in the direction the man pointed out. It was a long time until he came to wider streets with better looking houses and shops, ones that were still intact although there were gaps, like knocked out teeth. He began to breathe more freely but he had no idea where he was going except he wanted to stay out in the open where he could see what was going on.

A piercing shriek made him duck and cover his ears. Everyone was running. A man in a white helmet grabbed his shoulders and shook him. He put his hands either side of John Norman's face and turned his head sideways. 'Down those steps.' He stumbled down them, gagging with the press of people crushed against his ribs. If he tripped here he would be trampled. As he reached the bottom the weight of bodies eased a little. His arm banged against something hard. A cigarette machine of all things, set against the wall. He squeezed himself against the brickwork and closed his eyes, willing himself to think of home. Not the lurching sea but the still mountains. After a moment he groped in his pocket for a cigarette.

'John Norman, isn't it?' The sudden voice jolted him so that he dropped the cigarette. He fumbled for it and turned, frowning.

'Fancy seeing you here. It's a small world isn't it?' Now he recognised the posh English tones. Why here? But he wasn't surprised. In the last few months he had learnt that anything could happen.

'Come on. Surely you recognise me? I've not changed that much.'

'No. Hello Felicity. How are you?' She did seem the same, hunching up to hide her height. But different too, not as gaunt. Her face had altered too, her nose was less beaky. She had grown into her features. Grown up altogether, he supposed. He wondered if he seemed different to her.

'I'll be fine when we can get out of here. I've not been caught in an air raid before, have you?'

He shook his head. 'Want a fag?'

'Why not? I don't usually smoke but I need something to steady my nerves. I thought I'd be flattened by the crowd.'

He busied himself lighting up for them both. She inhaled and started spluttering.

'I can tell you're no smoker.' They both laughed.

'I was thinking about Skye, trying to compose myself.'

'Me too,' he said but his words were swallowed by a siren.

'That's the "All Clear". We can go now,' Felicity said. He reached out to guide her up the steps but she was already charging ahead. He hurried in her wake and followed her as she strode down the street, not knowing what else to do. She half-turned. 'I need a cup of tea after all that excitement. We'll find a Corner House somewhere.' She rushed along, not waiting for an answer.

There she goes again, taking charge, he thought, but he didn't mind. He was still feeling amazed at her sudden appearance. Relieved too to see a familiar face in this huge, unpredictable city.

'What's it like being in a convoy?' she asked him once they

were settled at a table. He didn't know what to say. He was scared he might burst into tears.

'Not so bad. It has its moments. We got through it.'

She waited, as if expecting more. 'What are you doing?' he asked.

'Oh, clerical work for the Foreign Office, you know.' She shrugged.

She seemed to be holding back too. He gulped down his tea. His swallowing seemed loud in the silence. 'Not anything dangerous, then?'

She glared at him. 'It's still important war work.'

He stayed silent. She was as touchy as ever.

'It's not just typing, like people think, but recording vital information.' He could see she was getting steamed up. 'It's cracking German codes to help the Navy and...oh.' Her hand flew up to her mouth. 'My goodness I'm not meant to talk about it. I'll be hung, drawn and quartered as a traitor.' She was all red in the face and looked as if she was about to cry.

'It's safe with me. I'm not going to tell anyone.' His hand surprised him by shooting out and landing on hers where it lay clenched on the table. 'This war's no joke, is it?'

'I don't know what's the matter with me. Well, I do, I suppose. I heard today that a girl I used to know was killed. She was an agent abroad, I think. Her mother was out of her mind with grief and yelled at me. As if it was my fault she was dead.' He was amazed to see a waterfall of tears streak down her cheeks and drip onto the tablecloth. Just like Lexie when she was feeling hurt. More than anything else he was aware of her turning her hand over so that her fingers squeezed his.

'Silly me,' she sniffed and pulled out an embroidered handkerchief with her other hand but she still held onto him. 'You don't expect it to happen to someone you know.'

'Do you want to go outside for some fresh air?'

She nodded. He released her hand while they stood up. She

blew her nose and headed for the door while he paid the bill.

'I don't know London. Where do you want to go?'

'One of the parks. I know – St James,' she replied. He remembered her as having plenty to say for herself but now she fell silent. What could he talk about that wasn't upsetting stuff about the war? He spoke about Montreal, finishing with the story of the wonderful doughnuts. She perked up at hearing that. 'Sounds better than the grey stews we get at work. Mind you, Winnie, my landlady, makes delicious rabbit pies. She's very kind.' Suddenly her face shuttered again.

'Like Grandad Duncan. He showed me the ropes.'

By the time they reached the park he felt more at ease. There was plenty to see and talk about. They smiled at the noisy, grumbling ducks. 'They're just like my old aunties, waddling and clucking on their way to church,' John Norman said. 'But what on earth are those funny big birds over there?'

'The pelicans? You must know the rhyme? A wonderful bird is the pelican, his beak holds more than his belly can.'

He shook his head.

'Everyone learns that at school. Edward Lear, isn't it?' She looked at her watch and gasped. 'I must go. I need to get back before Pa arrives.' Her fair skin reddened. 'I got your note. Well, Pa did. It's best if you write to me care of Winnie. I'll give you the address.'

She scribbled it down for him and then she was off in a flurry. He felt dismissed, a delivery boy again. Being with her was like bracing yourself on a rolling deck against a gusting storm. Never mind. Tomorrow he would head for home and the family again. He hoped that Iain would be back. They would have so much to talk about.

Chapter 24

November 1940

The journey home took nearly three days. Three days of tripping over kitbags piled in the corridors of carriages, standing in crowded lurching trains and waiting in grubby stations. But at last he came ashore from the steamer in the evening, shouldering his kitbag and heaving the case. It must be all the presents that weighted it down, especially the tins of ham. Why not call at Uncle Rob's first before climbing the brae? He would be sure of a welcome there and would find out if Iain was at home. After that he could brave Mamma and see if she had forgiven him. He whistled as he reached the door and called out a welcome. The door was flung open. 'Have you no respect, at all?'

He tripped backwards. Auntie Cathie's eyes were flickering everywhere like a snake's tongue, her hair tangled and the buttons of her blouse done up wrong so that the collar gaped.

'I'm just off the steamer. What's happened?'

But he knew of course. Not Murdo, not Archie but the one he had never suspected. His big, brave cousin.

'We had the telegram last week. Lost at sea. Not even a body to put in the earth.' Auntie Cathie spoke in a flat whisper.

'Did the engines fail and the boat go down in a storm?'

'They haven't told us. What difference does it make? He's gone.' Her voice rose in a wail and she clamped her hand over her mouth. 'Go home, John Norman. Your mamma's lucky to still have a son.'

She shut the door in his face. He stood staring at it and scratched with his nail at the peeling paint. It must be a mistake. The government had got the wrong name. It was a stranger who had died, not Iain. As he stumbled up the hill an unbearable thought almost felled him so that he had to lean against a wall.

Had his vision caused Iain's death? Could he have stopped it happening? Would Iain still be alive if he had protested at Duncan's faithless words? If he had prayed instead of staying silent? He picked up his case and trudged up the hill. He would have to batten down those notions. He couldn't speak to anyone about them. It would cause too much pain. Make him sound crazy.

When he walked in Mamma fell into his arms. 'Thank God you're safe,' she kept saying. No reproaches as he had feared. No fatted calf either. It was a household reduced by mourning. But a space was made for him by the fire, in the middle of them all. Reduced in numbers, Lexie the only one of his sisters there. Reduced in spirits too. Mamma was subdued, curled in on herself. He would have preferred her as she used to be, fists up and fierce. Murdo, Donnie and Angus all away. Archie too, and safe as far as anyone knew.

'Why not come along to the Home Guard tonight?' Pappa asked him the next day at breakfast. 'You'll see some faces you know.'

John Norman shrugged.

'Go and keep your father company. Better than mooching around the house.' Mamma seemed to have recovered some of her fire again.

'You should see them parading – with broomsticks,' Lexie giggled with her mouth full of porridge. 'Some of them in their coms with old army tunics on top. And some had old uniforms but they were too fat for them and had a piece added to the back in a different colour. I feel really safe in my bed with them to protect me. They'd scare any Germans witless.'

'Don't speak with your mouth full. They were doing their best.' Mamma told her.

Lexie pouted. 'I wish I was old enough to do something.'

'I hope the war will be over before you're old enough,' Pappa said, getting to his feet and turning to John Norman. 'I don't suppose you want to come out fishing?'

'Not today. I've had enough of boats for now.' But John Norman found that he couldn't settle. He couldn't believe that he wouldn't see Iain again, couldn't talk to him about what it was like in the Atlantic. He felt aimless, hauled up on the beach. He walked with Lexie to school, hoping her chatter would cheer him up. She skipped along beside him, still talking about the war.

'Miss MacLean makes us go and collect stray bits of wool from the fences to spin for knitting. "Waste not, want not", she says. My friend Maryann thought she saw silk from a parachute caught in the wire. She shrieked her head off. "The Germans have landed. They'll shoot us all dead." It was only a piece of old rag. She's a scaredy cat. Miss MacLean says we mustn't help anyone asking for directions 'cos it might be a spy. "But my mamma says it's rude not to answer a grownup. I'll have to run away if I see someone I don't know," says Maryann. I think a foreigner would stand out, like a parrot among seagulls, don't you? A spy would have to sneak around at night. Dressed all in black, like a Wee Free. Maryann's mamma's always listening to that Lord Haw Haw and it puts the wind up her. He keeps saying Mr Churchill is lying about how many of our soldiers are being killed and...'

By this time they had reached the school gates. 'Aye, I'm sure you're right. Off you go now or you'll be late.'

After tea John Norman went out in the garden for a smoke. Pappa joined him and stoked up his pipe. 'The platoon's doing an exercise tonight – a raid against the North End lot at Kendram. We're getting some fast boats from the Navy but we're short of sailors to steer them.' He took a puff and waited.

John Norman sighed. 'Alright, I'll give you a hand but only on a boat. I'm not charging up the hill with a lot of *bodachs* and watch them keel over with heart attacks.'

'Well, I'm not a *bodach* yet awhile. The older ones are going in a truck over the *Bealach*. We're landing from the boats at Staffin bay. They'll be expecting us to head for Score Bay and come in the other direction. Dougie and some of the other lads helped build that NAAFI place and know the way in.'

Out in the moonless dark, steering a fast motorboat towards the broad U shape of Staffin Bay John Norman enjoyed himself more than he had expected. It was like being in the Boy Scouts again. Adventure without the bowel loosening fear. Like all those trips out with Iain but no Iain to share it with. He still couldn't believe he had gone for ever. He must be out there somewhere and one day he would do his old trick of sneaking up from behind, pouncing and covering John Norman's eyes. 'Caught you!'

He was glad that it was so dark that no one could see his glistening cheeks. He recognised a few of the sailors but they were mainly strangers, naval men in dark jerseys. They dropped the Home Guard soldiers and stepped ashore to stretch their legs before leaving. The men would march back later to base or return in the truck. As the sailors got ready to board John Norman hung back. He was wondering whether it might be better to join the raid after all, rather than sail back alone in the grip of his dark thoughts. As he waited undecided, he noticed one of the sailors standing watching him. The man came up, raised his balaclava and spoke.

'Excuse me. You look familiar. Are you Margaret MacPherson's brother by any chance?'

John Norman stared at the tall Englishman, with his confident smile. Then he gathered himself together. 'Aye,' he said.

'Pleased to meet you. I'm Simon Presnail, based at Kyle at the moment.' He thrust out an eager hand. 'And you must be John Norman. On leave from the Merchant Navy?'

John Norman found himself won over by Simon's grin. 'I don't think Margaret would be pleased to think she and I look so alike.' He was itching to ask if Simon was her boyfriend but before he could find the words another man came over, tapping at his wrist.

'Can't wait, I'm afraid. Go with the others if you want to. We can get your boat back,' Simon said.

John Norman nodded and ran after the others who were marching along the road much faster than he had expected, so fast that he got a stitch keeping up with them. Not that he would admit to it. Once they got close to the ruins of Duntulm Castle they turned up the back way, down through the gully towards the camp. They crawled along on their bellies while those who knew the layout ran ahead to cut through the barbed wire. Then they all charged into the building and up the stairs, blown by gusts of excitement. They found a handful of men there and tied them up.

'Better to be caught by Germans than by you lot. You'll be wanting revenge for us beating you at shinty,' one of them joked.

'No joking around, men. Go and find the rest of them,' Matheson the officer ordered. The platoon surged out and rounded up the others who were standing guard outside and looking in the wrong direction. They groaned and surrendered readily enough.

'Well that was a sneaky thing, coming up the back way like that,' their sergeant complained.

'All's fair in war,' Pappa said.

'One drink from the NAAFI. That's your lot. Then we'll go back to Portree,' the officer said.

'Aye, Sir. But there's no sign of the truck,' someone called out.

Soon there was a flurry of voices. 'Or of the *bodachs*. Where have they got to?'

'This lot must have got sick of army rations and put them in the cooking pot.'

'Must be desperate to eat those old boilers.'

'The truck maybe broke down on the way. They'll be huddled somewhere like lost lambs.'

'Aye but lambs with hip flasks.'

Matheson raised his hand for silence. 'We can't wait for them. They'll need to find their own way back.' He frowned. 'Finish the drinks. We'll have to set out at once to get back by daybreak.'

His order was met with muttering. 'Just let me go and have a look around,' John Norman said. He expected to hear digs about sending the blind to find the halt and lame but none came. 'He's got a good nose, this lad,' Pappa said.

'Very well. Have a scout round but we can't wait long.'

'It was odd how they were all such good losers. I think they've captured the truck and hidden it,' John Norman said as he and Pappa prowled around outside. He sniffed the air, lifting his head from side to side. 'Let's try down there.' He pointed towards a dip in the ground ahead, shadowed with trees. They slid down the slope and John Norman swept his torch beam across the rough grass. He plunged a fingertip into a darker patch and held it out for Pappa to sniff. 'Oil.'

They crept forward to a broken-down sheep fank and a ruined shed. The earth was churned up and behind the shed something jutted out, like a blunt snout. All was silent as they tiptoed towards it.

'There's the truck!'

'Watch it, lad. They might have posted guards.'

John Norman put his fingers to his lips. 'What's that noise?'

He ran behind the shed, jumping up and laughing as he lifted the tarpaulin at the back. There were the *bodachs,* snoring like cattle in a byre. Charlie Fraser started spluttering and coughing, waking the rest.

'It's yourself, John Norman. Back home from the sea?' He turned to the others. 'It's fine lads. It's our side here.'

'What happened?'

'They were lying in wait for us on the road. Saw our lights and took us as hostages. Drove the truck down here and tied us up.'

Old Donnie piped up. 'We whispered loudly that the rest of you were coming up in another truck. That confused them.'

'You could say we saved the day,' Charlie wheezed. 'All this excitement's not good for my heart, you know.' He tapped his chest on the left side. 'I get palpitations here.' Then he touched the right side. 'And here. Awful bad.'

'Well, Charlie we'll just have to call you *'dha chridhe'* (two hearts) from now onwards,' Pappa said. 'Let me untie you. Then you can get a dram before we head back.'

Chapter 25

The next day

'Well son, you did fine for a man who didn't want to come. That raid will get burnished into a grand tale. Maybe even a song.'

'But why didn't they just throw them out of the truck and make them walk home? Why keep them as hostages?'

'Aye, they wouldn't get much ransom money. Their wives would be glad to be rid of them. But they couldn't be hard on *bodachs*, could they?'

'Especially if they've two hearts.'

There was another surprise the next day. 'Margaret's bringing her young man over to meet us all,' Mamma told them.

'Young man?' John Norman said.

'And why not? She's a good-looking lass. Knows how to dress well too.'

He admitted that this was true. She had high cheek bones and clear blue eyes, like Pappa's. But the look in them was so different. Haughty, beautiful but untouchable, like a hawk when it turned its head to glare at you.

'What about your girlfriend? The posh Miss MacDougall?' Lexie grinned.

'And what about her? She went down to England long ago.'

'But she wanted me to give you her address. Did she write to you?' He kept quiet but Lexie kept probing. 'Have you seen her?'

'What gives you that idea, nosey miss?'

'Hush, the pair of you.' Mamma sounded tetchy. 'I need to think. What am I going to give them to eat? It needs to be something special.'

'Don't fret,' Pappa told her. 'What's wrong with herring and tatties?'

'I'll bake some rice pudding and scones, too. But first I must clean the house from top to bottom.'

'He's not an admiral coming to inspect us,' Pappa laughed.

'I suppose he will be from the Base? Only an officer would be good enough for Lady Margaret,' John Norman said.

'We'll know soon enough. I'm off out before your mother turns me upside down too.'

Mamma had just finished pushing the cushions into line when Margaret arrived with a burly, fair-haired man in uniform. 'This is Simon, Lieutenant Simon Presnail, I should say,' she announced.

'How kind of you to invite me. I'm so pleased to meet you all. But I've met you already John Norman on that exercise. I heard it went well, thanks to you.'

'But how did you recognise him?' Margaret asked.

'The family good looks, of course.' Simon said.

Margaret bridled. 'I've not got a nose like his.' But when Simon smiled at her she flushed and looked almost shy. He had an English voice but a clear one, without an accent. Once they had sat down Margaret was bursting to tell them all about him, how he came from Kent, used to be an accountant and went to a boarding school.

When she paused for breath he shrugged. 'None of that matters much when we're in the middle of a war, does it? Still, one good thing that's come out of it is being stationed in this lovely part of the world.'

Mamma glowed and even more so when he praised her food.

'Why have you given me cutlery when everyone else is using their fingers? Much more sensible with bony fish, isn't it? I've never eaten anything so tasty, especially after all the tinned stuff and stodge on board. One of the jobs I've been given for my sins is working out the menus. Everyone complains about the food aboard ship, don't they John Norman? In the end I took some of the biggest moaners, both officers and ratings, and showed them the stores. "You lot take charge and see if you can do better."'

'And did they?' John Norman asked.

'No chance. But they stopped grumbling so much, especially once they saw everyone on board was getting the same. I couldn't stand that nonsense of better rations in the Officers' Wardroom.'

He made John Norman feel as if he had always known him. Like sun spilling through the window, he made you want to smile, stretch out and loosen your collar. They were all affected by his easy ways but especially Margaret. She had changed into another being. Not a butterfly exactly but one of those delicate moths that hovered in the doorway when the lights were switched on, the ones with the soft pelt on their bodies and the frothy patterns on their wings.

Later the three men went out for a smoke and a walk. Simon offered them a fat cigar each. 'We get them for next to nothing.'

'It smells good,' John Norman said but after a deep puff he started to splutter. 'Are these the ones Churchill smokes? They must be what keep the old man going.'

Without the women there they talked a little about the war. 'It's you merchant sailors who'll win the war. Before it started I was a weekend sailor. Joined the Wavy Navy with notions of big sea battles. Some of the old hands thought convoy duty beneath them but convoys are our lifeblood. Without them we're beaten.'

'Aye, but our skipper couldn't stand your lot. He turned the air blue, cursing the naval commodore for ordering him around.'

'I bet he did. Some of those old fogeys must have served in Nelson's day. You've been on the Atlantic run?'

'Aye, I don't know where I'll go next. You get told your berth by the Pool. Avoid the Arctic runs if you can is what I've heard.'

'That's sound advice. You're chipping the ice away all the time. I've come back from the Med. We all cheered when we sank a U-Boat. That must be the worst death, though, trapped in a tin can at the bottom of the sea.' Simon shuddered.

'It's an odd thing. I always thought the sea was the enemy, your boat fighting the waves. I can't get used to the idea of other vessels turning on you.'

'I'm glad I only have to worry about catching fish,' Pappa said. 'Would you like to come out with us, Simon? It's a wee boat, I know, no engine, not as tidy as a naval ship.'

'You can say that again,' John Norman laughed, 'and it stinks of fish.'

'I'd like to but we're upping anchor tomorrow. We'll take that trip another time.' They all smiled but John Norman caught a wintry flicker in Simon's pale eyes. They turned back inside to have a dram. Gulping down hope.

Part 4

Felicity's Story

Chapter 26

December 1940

'I hope your father's fully recovered.'

For a second Felicity looked blankly at him before recovering and putting on a plucky smile.

'He's on the mend thank you, Commander Harrison. But he needs a long convalescence. He's thinking seriously about shutting up the London house and living in our home in the north of Scotland. It's such a distance. I was wondering if there might be any chance of me getting a transfer to work nearer him.'

The officer frowned.

'I know it's inconvenient but I do need to keep an eye on him. I'm his only family.' She looked down, biting her lip.

'It's extremely inconvenient. Most of the listening station jobs are reserved for uniformed personnel.'

'I understand. I don't want to be a nuisance.' She blinked at him and let her voice falter.

His eyes widened as she released a discreet sob. 'Now don't take on. I've not said a definite "No". You've worked well here after a shaky start. Leave it with me.'

'Thank you so much for your kindness.' She kept a subdued front but behind the blackout curtains her heart was dancing. What had come over her? She hadn't planned to lie like that. It was as if she had been taken over by a secret agent. Maybe she had been convincing because she hadn't planned it.

Felicity had returned to Winnie's house on Saturday, two days earlier, her nerves jangling after her trip to London. She had been so startled to see John Norman. Not an awkward delivery boy but a grown man. It felt like meeting him for the first time. She found herself worrying about what he thought of her. They were two figures stepping out of a canvas, their colours drying in the sunlight. But a sudden chill whipped up when she realised she could never take him back home and face Pappa's disapproval. How could she explain that to him without causing offence?

On the train back to Bletchley she had looked forward to seeing Winnie again and slipping back into her old routines. But like Alice in Wonderland she had sipped some strange potion and found herself bursting out of her old life. Winnie had smiled and hugged her but it wasn't the same. There was a gulf between them that was too wide to jump over. On Sunday morning she couldn't bear to go to Chapel and face Ted and his mother but she didn't want to offend Winnie by avoiding church. She had pretended to have a cold and stayed miserably in bed when Winnie left for the service. It wasn't just the awkwardness over Ted; she had felt she couldn't confide in Winnie about bumping into John Norman. She hadn't mentioned him ever before and now it felt too late. Her confusion and guilt took away her appetite and she struggled to eat much of the rabbit stew and apple pie at lunchtime.

'You must be feeling poorly, my dear. It's not like you to pick at your food.'

Felicity could hardly bear to look at Winnie's concerned face. 'I don't know why I'm not hungry. Maybe it's all that smoke and dirt on the train.'

'Back to the Park tomorrow, then?' Winnie said with forced brightness.

She nodded, too full of jumbled sensations to answer. All she wanted to do was to escape from this tight little life, the tedium of the endless filing, the disruption of ever-changing shifts that left her deflated but restless. John Norman had brought with him the salt taste of the sea. She was sick of pottering in a pond for toy boats. She wanted to go back to Skye, the only place that felt like home.

She battened down her hopes, just like the old days at school

and tried to make the best of things. Her friend Susan was all
fluffed up now that she had found a beau, a rather weedy one,
Felicity thought. He was a naval officer with a wobbling Adam's
apple and a weak chest. 'A fine mind,' Susan told her. 'That's
why he's been sent to the Park.'

'You can rub goose fat on his chest. That's a good remedy,'
Felicity had suggested.

Susan gave her a hard stare.

'Only jesting. Will he come to Scottish Country Dancing?'

'Maybe. He doesn't have a kilt.'

'I don't think that matters. He can always ask around for
one.' Felicity kept her face stiff as she imagined his legs, bent
twigs with lumpy bosses of kneecaps.

There were still the small pleasures of life even though they
weren't enough to stop her restlessness. She still enjoyed cycling
fast, whooshing downhill with her heart jumping as her feet
lifted from the pedals. Winnie was as kind as ever.

'I don't want you getting too thin so I've made a lardy cake.
Not much fruit, I'm afraid.' She shared her two ounces of
chocolate ration with Felicity to eat with their bedtime cuppa.
Her generosity made Felicity feel uncomfortable. They didn't
discuss Ted again and Winnie didn't suggest Felicity go to
Chapel. Instead she set off on Sunday mornings, calling out,
'Goodbye then. I'm off now,' in a too chirpy voice that didn't
mask the sigh at the end.

'Plod on. Chin up. Make do,' Felicity told herself as she
looked out of the window of the draughty hut on a rain plastered
afternoon. She glanced again at the seemingly fixed hands on
her watch.

'Ah, Miss MacDougall. Come to my office.'

How long had he been watching her? Was she to be
reprimanded for slackness?

'Further to our conversation...' The Commander sounded
like a legal letter. She was poised for disappointment. 'We need

fluent German speakers, ones who can follow the spoken word. You don't come into that category.'

Here we go, she thought. Her spirit slumped, like a dog disappointed in hopes of a walk.

'But you have shown a certain facility for filing code words quickly and accurately.'

The tip of her tail flickered.

'We also need a different sort of operator.' He paused to draw on his compost-smelling pipe.

Who is this royal "we"? He talks as if he was the government, Prime Minister Churchill himself. Felicity kept her eyes downcast to hide her frustration.

The disgusting tobacco was alight and reeking again. 'Those who can listen to another sort of language.'

Now he was talking in riddles, making no sense at all.

'Morse code. It's used for thousands of messages and picked up in various places away...'

She jerked her head up. 'Which various places, Sir?'

He frowned at her interruption. 'Where you would expect. Near the coast.'

'In Scotland, perhaps?'

'Possibly. Certainly well north of here. Now listen, young lady. I went to a great deal of trouble to arrange this. Do you realise that most of the women in these stations are ATS? It's only because of the urgent need for training more radio operators that they agreed at all. I expected more gratitude.'

'Sorry Sir. It's only because I'm so concerned to be nearer Pa.'

'That's why I pulled out all the stops on this occasion.'

It was amazing how a tremor in her voice could soften him. Time now for a brave little smile.

'Thank you, Sir. I won't let you down.'

'I trust not. You'll be sent your orders shortly. You'll have a period of intensive training before you're allocated to a station. Work diligently and you might have a say in where you're posted. That's all. Return to your desk now.'

'I'm so grateful to you.' This time she smiled with her whole face. His eyes brightened but he stayed tight lipped.

'Remember you mustn't mention anything about this posting to anyone else.' She was already going out the door as she mumbled agreement.

Chapter 27

December 1940–January 1941

Telling Winnie was tougher than she had imagined. 'I knew this would happen once you finished with Ted,' she sniffed, rummaging for her hanky in the folds of her pinny.

'Don't take on so.' Felicity's voice was gruff.

Winnie wiped her eyes. 'I knew you wouldn't settle again after that. I'm so cross with that fellow – and his snooty mother. She's spoilt him rotten. Too used to getting his own way.'

Felicity gaped. 'But I thought you were angry with me for turning him down and making things awkward.'

'Not at all. Would it have made a difference if I'd had told you that?'

Winnie looked so desolate that Felicity put her arms round her sloping shoulders, 'I don't know. Maybe it was going to London that changed things – put me on edge.'

'You were worried about your Dad being bombed?'

Felicity sighed. 'Yes, but he made light of it all. Said he couldn't leave his work. He was glad I was somewhere safer. One thing he let slip, though. It's haunted me ever since. He said that walking to work after a raid, it wasn't the bombed houses that were the worst, it was the dead bodies lying around the chimney stacks, like huge roosting birds. I suppose they were thrown up by the blast and caught there.'

'What a terrible thing, the poor souls.'

'But I've not told you the whole story. Let's have a cup of tea and I'll explain.'

They sat down in front of Winnie's fire. 'Look, I've found a few mint imperials,' Winnie said, delving into her pocket. 'They're only a little bit fluffy.'

'And I'm not fussy at all.' They both laughed and scrunched

the mints while Felicity told her about meeting John Norman. 'Seeing him again – how he's changed, made me restless. I want to get back to Scotland. It's the only place where I've really felt at home. I'm cut off from the real world at the Park.'

Winnie's eyes clouded for a moment before she said, 'And this wish to go to Scotland has nothing at all to do with this young sailor?'

Felicity snorted. 'Of course not. He's just a boy from a fisherman's family who I knew before the war. I only told Ted he was my boyfriend to annoy him. Then he dared to accuse me of being a slut.'

Winnie patted Felicity's hand. 'Well, you must do what's best for you. I shall miss you. Goodness knows what my next lodger will be like – one of those la-de-da types, I expect.'

'Well, I could mention it to Susan. She's always moaning about her rotten digs. She's not a bad sort. Even though she's got this boyfriend who looks like an overgrown thistle with a big spiky head.'

'He sounds like a sight to behold,' said Winnie laughing. 'Would you like another cuppa?' Felicity nodded and Winnie busied herself with the teapot. 'I know you can't say where you're going or what you're doing but you'll write to me, won't you, my dear?'

'Of course I will. I'm sure I shan't be going until after Christmas. I dare say Pa will be busy so I could stay here with you.'

'We could have a tree. I've got decorations from before the war in a box up in the loft. And we could ask the neighbours over,' Winnie said, her face lighting up.

'And I shall come back to see you. And to eat your apple pie.'

'I'm sure you will.' Winnie blew her nose. 'Talking of pies I must get dinner on.'

Christmas and New Year went by with no word of Felicity's new posting. If 1939 had been the 'phoney war' she was enduring the 'phoney job'. Everything carried on as usual. Every day she rattled the letter box to see if an envelope had got trapped in it. 'You'll break the spring if you keep doing that,' Winnie grumbled.

She had been hoping she would be away before the next night shift came round. Instead she found herself pushing her bicycle back home at 8 o'clock in the morning. She was so shaky with reined in frustration that she couldn't trust herself to balance on it. As usual Winnie had set out breakfast for her, thick slices of crusty bread although the butter was painted on these days rather than plastered. And there, propped up against her cup, was a buff envelope. She ripped it open and had to read it several times before the words stopped flickering. She was to travel to the Isle of Man for training in Morse code transmission.

'That's near Scotland, isn't it? Nearer than here anyway?'

Felicity laughed as she pulled Winnie round the kitchen in a clumsy jig. 'I'm leaving in three days' time. I'll write to you as soon as I'm settled in.'

'You must do that dear. How I'll manage with a new young lady, I don't know, what with the rationing getting so tight.'

'I saw you were eking out the butter. Never mind, you'll manage, Winnie. You always do,' Felicity shouted down as she ran up the stairs, her legs suddenly strong again and her head brimming with fresh hopes.

Chapter 28

February 1941

Felicity stood on the deck of the boat all the way to the Isle of Man. The wind and spray revived her. I'm not suited to stuffy inland places, she decided. The boarding house where she was billeted stood on the seafront of Douglas. There were ten women there, girls really. Most of them had just been called up from their homes in landlocked Midland counties. They bounced in excitement when they saw the sea, making Felicity feel quite middle-aged as she smiled at their squealing. Her bedroom was tiny but at least she had to share with only one other person. The other occupant was already there, unpacking a battered holdall. She had a solid body and looked older than Felicity. She lifted a square, heavy face and stared without smiling.

'How do you do? I'm Felicity.'

The woman peered suspiciously at her outstretched hand. 'I'm Bertha.'

Felicity looked around at the two iron bedsteads with their slumped mattresses crammed together into the attic space. 'Oh my goodness, it's like a maid's...' she blurted out before coughing to hide her mistake. Bertha gave her a funny look. Odd really. Before the war she wouldn't have stopped to think at all about what she said. She had got used to mixing with all sorts of people, she supposed. She didn't want to sound like one of those Debs at the Park who snickered about trips to Claridges.

She tried again. 'You're not in uniform, the same as me. The rest of them seem to be ATS or Wrens.'

Bertha grunted and carried on rummaging in her bag. Felicity almost gasped as she saw Bertha's left hand. It was scored with raised weals, cross hatched as if for a game of noughts and crosses. Worse, there were blotchy, purple bumps where the last three fingers should be. Felicity looked away but not quickly enough.

'Why don't you ask – instead of pretending you've not noticed?'

Felicity backed away. 'I'm...m sorry. I was rude to stare. How did it...?'

'How do you think? A bloody typewriter jumped up and bit me?'

Felicity flushed. She was struggling with Bertha's anger and her strange accent. The other girl seemed to relent. She sighed and said, 'Me job was in munitions. Out near Wolverhampton – a filling factory.'

'Filling?'

'Putting detonators into bombs. Good pay and me Da said it would be safer than the army.' Her laugh had a bitter ring. 'Me hand slipped.' She shrugged. 'But I could have been blown to smithereens.'

'Oh. How dangerous.'

Bertha gave her a funny look again.

'I was doing clerical work before.'

'You would be.' Bertha's voice was loaded with contempt.

Felicity drew herself up to her full height. 'It's important work but I'm not allowed to talk about it. I'm surprised to hear you speaking so freely.'

Bertha grinned. 'Good on you, our kid. You're not such a drip, then. "Be like dad, keep mum: careless talk costs lives,"' she chanted. 'They had that on the factory wall. It's all a plot to keep the workers down. That's what me Da says.' She laughed at Felicity's open mouth. 'Stop catching flies. You'd better hurry up and unpack your stuff.'

They went downstairs where they had to line up for a doctor to test their hearing. Next, they were ordered into what had been the dining room of the boarding house. The tables were all piled up in a corner and covered with dust sheets. The girls unstacked the chairs and sat waiting in a row. A brisk ATS officer marched in.

'I'm Captain Turner. We're by the sea but don't imagine you're here on holiday. You have a few months to become proficient in Morse Code. You will need to work hard. No time for paddling your toes in the sea.' Her smile was a grim parody of humour. 'Morse Code is a universal language that can be transmitted over great distances. You've all been selected because you are supposed to have some ability to listen and learn.'

She scanned the faces before her, skewering each in turn. It felt like being the guilty member of an identity parade. Felicity held her breath until the searchlight moved on.

'You will need to study in your free time and will be tested at the end of each week. Failure is not tolerated. I don't expect any of you to have to repeat the course. I shouldn't need to remind you that you've all signed the Official Secrets Act. You must not utter a word to anyone about your training here.' Again her deep-set glittering eyes burnt into their faces.

No one spoke or moved. We can hardly tell any tales when we don't even know what we're to be doing, Felicity thought. Then Bertha put up her hand. 'What happens when we finish the course? Where will we be sent?'

The silence was thunderous. It reminded Felicity of when Oliver Twist asked for more gruel. Everyone stared at Bertha, in amazement at how foolhardy she was. Would Captain Turner's gorgon stare turn her to stone? Or would her dragon breath sizzle her to ashes? Felicity, like the others, looked down, not wanting to be involved. She had wanted to ask that question too but the experiences of the last year had made her more cautious. No one moved or spoke. Felicity risked peeping sideways at Bertha. She was sitting bolt upright, staring at Captain Turner. She slowly raised her left hand and scratched her nose with her forefinger.

'You're not here to ask questions,' Captain Turner said. Her sallow face was flushed. The girls beside Felicity stared at

Bertha's mutilated hand. Everyone was holding their breath. The officer swept her gaze over them all and raised her voice.

'When and if you finish the course you will be told. Now the first thing you do is fetch your headphones.' She pointed to a table in the corner.

They all trooped over. Moving released the tension in the room but no one risked speaking. Felicity picked one of the heavy metal objects up, turning it over and feeling its weight.

'Put them on,' Captain Turner ordered. Felicity noticed that her face had lost its pinkness. They all obediently clamped the heavy metal cups over their ears. Their first task was to listen to a slow pattern of dots and dashes, each representing a letter in Morse Code.

'You will need to learn each letter by heart this evening. Tomorrow you will start to listen to whole words,' Captain Turner told them. By this time Felicity's ears were throbbing with the pinch of the metal. After she removed the headphones she had to massage life back into her sore lobes.

'It'll take me a while to get used to those,' she said to Bertha.

'Baa! You're always wearing diamond earrings, aren't you?'

'Oh, yes all the time, I don't think.'

'Never mind, our kid, you'll get used to it.'

Felicity was so anxious not to fail that she decided to practise at every free moment. She was busy tapping letters out on the table while eating dinner. Bertha laughed when she came to join her.

'I wish I knew shorthand. It would maybe help with learning this,' Felicity said.

'Didn't you do Greek at the posh school you was at? That's another alphabet, isn't it?'

Felicity shook her head. 'No. Boys learnt Greek, not us. We had to learn to be ladylike.'

Bertha snorted. 'Well, that's a lot of bloody use in wartime, "Please Mr Jerry, don't put me up against the wall and shoot me."'

Felicity shrugged. 'So, tell me what it was like in the factory.'

'It's better 'ere than in the munitions. It was boring as Hell but you had to keep your mind on the job, using tweezers to pick up them detonators. The Blue Bands – that's the supervisors, always on your back, checking you. Woman next to me got suspended for having a small Kirby grip in her hair.'

'Really?' Felicity looked round to see if anyone was listening to this dangerous spilling of secrets but the other students were all talking among themselves.

'It was so easy to set off an explosion. A tiny spark from metal could do it. We had to change all our clothes at the start of each shift. Put on white overalls and a turban. I never saw a big explosion meself. High-ups tried to keep them secret – as if you could.'

'And how...?'

'Did this happen?' Bertha held up her hand and wiggled the remaining fingers. Felicity could look at it now without wincing.

'Blood everywhere. Like a fountain. The foreman found me fingers under the table but they was too mangled to stitch back on. Hurt like the devil when the stumps were healing and all swelled up with pus. Doctors thought they might have to cut me arm off.' She paused and grinned. 'Am I putting you off your grub?'

Felicity smiled weakly.

'Anyways, it meant they 'ad to let me leave that God awful job. Gave me an aptitude test. Handpicked I was. "It appears you might be suitable for a technical role, despite your lack of education."'

Felicity spluttered over her mouthful as Bertha mimicked an upper-class accent. 'A buggered hand 'as its uses. People think twice about being nasty to a cripple.'

The days were long and tiring, a constant effort of concentration needed as coded messages ground into their ears.

Bertha was as keen as Felicity to get through the course so they paired up in the evenings to test each other with the dots and dashes. The practice transmissions they were given every day were gradually speeded up. A few of the girls were sent back to restart the course but Felicity and Bertha kept up. Even when fast recordings were used they passed all the tests.

'Twenty words a minute. Beat that if you can!'

'I will, Bertha, or eat my hat.'

Felicity had heard the other girls whisper about the 'Oddballs' behind their backs but she didn't care. They were just childish, jealous of her and Bertha being top of the class. Felicity had made a friend and found something she could excel at. When they weren't practising and competing at being top Morsers, Bertha introduced her to smoking. 'It's a pity we don't have a wireless here.'

'I never really listened to it. What do you like? Music?'

'What, you mean the likes of "Workers' Playtime"? "Opium for the masses" my da says.'

Felicity frowned.

'I thought you was the educated one. Karl Marx – he said religion was a way of keeping the workers quiet. Same with those daft programmes. Ever heard, *Germany calling*?'

'Lord Haw Haw? But he's a traitor!'

Bertha shrugged. 'He's funny though. Not like the boring stuff from the government. Doesn't care what he says – "Mr Bleeding Bevin" and "to Hell with Churchill and his lousy gang of crooks."'

Felicity gasped.

'Shocked you, have I? Ever asked yourself who's expected to die for King and Country? Not the nobs. It's the poor. That's what my da says and he's right. Workers on both sides have more in common with each other than with the officers. That's why they stopped the football games between our lads and the Germans in the First War. They was scared that once the soldiers on both sides got together they would know who the real enemy was and turn on them – their officers. Did you know that men on the dole get a better deal in Germany than they do here?'

'Shush. You're a Red, a communist! You'll get us both in hot water with talk like that.'

'No, you fool. I'm not a communist. I'm a socialist, like me Da. We want a fairer world. One where people don't have to live in slums. Folk like you don't know what that's like.' Bertha's face was red now.

'But I do! I know a boy from a fisherman's family in Scotland. I don't think they have much money.'

'One of your servants, eh?'

'No, he's a friend. And when I lodged with Winnie I had to use an outside lavatory. It was full of spiders.'

'Did you have to share it with ten other families?'

'No, of course not.'

'You don't know you're alive, me ducks. One day I'll show you the back streets.'

Felicity felt her own face redden. She bit back an angry retort and spoke quietly. 'I can't help the family I was born into, any more than you can. We all have to pull together to win this war. Anyway, just because your family's well off it doesn't mean you're happy.'

Bertha shrugged. 'Maybe, but money oils the wheels, don't it? I'll tell you something else about Lord Haw Haw. He gives out the names of POWs, even before their families have been told by the government here.'

'That's to get people to listen to his broadcasts.'

'And he's given warnings about where bombing raids are going to be.'

Felicity snorted. 'Are they accurate or is he just playing tricks?'

'Listen yourself and make your mind up.'

Felicity shook her head. She was both scared and intrigued by Bertha. She was like a tank, trampling over the scenery of the world she had known, making it seem like a theatre set, just flimsy curtains and balsa wood props.

Chapter 29

May 1941

Captain Turner remained silent about their destinations and no one dared ask her, not even Bertha. The officer reminded Felicity of the Matron at her boarding school, a woman so forbidding that no pupil would approach her unless they were in unbearable pain. One girl had carried on with a broken wrist for several days until a teacher noticed her swollen hand and marched her off to the sanitorium. The officer stayed as stiff as she was at the start, frowning at mistakes and never praising. The nearest she managed to encouragement was a nod and raising of the eyebrows, if one of the girls was especially fast at her decoding. If the student happened to be Bertha she didn't even get that recognition.

'She don't like the proles doing well – we might take over the world.'

Felicity was used to her friend's way of talking by now. 'She might put you against the wall if you come top in the final tests?'

'If looks could kill, I'd be dead a hundred times. She'll fiddle the marks if she can.'

'Surely not.'

Bertha shrugged. 'Well, I'll do me best anyway, to beat the nobs.' She said it with a grin but behind the joking Felicity knew that they were rivals. They were the best Morsers in the group by far and they both wanted to win. After they sat their final tests Captain Turner made them all wait in the old dining room. They sat in an anxious line, with Bertha and Felicity nearest the door. It seemed odd not to be wearing headphones. They were lying on the table like discarded jumble.

'I'll call you in turn to my office. Then you must come back to summon the next one,' Captain Turner said, nodding at a girl at the far end of the row whose face turned ashen as she scrambled to her feet. They all waited, too tense to speak but the girl didn't come back.

'She'll be boo-hooing in the lavs 'cos she's failed,' Bertha boomed, making everyone jump. Some of the other girls glared at her. At that moment, Captain Turner appeared at the door and called out the next name. 'Told you so. The old bitch wants to make us all suffer,' Bertha said once she had left.

'I don't think so' said Felicity, 'Gillian's surname is Atkinson. And Captain Turner's just called out Joyce Baker's name. She's going through the list alphabetically.'

'We'll see then,' Bertha said, 'It should be Anne Bates next. But it won't be. We all know those two are useless, Gillian the Ass and Joyce the Bloody Fool. They'll have to repeat the whole course if they've not been thrown off it altogether.'

'Shhs, Bertha,' Felicity muttered. At that moment the door opened a crack and Joyce stuck her head round it to croak 'Margery Simpkins' before scuttling off.

'Told you so. That's blown your theory out of the water,' Bertha crowed. The others all glowered at her while Felicity looked away.

When Margery returned, she was smiling in relief. 'I passed,' she said.

'What mark did you get?' Bertha asked but the girl ignored her and sat down to talk to her friends.

'Not that good, eh – just a scrape through?' Bertha added. As each girl returned, the others congratulated her and ignored Felicity and Bertha. When the last one went for her turn, Bertha punched Felicity on the arm. 'Well, it's you or me, kid. I'm not waiting here any longer.'

She marched along with Felicity in her wake. They waited in the corridor outside Captain Turner's office. Bertha pointed at the name board on the door. '*Captain Turner,* my arse. I bet her office was a broom cupboard before and she was a stuck-up supervisor. We'll see who she calls in next.'

'Well. If you're right, we've both done well.' The door opened. A surprised looking girl came out and walked up to them.

'We got fed up waiting,' Felicity said. 'I hope that congratulations are in order?'

The girl smiled thinly. 'Yes, thank you. You're to go in next,' she said to Bertha.

'I've shown them what the girl from the back-to-backs and the Board School can do,' Bertha said. 'But it's a pity if you've pipped me to the post,' she added over her shoulder as she strode up to the door. Felicity paced up and down as she waited. She didn't know what to think. Would it have mattered if Bertha had beaten her to the top place? Not really – she was pleased to have done well, for once. She would have to tell Daddy, without going into details, of course. Would he be proud of her? Probably he wouldn't be that impressed, she thought and felt her confidence deflating. What if Bertha was right and Captain Turner had fiddled the marks so that Felicity came first? Would that really happen?

She stopped pacing as she realised that Bertha had been in there a longer time than the others. She moved nearer the door. She could only hear muffled voices despite straining her ears. She jumped backwards as the voices rose. She could hear Bertha's roar. 'You're saying I can't get the best posting even when I got the best marks?'

'It's not just a matter of your marks but about your suitability and background.' The captain's voice was booming now.

'I didn't go to the right school, is that it? Me family's not posh enough?'

'I'm warning you not to be insubordinate. You've shown the wrong attitude from the start.'

'What? Because I dared to ask questions?'

Felicity was boiling inside. She was furious to hear how unjustly Bertha was being treated. Her friend was right about the captain's prejudices. At the same time she wished Bertha would stop inflaming the situation. She was always saying that she wouldn't 'bite her lip for anyone'. Felicity groaned and muttered under her breath. In her turmoil she found herself swearing, every bad word she knew, in English and then in French. Words she didn't realise that she knew or understood. A pent-up tide of frustration poured out of her mouth. 'Blast and damn. Shit and bugger – *Sacre bleu, Merde, va te faire foutre, putain de merde.*'

The door swung open. Bertha stood there, red-faced and chin jutting forward beside a grim-faced Captain Turner, her jaw clenched so tightly that her lips had disappeared. 'Go to your quarters,' she hissed at Bertha. 'And you come in,' she barked at Felicity.

She tried to catch Bertha's eye but her friend stared ahead. I'm for the high jump too now, Felicity thought. After she sat down the captain stared at her silently. Although she was cringing inside Felicity returned her gaze.

'I apologise for swearing, Captain Turner. I don't know what came over me.'

'What?' Captain Turner sighed. 'That girl is a troublemaker and a bad influence. I'm not sure how much she has corrupted you.'

'Corrupted me, Ma'am?'

'With her dangerous opinions and refusal to accept orders.'

'I'm not corrupted. I've not turned into a Communist.' She took a deep breath and continued. 'But Bertha hasn't had the chances in life that I've had. And she had that horrible accident so she must be really clever to have done so well in the tests.' She looked down at her hands, unnerved by her boldness.

'Hmm.'

'She does get carried away. Maybe if she apologised?'

'I doubt that's in her nature.'

Felicity silently agreed. 'What will happen to her?'

'None of your business.' Captain Turner's voice had stiffened again. 'The question is what we do with you. There's a vacancy at a station in North Yorkshire.'

'Yorkshire? I was banking on a posting in Scotland. My father's there and his health...'

'We all have to make sacrifices in wartime. You can't expect special treatment.'

Felicity blinked hard to stop the shaming tears.

'However, you have some pluck and you can speak French in a very convincing way.'

Felicity found herself blushing. Had Captain Turner not understood her words? 'Er, thank you.'

'There might be another opening.' She raised her hand. 'No questions. I shall pass your name on and see what happens.'

Felicity stumbled to her feet. 'Ah, by the way, you achieved the joint highest mark in your final test.'

She nodded and left, thinking what a burst balloon of an achievement that was.

Part 5

John Norman's Story

Chapter 30

Winter 1941

'Double pneumonia, I'm afraid. Both lungs congested.'

They thought that he couldn't hear them whispering outside the bedroom door. They didn't know how being at sea sharpened the senses. As a hunted creature your life could depend on detecting anything unusual – a sound carried on the wind, a smell rising from the sea, a shifting in the bowels of a boat.

He could hear Mamma sucking in her breath to stop the cry from escaping.

'Better to keep him at home for now. I'll be back later.'

After the doctor left John Norman's senses went to ground. Time – minutes, hours, days lost in a fug of delirium. Roasted in a furnace from within he believed the inferno was outside his body. He was swallowed up in a fireball, desperate to plunge into the cold sea. But when he dived into the waves they were black and sticky, clogging and choking him.

Until the day he knew he was back in harbour, his bed a raft swaying at anchor. Faces peering down at him, Mamma and Pappa, Lexie and Margaret. He prised his cracked lips open. 'You look as if you're at a funeral.'

Mamma sobbed. 'Thank the Lord you've been spared. You won't have to go away again.'

Pappa nudged her. 'The important thing is that you're getting better.'

Lexie, who was kneeling at the side of the bed, reached over to hug him. 'Don't squeeze him,' Mamma said.

He had never been ill before. It was the weakness that shocked him. He was a new-born creature, too frail to tend to himself. But he latched onto life, like an orphan lamb tugging at the bottle. Each day he set himself a new task. The first one was levering himself out of bed and crawling to the bathroom. Afterwards, exhausted and shivering he clambered back into bed. His body horrified him. Always lean he had become skeletal, as skinny as when he was a boy. His clothes swamped him, his trousers sliding down even after he asked Pappa to make a new notch in his belt. Always he had to fight against the longing to sink back into the feathered nest.

'Shut that door, Lexie. John Norman mustn't sit in a draught,' Mamma would say, tucking the blanket around him as he sat in front of the fire like a *cailleach*, nursing his milky cup of tea. Pappa and Lexie blew in with tales of the outside world that encouraged him to flex his wings, practising to launch himself. He expected the doctor would sign him off once he had gained strength and weight.

'You've recovered from the pneumonia,' he said, peering over his half glasses after sounding John Norman's chest. 'But it was touch and go. Your lungs have been weakened and in that condition there's a risk of TB setting in. You need more time to convalesce.'

John Norman's face fell. 'How much time, Doctor? I feel so much better in myself.'

'Aye, I'm sure you do. We'll take it a month at a time. Then you'll need an X-ray to make sure there's no shadow there.'

A month at a time! How would he survive? None of his friends were on leave. He had a drink with some other lads he knew from school but it wasn't the same. They were only home on leave while he was hauled up beyond the high tide mark.

One day a letter arrived from Felicity. Luckily Mamma was out at a neighbour's when the postie came.

Dear John Norman,
Wasn't it strange us bumping into each other like that in the Underground? As they say, 'It's a small world.' I don't know when this letter will reach you as I'm sure you're away at sea again. I've

changed jobs. I'm training in the North of England now. Can't say what I'm doing, of course. They're keeping our noses to the grindstone. No time to relax at all. I don't know where I'll be posted. I hope it will be up in Scotland. It's the only place I've ever really felt at home. I envy you being brought up there. That might sound odd but one thing I've learnt from this war is that a loving family is the greatest gift you can have. It's much more important than wealth, schooling or anything else.

I think about you sailing the oceans and how dangerous that must be. I pray that you stay safe and I trust we shall meet again before too long. I hope your family are all in good health.

My warm regards,
Felicity

He was so surprised that he read it twice more. Like him she didn't go in for epistles but this one was so much warmer than anything she had written before. She must be feeling lonely. The letter made him angry too. It was only ever rich people who claimed that money didn't matter. And a close family wasn't that wonderful. He had fought Mamma to go to war and now he was going to have to cut himself free from the net to leave home again. How he envied Felicity, a far speck out at sea, out in the world. He screwed the letter up.

He was feeling lonely too. There was so much open water between him and people who hadn't seen fighting and death. How could he burden anyone with his nightmares? But a line was thrown to him from an unexpected hand. Margaret had some time off from the hotel in Kyle and came back home. She looked wan. He surprised himself by suggesting they go for a walk together on the Scorrybreac shore. He couldn't remember when the two of them had last been together without the rest of the family. Usually he let the spate of her words flow over him but she was subdued this time. What on earth could they talk about?

'How's Simon doing? I really took to him. He isn't snooty like so many of the other officers.'

'I've not heard from him for a while. I wish he would write more often. He must know I'm worried.'

'It's hard to find time to write. Then if you do it can take for ever for the letter to arrive.'

'How would you know? When have you ever written to anyone?' She had found her sting again.

'You've no idea what it's like at sea. You're safely tucked up in bed but at sea you're on edge all the time, living on your nerves. Listening and waiting for an attack – from above or below.'

'That's why you should never have signed up when you didn't have to. Scaring Mamma to death and it was my ear she bent all the time about her beloved only son in such danger.'

By this time they had reached the Black Rock, a finger of land reaching out into Portree Bay. As he gritted his teeth he looked out and saw that the high tide had turned it into an island. Like between him and Margaret there was no causeway where they could meet.

'I had to go. I didn't feel I was a proper man, hiding from the war. And I'll go back as soon as the doctor says I can.'

'At least you have a choice,' Margaret hissed.

John Norman had turned on his heel to walk back the way they had come. Now he stopped. 'What do you mean?'

'I wanted to join up. Can you imagine what it's like, stuck in Kyle with all those naval people. It keeps reminding me of Simon. Will he ever survive? Will the war ever end? Will we ever marry? I hear them talking about ships being sunk and hundreds of men drowning.' She clenched her jaw but her eyes looked desolate.

'What do you mean about joining up?'

'I want to escape. I'm sick of being the good eldest daughter, comforting Mamma all the time.'

'So, what happened?'

'They wouldn't take me because of my asthma. And being in

a reserved occupation. I tried the Wrens and the ATS. Not strong enough for manual jobs they said. And I don't have my School Cert so I can't do an office job either. And why didn't I take my exams...'

She was starting to cough. John Norman took her arm. 'Don't upset yourself and bring on an attack. You didn't take your exams because you missed too much school.'

To his surprise she came closer and rested her head on his shoulder. He waited until her fit of coughing stopped. 'What a pair we are. Me half-blind and you with not enough breath. We would make one healthy person between us.'

She stepped back and blew her nose. 'Don't tell Mamma – or anyone else about me trying to join up.' The old fierce glint was in her eyes again.

'Don't worry. I can keep secrets.'

'You have to in our family.'

They walked on. 'I can write letters, you know,' he said.

Margaret smiled. 'Wee scribbled notes, just like Iain used to do.' She stared at him. 'You've been writing to that Felicity MacDougall, haven't you?'

He nodded. 'But there's nothing in it. Her family's upper class.'

'Well Mamma's always wanted us to better ourselves.'

'As if I didn't know! Jeannie getting to the university and becoming a teacher is one thing. So is you marrying a naval officer. But me marrying into the gentry is way out of reach.'

'But this war has shaken everything up. We can't go back to how it was before.'

'If it ever ends. Well, you and I are quits now. Each of us with a secret.'

They walked home, easy in each other's company. Maybe he would reply to Felicity after all, even if there wasn't much to say.

Chapter 31

Winter 1941–Spring 1942

John Norman had to wait some months before the doctor would sign him off as fit for any work. At first he would only allow him to go back to fishing part-time.

'When can I get a berth and go to sea properly again? I'm tired of kicking my heels.'

'Not until I'm sure that your lungs are fully recovered. I've looked up the records and there's TB running through your father's side.'

'Aye, but that was long ago and all my family are fit as fleas.'

The doctor's gaze was sympathetic but his voice was firm. 'I used to work in a sanatorium. We send patients there to get better but often they're not cured. We just delay their deaths. Your chest's still rattling and I won't have your death on my hands. If you continue to improve I'll give you permission to work in home waters, on lighter duties. I know that's not the front line but it's vital war work – and it'll give you a chance to get away from home,' he added with a smile.

John Norman stood up and nodded. He didn't trust himself to speak.

'The war won't be over quickly, you know. You'll get another chance to be in the thick of it,' he said to John Norman's retreating back.

What a comedown to be working as crew on a rusty old puffer – chugging around the islands, mooring on the beach and waiting for the tide to lift the boat out to sea again. Light duties! What a joke. All hands were needed to shift the cargo ashore. What did the doctor know about it, up from Edinburgh as he was? John Norman felt too angry and disappointed to go straight home and endure Mamma's delight without grimacing.

He walked down to the Scorrybreac shore and looked over to the wide gape of the busy harbour, full of boats of all sizes. He remembered how Pappa had told him about the days before the war when the sea was stiff with herring and the harbour so packed with vessels that you could cross the water with dry feet from the beach of *Camus Bàn* to the pier by clambering from one boat to the next. He had always been around boats from when he could first totter after Pappa as he strode down the Pier Brae. Then a few years later he was grasping Lexie by the hand as they went to Grandma's house down at Bayfield on the shore, bringing a herring for her tea. One time he forgot about how nervous his wee sister was of ships and they arrived the same time as the steamer with her bellowing hooter. Lexie had dropped the fish and stood rigid, screaming her head off. When he tried to pull her along she had started her trick of clicking her knee joint in and out. That always made him feel sick so he looked away and waited for her to calm down.

'Have you been pinching your wee sister to make her cry like that?' a nosey *cailleach* had tutted at him.

And then there were the boat trips with Iain, as close as a brother, the best friend he avoided thinking too much about. What would Iain say to him now?

'You're alive and kicking, man. Make the most of it.'

John Norman began to ask around for inshore work. Someone told him about how the Royal Navy had commissioned Victualling Inshore Craft or VICs, up to date puffers that were used to supply naval bases.

'Does that sound a good idea to you?' he asked Pappa.

His father was never one to hurry an answer. He took out his pipe, filled it with tobacco and lit it before replying. 'I reckon that could be a very rushed sort of job. It's hard work too on the old puffers but you can have some fun too travelling around the islands if you get a fair skipper.'

'I'll do that then.'

And Pappa was right. John Norman found a berth with the four-man crew on the *Fair Maid,* a misnamed vessel if ever there was one. She was rounded and lumbering and a devil to steer but Captain Sullivan was a jovial man, an experienced sailor who had spent years on the Clyde puffers. They pottered around the islands, delivering timber, coal, slate and every sort of heavy cargo. Local people would come down to the pier, or the beach if there wasn't a pier, ready with their horses and carts. It had a deep-bellied hold so it was tiring digging through the piled up cargo but afterwards there was the chance to rest and have a few drinks ashore. John Norman wondered if he might bump into Archie but no one seemed to have seen him. He would probably be on convoy duty now while John Norman had been downgraded to an old puffer. Archie would have a laugh at that.

It was in the spring of the next year that John Norman found himself travelling down the coast of Kintyre and ending up at Gigha, a Hebridean island that had slid down southwards to Argyll. How flat and green it was, he thought, as he stepped ashore. After they had unloaded the cargo of cattle cake and fertiliser, John Norman started talking to one of the local farmers. One of the pleasures of travelling around the islands was the chance it gave him to speak Gaelic all the time, without tacking between it and English as he usually did.

'That's a fine Clydesdale horse you've got there.'

'Aye. We're noted for our horses here. Is that a Skye accent you have?'

'It is indeed.'

'Well, if you've time you're very welcome to come back with me. I work at Achamore Farm.'

John Norman accepted the offer and as Fergus the horse trotted along, James MacNeill told him about his family.

'I lost my wife Isobel a few years back. My three sons are all off at the war but my daughter Chrissie helps on the farm.'

'I'm a Merchant Seaman myself but the doctor won't sign

me off yet for convoy duties.' John Norman always felt uneasy when people spoke about the war, in case they wondered why he wasn't away fighting. He always wore his Merchant Navy badge on his lapel so that they would know. 'I can give you a hand unloading the cart,' he said.

James smiled. 'Thank you but you'll find that Chrissie's a strong lass.'

John Norman imagined that she would be a hefty girl with washer woman arms but he was greeted by a tall, slender young woman with glossy black hair tied back with a red scarf. The three of them made short work of unloading the sacks even though they weighed 112 pounds each. So much for the doctor saying that he should stick to light duties, John Norman smiled to himself. He knew that he had become much stronger since his illness even though he had stayed wiry. Then Chrissie fetched them a drink of oatmeal mixed in water. John Norman was suspicious. He would have preferred milk but the concoction was surprisingly refreshing.

Then she took Fergus away for a feed and rubdown while her father showed John Norman the farm.

'We've good soil here and plenty of sunshine,' he said. 'We keep cattle as well as growing turnips, oats and potatoes. And there's a man nearby who breeds pit ponies, those wee Shetland ones. When they sent a stallion over last year all the children had a go at riding him. Much easier to ride than the big horses.'

'When do you sail?' Chrissie asked him when he came back to the house.

'We'll catch the tide early tomorrow.'

'Well, that means you can come to the dance at the Iron House tonight. We're short of men so you'll be very welcome.'

'The Iron House?'

She shrugged. 'I don't know where the name comes from. It's on one of the farms.'

Before the war John Norman would have run for the hills

rather than go to a dance. He had felt clumsy and tongue tied, especially with girls who had known him from when they were at school together. But he surprised himself by looking forward to visiting the Iron House. Even if he made a fool of himself they were strangers and he wouldn't see them again. But maybe he would see Chrissie again? He was very taken with her straight way of speaking and her capable ways. She was very pretty too, of course.

Chrissie was right about the shortage of young men. They were outnumbered by schoolboys and a scattering of older farm workers. Many of the girls had to partner each other. A couple of elderly fiddlers provided the music and there was plenty of home baking but little in the way of alcohol. John Norman would have liked to dance with Chrissie the whole time but after a few sets she nudged him towards the girls who were sitting on the edges of the dance floor trying not to look neglected. Suddenly he thought of Felicity. What was it she had said to him about it being so much worse for a girl having to wear spectacles? Yes, he remembered now. She had said how she was forced to be a wallflower and no one would ever marry her. That was her being over dramatic as usual.

When he had done his duty by dancing with the other lassies and the fiddlers were taking their break he asked Chrissie, 'Shall we go outside for a wee walk?'

She hesitated and his hopes wilted but then she agreed. The dusk and the realisation that he had little time made John Norman bolder than usual. He reached for her hand and squeezed it as they strolled along. She let him hold her hand for an instant but then withdrew it and turned to face him.

'I hope I haven't misled you, John Norman. I've enjoyed your company but I'm spoken for already. Alan's away in the army.'

'I should have guessed that a pretty lassie like yourself wouldn't be free.' He tried to speak lightly but there was a crack in his voice.

'And I would expect that a well set up young man like yourself would have a sweetheart.'

'Would you?' He was astonished and suspicious of a joke at his expense but her open face looked puzzled.

'Of course,' she said.

Then somehow he found himself telling her all about Felicity from their first meeting to their bumping into each other in the Underground. She listened keenly and when he stopped, suddenly embarrassed, she said, frowning, 'You say she's not your sweetheart but everything in your voice tells me that she is.' .

'But how can she be? She's from a wealthy family and they would never accept me.'

'Come on, John Norman, what's that saying about "Faint heart never won fair lady?" You're surely not giving up that easily? Write to her and explain that you've been ill. She'll have been worrying about not hearing from you.'

Chapter 32

Summer 1942

He returned home with Chrissie's words still buzzing in his ears. This time when he saw the doctor he signed him off as fully fit. While he was waiting to be summoned to report to the Pool again he decided to write to Felicity. She was moody and not a proper girlfriend whatever Chrissie had said but he did feel some link with her, beyond them both having bad eyesight. He supposed that they both needed to free themselves from their families.

> *How are you? I know its a long time since I last wrote but there's not much to say I was ill and kicking my heels when i came back from my trip. Ive been working on a puffer carrying cargoes round the islands some I had never been to before like Gigha Its very flat and green.*

What else to say? He scratched his head in frustration but then he remembered what Mamma did when she was writing one of her endless letters to relatives who had moved away. If she was stuck she re-read the last letter she had received from that person and replied to something they had said. But where was Felicity's last letter? He found it eventually, tucked away in an old tobacco tin at the back of a shelf in Pappa's shed, the only place where Mamma or Lexie wouldn't find it. A quick read through of her letter and then he took up his pencil.

> *You're right that my family are loving but they want to know everything. Mamma was furious about me going away at first she's got used to it I think You'll have your new posting now and I hope its what you want It was odd us bumping into each other in*

London. What's that song say we'll meet again don't know where
don't know when. I hope we do
   Kind Regards,
   John Norman

He even told Margaret that he had written to Felicity when she
had her next day off and came back home.

'I've just heard from Simon,' she said. He's included a note to
you. Here it is. I've not read it.'

John Norman smiled and put the envelope in his pocket.

Later, back at home he opened it.

I'm back to the Med. I sailed from Alexandria last time. I might get
the western end from Gibraltar next. They call it the 'Ladies' End'.
I think that's a bad joke. It's probably even worse than the eastern
end. We're sitting ducks either way.

'It was just sailors' talk,' he told Margaret later. 'The Med sounds
much better than the Arctic convoys. At least they won't get
weighed down with ice .'

What sort of ship awaited him? he wondered. When the letter
from the Pool finally arrived he felt relieved. He would soon
know and that was much better than all the waiting. At the docks
in Greenock he was told to board the *Port Chalmers*.

He found the vessel and stood watching her being loaded.
'What's she carrying?' he asked a docker who straightened up
and replied, 'All sorts. Food – wheat, corned beef, cloth, tobacco.
And shells and aircraft parts.'

'What's in the drums over there?'

'Fuel.'

That's not so good, he thought. The ship could turn into a
furnace very quickly if she was hit. He walked along to King
George's Dock. Under the big crane lay a huge ship. It must be a
naval vessel he thought as he counted the guns. Two in the bows,

a Bofors gun aft near the squat funnel and six other guns spread around the ship. A good-looking vessel, long and sleek but no, not a naval vessel. A tanker surely but not like any he had seen before. He went back to the *Port Chalmers* to find his berth. No one else about yet so he decided to write again to Felicity, to tell her he was off to sea again. What a shock, getting two letters at once after months without a word from him. She didn't make sense, like that ship he'd just seen. She had seemed pleased to see him in the Underground and then turned all haughty. She wasn't a proper girlfriend but she was the only person apart from his family he kept in touch with. He would have to hurry up if he was to get it posted before they sailed.

> *Dear Felicity,*
> *At last I got my new posting its not a bad one and I'm glad to be off to sea again Mamma didn't complain this time but I know she's not happy about me going. we all have to do our bit, don't we?*
> *Kind regards*
> *John Norman*

By the time he came back from posting the letter the rest of the crew had arrived. There was no one he recognised.

'What's the big boat, the one with all the guns?' he asked another man.

'The *Ohio*? An American tanker. But the crew's English.'

'The kind Yanks bringing us petrol. Why don't they send us troops?' someone else snorted.

'So is she off back home?' John Norman asked.

'God knows. The odd thing is she's loading up again. So why are we sending fuel to the Yanks?' the first sailor asked.

'Round the Cape to Suez? Or help to the Russkies? Kept in the dark we are, like mushrooms.'

'And we have shit thrown on us.'

They all laughed.

They set off in the light of the mid-summer evening in a tight group of fourteen ships. The sun was setting as they reached the open sea. John Norman let the waves rock him asleep but his body jerked awake in the small hours. Why hadn't he thought of it before? The tanker was full. So was their boat. Why were they carrying goods on the outward journey? Last time they went out in ballast and came back with a cargo.

The next day as dawn lit up the sky he went on deck for his watch duty and gasped at what he saw across the rolling Irish sea. Two long strands of convoy ships and on each side of them the grey outlines of warships rocking on the waves, not just destroyers and cruisers but towering battleships. Streaming above were Sunderland aircraft. Plenty of protection but it made him feel uneasy rather than safer. What was going on? In the second dog watch they were all called to hear Captain Higgs read out the message from the Admiral:

For over twelve months Malta has resisted all attacks of the enemy. The gallantry displayed by the garrison and people of Malta has aroused admiration throughout the world. To enable their defence to be continued, it is essential that your ships, with their valuable cargoes, should arrive safely in Grand Harbour.

So now he had his answer. Not what he wanted to hear but at least it ended the uncertainty. The captain's voice rose as he neared the end of his speech.

'Remember that the watchword is: THE CONVOY MUST GET THROUGH.'

The captain smiled. 'Here's the Admiral's little joke':

We'll be at the Skerki channel on the 12th. The Glorious Twelfth, of course, for the grouse shooting. And we should bag some birds in the Med.

There was a ripple of laughter. What had toffs shooting birds got to do with anything? John Norman wondered.

'What's the channel the captain was talking about?' he asked the others when they were eating.

'It's shallows between a wee island off Sicily where the Ities have a bloody big fort and the African coast where the frigging Frogs are. We're buggered whichever way we go,' an older sailor said as he chewed a mouthful of meat. He tapped John Norman's arm. 'Don't fret, lad. You've a few days sunbathing before we get there.'

'And we've the miracle of radio so the captain hears about an attack before the torpedoes arrive.'

'Eh, the wonders of science,' another one added.

As they sailed towards the coast of Spain there were plenty of drills to make John Norman forget his fears. Carrying ammunition for the army gunners, playing out ropes, practising turns and zigzags with the steering. On the ninth they all cheered when four aircraft carriers appeared. Their arrival meant that the convoy wouldn't be sitting targets for enemy planes. The merchant ships had to get into line in four columns, like classes in the playground before school started. Lots of signals and radio messages to sort out the long-distance manoeuvring. Then more jostling and herding as the ships formed two columns and finally one. Meanwhile Fleet Air Arm planes swept overhead making dummy attacks. Maybe Angus was flying one of them. John Norman had heard nothing about him since he joined up. Finally, aircraft from the carriers flew slowly overhead, waggling their wings. First were the slower Fulmars which provided lower level cover. Then came the faster Hurricanes and Martlets.

'Can't risk our lads shooting them down by mistake,' the third mate said.

But John Norman wasn't listening. He was thinking how the planes were like different sorts of seabirds. Some, like gulls, hovered closer to the sea while others, like gannets, swooped down from above.

As they neared Gibraltar a protective fog came down. The great rock vanished in the gloom, like the Cuillin when the mists smothered it. As they groped their way between the Rock and Cape Spartel on the African coast lights began to glimmer. The fog blurred them into glowing snowballs.

'What on earth are those?' John Norman asked the mate.

'Bloody Dagos. Fishing boats.'

'Are we fighting them too?'

'Not officially but they're like the sodding Irish. Call themselves neutral but they're bloody liars. You can bet your life they're counting the number of ships and telling Adolf.'

John Norman shivered. It was hard to believe that the welcoming flutter of lights meant danger. The next day they were into the Mediterranean and the fog had lifted. Their boat was going flat out, shaking and rattling with the effort. Like John Norman as a wee boy, legs burning and chest gasping as he struggled to keep up with Iain. The memory stabbed him, like a stitch in the side from running. The mate, Tom Evans, told him how the captain of a cruiser had reprimanded *Port Chalmers* for not keeping up.

'Like being back in bloody school. Do your best and you still get into trouble. But this ship's lucky. Got through last time when most of the others didn't.'

Ahead, on the starboard side, was a line of their escorts, seven destroyers and the carrier *Eagle* at the back. John Norman watched as the carrier's planes took off, a horde of hornets ready to sting. He wanted to cheer. Suddenly a boom vibrated across the sea. Gouts of water spouted skywards, three times higher than her masts. Black smoke erupted and smothered the vessel. When a gap appeared in the smoke he could see how the carrier was tilted onto her side. Aircraft were sliding into the sea like discarded toys. She was rolling right over at 45 degrees. What was that movement? He strained his eyes to see and was horrified to pick out members of the crew scrabbling on the sloping deck and sliding off the edge. The ship sank within a few moments, silently giving up the struggle to right herself, turning over with a terrible grace. She disappeared completely. Trapped in the spreading pool of oil were rafts, boats and the bobbing heads of swimmers. The nearest vessels were launching boats to pick up survivors. But how many men would have had time to jump overboard? What about the stokers trapped in the engine room as steam burst through broken pipes? Only those already on the deck had a chance. Even if they did manage to jump how many would get sucked down by the stricken ship? Or trapped in the oil, swallowing its poison? He closed his eyes but knew that it was hopeless. Those terrible sights burnt into his brain.

The bright sun and the warm wind mocked the convoy. Perfect sailing weather meant there was nowhere to hide. To the north, cloud marked the position of the island of Majorca. To the south mist grazed the flat North African coast, held by the Italians. He had asked the mate how much further it was to Malta. 550 miles. He wished he hadn't asked. Everyone watched if they weren't busy down below. They scanned the skies, ears strained for the hum of engines. They peered out to sea, searching for the white tracks of torpedoes or the beak of a submarine periscope. Meanwhile their ships zig-zagged, like hares chased by a fox. In the early afternoon the warning came, *Enemy aircraft approaching from the starboard beam*. The buzz of the aircraft disappeared as the big guns fired and crackled. But there was no sign of the aircraft. The battleships silenced their guns.

'Just taking a butcher's at us,' one of the sailors said. As the day drew on, the sea darkened and the sun sank to douse itself in the water. They began to breathe more easily. Surely it was too late for an air raid now? Then out of the dusk streaked Junkers and Heinkels, diving and screaming. The sky was lit up with the fireworks of coloured tracers and bursting shells. Everyone cheered when the bombers fell like firebombs into the sea. The naval vessels spun and twisted with the merchant ships struggling to follow them. The howling planes, the rattling guns and the thudding bombs hurling into the sea. Then suddenly it was all over.

The night became cool and peaceful. John Norman, like many of the crew, slept on deck. At sunrise they saw fighters from the Fleet Air Arm take off from the carriers. German and British planes circled and fought each other over their heads, rooks against seagulls. The seagulls returned to their roosts. Again the eerie peace. They steamed ahead until the next attack. Eight Italian bombers this time and amidst all the smoke and noise they had to follow the rest of the convoy as they banked into an emergency turn. No one knew why. By the evening they were nearly at the Skerki channel where the enemy would make an all-out attack. How could they endure more after this endless day? No one could rest, sleep or eat. He could see the caved in faces, sunken eyes and slumped shoulders of his crew mates and knew he must look the same. Deafened, choked and beaten down. The captain told them that the battleships with the remaining carriers were turning back to Gibraltar. He said that had always been the plan but as the big vessels swept away, escorted by their cruisers and destroyers, it felt as if they were being abandoned.

Chapter 33

Summer 1942

With night coming on the convoy approached the Narrows. The merchant ships slowed down so that they could shuffle their four lines into two. As John Norman peered ahead he could see the cruisers racing forwards, with the destroyers taking the lead at the front. He wasn't a religious man. He found Mamma's Sabbath observance hard to bear. Not working he could understand but not being allowed to do anything enjoyable either seemed such a waste of time. But now he found his lips muttering in prayer. Peace tonight, please God. We can't keep going like this.

He gasped as he saw a burst of red. Had his words conjured up a bolt from heaven? Spumes of water sprayed ahead of them, tossing lumps of metal into the air. Another explosion. That was two cruisers hit.

'They've got the *Ohio* too,' someone shouted as their own ship twisted sideways. The convoy was scattering. One of the stricken cruisers was going round in circles, her steering jammed while the *Cairo* was tilting and sinking fast. Their boat swerved to starboard. So did several others. The admiral must have sent new orders. But other ships were milling around and scrambled together. Another lurch at speed to avoid crashing into them. Thank God the captain knows what he's doing. Then a cry, 'Men in the water!' They must have reached the front of the convoy where some of the *Cairo's* crew were still floundering in the waves.

They hauled them aboard. Dazed and shivering, vomiting as they crawled onto the deck. Some had clothes dyed pink with blood diluted by sea water. Others lay still, eyes glazed and beyond help. They hardly seemed human. It was as if the sea had spewed up all the shipwrecked sailors it had ever held in its depths. He shook his head. Exhaustion was putting sick fancies into his head. The injured men were carried below while the fitter ones hunched together on the slopping deck. 'Here you are,' he said, holding out a cup of tea to a slumped figure. The man looked up, hollow eyes sunk in yellowish skin. He managed a lopsided smile. There was something familiar about the grin.

'Simon, it's yourself.'

'It was, last time I checked. What are you doing here? Sorry, silly question.' He coughed and spluttered up oily water.

'Drink up. I'll talk with you later.' John Norman had to swipe away the moisture from his eyes as he turned to help the other survivors. How silly to weep over seeing a face he recognised, one familiar face among the many. An officer ordered him below to work with the stokers. Apart from the gunners with their special skills, everyone else had to turn their hand to whatever was needed. He hated being trapped like a rat in a hole. He'd heard too many stories about stokers being boiled alive like lobsters when the engines were hit. He kept shovelling, staring at each glossy spadeful of coal. He was too busy to talk to Simon that day or night. The attacks from sea and air continued but were aimed at ships further away. The mate said that the convoy was scattered over twenty miles of sea. They could all be picked off one by one. It was hard not to pray that it would be some other ships that would be attacked. That night as he lay tense in his bunk it was quiet apart from the splash of waves against the hull and the thrum of the engines. It felt as if they had the sea to themselves. The captain had told them that the head of the convoy was turning south close to the Tunisian shore. There they would be on the lookout for the small Italian E-boats, fast as ferrets. Once through the Narrows they would be in range of air cover from Malta itself.

'What about the big ships the Ities have?' he heard the mate mutter. Was the captain keeping back the worst from them? At least by the morning they were back in line and so were five other merchant ships. The fitter sailors among those they had rescued volunteered to help with the watches. There was no sign of the Italian Navy but they were expecting enemy planes, a locust plague of them. John Norman and some of his exhausted crew mates were able to stagger to their bunks. He could close his red-rimmed eyes that felt as if they had been scoured with sandpaper. He expected that his writhing thoughts would keep him awake but he fell into a stunned sleep. He dreamt that the boat stopped dead. Then she gathered speed and moved backwards. She must be docking. But no. She shuddered as he could feel rather than hear a muffled explosion. His legs were too heavy to shift. The engines throbbed back to life and he sank again, down, down to the depths.

By the time he was back on watch they had the sea to themselves. The enemy planes had fled and he could see Valletta, sparkling white in the morning sunshine. The smoke from the naval vessels streamed ahead. He looked around to see where the other merchant ships were. He squinted and shaded his eyes with his hand but he could only see one.

'Can you hear the band yet? They'll be welcoming us with *Rule Britannia*. He turned to see Simon behind him, washed and brushed but bruised under the eyes.

'I can't see the rest of the ships? Are they straggling behind?'

'Have a look through my telescope. It's *Melbourne Star* you can see. She's been badly scorched.'

'And the others?'

'Only one other, I'm afraid.'

'What? Just the three have made it?'

'There might be some stragglers, right enough.' Simon's face drooped but then he gathered it up again. 'Talking of stragglers, our captain sent a signal to yours earlier on. Did you know? "S stands for straggler – and sunk." But in the end it was us who sank. Wasn't it lucky you were straggling behind and able to pick some of us up?'

There was a warm breeze but John Norman shivered. They were close enough now to hear the cheering crowds on the ramparts. He gasped as he looked at the harbour below. Outside the entrance lay the crumpled and mutilated wrecks of ships. Among them was a flattened submarine, its conning tower shattered by an explosion.

'It's been very bad. The Germans are trying to bomb the island into smithereens. They even bomb ships that have reached sanctuary inside the harbour. Once we dock we have to unload at once before they catch us out. Will you meet me later? On the inside edge of the harbour? We'll find a bar that's still standing and have a drink together. I'd invite you to my mess if we had one.'

John Norman nodded. He thought what a fish out of water he would be in an Officers' Mess, unless as a steward. Simon wouldn't have thought of that.

Chapter 34

Summer 1942

They found a bar, a cave really, gouged out from the hillside. Simon came back with two glasses of a pale, cloudy beer. 'Cat's piss, I know, but the best they can manage. I still can't get over us meeting like we did. What a bit of luck. And it means we can both write home and let them know we're safe.'

'Aye.' John Norman sipped his beer. Warm and thin it might be but he was grateful for it. He stretched his legs out and sighed. Simon grinned at him. There was something so easy about him. It made John Norman want to say more.

'I seem to make a habit of bumping into people. When I was in London there was an air raid siren. I went down into the Underground and bumped into Felicity MacDougall.' He could feel his ears starting to burn.

'The young upper-class girl?'

John Norman nodded.

Simon took a gulp of beer. 'Can I ask your advice? I've not told anyone else...but you know how it is. We don't know what might happen.'

'Go ahead.'

'Well, Margaret and I, we decided not to get married until the war's over. It wouldn't be right to risk leaving her a widow, maybe with a child.' He scratched his ear and swished the beer around in the glass. 'But it's so hard when you see each other rarely. How can I put it? I stepped out of line. Got a bit fresh. Thinking about coming back here – maybe not returning home. Tried it on you could say. I didn't mean her any harm – I love her but...'

'She was angry?'

'Furious. She had cause but she wouldn't let it go. Then she froze me out and I had to leave before we could make it up. I've written to say how sorry I am but I don't know if she's got the letter or not.'

'You're wondering if she'll forgive you?' John Norman could imagine his sister's fury. She was good at sticking the barb in and making other people feel guilty. You had to abase yourself for a long time, dangling and wriggling before she wrenched the hook out of your gills. He rather liked the idea of a tousled Margaret getting all indignant and hoity toity. But she did seem fond of Simon and she wouldn't lightly let go of a good match.

'She'll be gracious in the end, I'm sure. Accept you're only a man with normal needs. What you maybe don't know is how strict our Mamma is. My Granny, her mother, was born out of wedlock. That was a terrible stain on the family. So any what you might call "funny business"...'

'Would really upset her.' Simon's usually pale face was schoolboy pink. 'Do you think she'll wait for me?'

'I'm sure she will.'

'You really think so?' He plonked his glass down on the rough table. 'You've helped to put my mind at rest. Will you be seeing your young lady soon?'

John Norman felt his own cheeks start to glow. 'I wouldn't call her that exactly. She's too posh for me.'

'Surely the war's changed all that class rubbish? Everyone's had to muck in together.'

John Norman shrugged and decided to change the subject. 'The people of Malta should be able to last out a bit longer now.'

'I don't know. For food yes but not for fuel. *Ohio* was hit. I don't know if she made it, with all the oil and paraffin she was carrying. There's no sign of her yet.'

'After all that hell we've been through...'

'But we have come through. What about the drama on your own ship?'

John Norman shook his head.

'No? The captain must have kept it under his hat. It happened when I did that watch and we had the final attack. A torpedo whistled past us. Or so we thought but turned out we netted it in the starboard *paravane*. Two of the lads found it nestling there when they wound in the wire. Not the sort of catch you want.'

'And the ship stopped, then played out the wire and let it explode?'

'You did hear the story, then?'

'No, I heard it happen but I thought it was a bad dream.' He clenched his fists. 'The captain let you officers keep the story to yourselves. The other ranks, the merchant lads, might get in a panic if they knew. Was that it?'

'Come on, old chap. Don't take on. It wasn't a secret but there was so much going on. I know there are some silly old duffers among the top brass but anyone who's been on convoys knows what good sailors you fellows are. I'm just a wartime amateur, part of the wavy navy.'

John Norman still glowered.

'We were all under such strain. Maybe the captain thought you didn't need any more. You lads were exhausted.'

John Norman grunted. 'Aye we're still two different tribes, though, aren't we? Not all mucking in together. I heard another story about the *Deucalion*. She was hit by a bomb and taking in water. Looked as if she would sink so some of the crew lowered the boats and made for a destroyer. Clambered up the scrambling nets to safety or so they thought. But they got their hands jumped on by the destroyer's crew. Sent back like naughty boys, they were. They all had to abandon ship later anyway when she was torpedoed.'

Simon sighed and rubbed his eyes. 'I don't know what's right or wrong any more. German planes machine-gunned our lads in the water so one of our gunners shot a German pilot coming down on his parachute. Could I have stopped him? Should I have?' He looked directly at John Norman. 'You're going to be my bloody brother-in-law. I don't want to fight with you. We're on the same ruddy side. Sit down and finish your drink, even if it's cat's piss.'

'Aye, aye, Sir.' John Norman laughed.

'Let's forget about the bloody war for a moment.'

'I'll get us another drink.'

'Are you going back to Alexandria?' John Norman asked when he came back with more beers.

'Yes and further east maybe. I want to get stones for Margaret's ring. I'll see what I can find in the souk. Have to watch the Arabs though – they're crafty. Then I'll get some leave, I hope. I'll have to see my mother first, in Surrey. She's a widow as you know. She worries about me. We have to keep the worst of it from the women folk don't we?'

They looked back towards the harbour as they drank. 'Have you seen the Maltese fishing boats with the magic eye painted on the side?' Simon asked, 'Not that there's many about just now.' He sighed, downed his beer and stood up, holding out his hand.

'It's good that we both survived in one piece. I'll see you in Skye, God willing.'

Aye. But it's my sister you want to see, John Norman thought as he ambled back to the Seamen's Mission. How different Simon was from his sister. They said opposites attract. Maybe each partner caught something opposite and worthwhile from each other, a sort of kindly germ. He sighed. The drink was making him sentimental. It might be cat's piss but it had gone to his head after being dry for so long. That's what he needed before he was back at sea again. More drinks under his belt. A chance to slough off all that had happened. 'God willing.' He hadn't seen Simon as the religious sort. The English usually kept their religion to themselves. He suddenly thought of his old Granny, her ruined arthritic hands curled up in her lap.

'I'll see you soon,' she would say. *'Ma bhios mi air mo chaomhnadh'* – 'If I'm spared.' At the time he thought what an old misery she was. Now that memory squeezed his heart. This was no good. A few more drinks were the answer.

Chapter 35

Summer 1942

'He promised to find some stones, rubies even, when he's in the Middle East. But who knows when he'll be back. I'll be waiting for ever.' Margaret glared at her naked ring finger. 'Did he say anything to you about them?'

John Norman took a deep breath before he answered. 'Aye, he did once he had got over being torpedoed and hauled out of the sea.' The image of Simon, spent and sodden, flashed into his mind. Better not say anything more, though, with Mamma there, knitting another of her endless khaki socks.

Margaret sniffed. 'He never says anything of any consequence when he writes. Just about Gilbert and Sullivan songs he listens to on records. And how brave and wonderful the people on Malta are. Maltese people, that's the word.'

'Maltesers, more like. Not that we get them now.'

'Shush, Lexie.' Mamma stood up. 'Who wants a cup of tea? Is your leg paining you, son?'

'Aw, not bad. More itchy than anything, under the plaster.'

'Did you trip on purpose to get a holiday?' Lexie asked him when Mamma had gone into the kitchen.

'Well, if I had I would have gone for a sprain, not overdone it with a break.'

'Can I sign my name on the plaster?'

'As long as you don't write anything cheeky.'

People at home had no idea what it was like. He could understand that with the youngsters. You didn't want to upset them. But the rest. They kept moaning about the same old things. Spread silly rumours. The *bodach* opposite had beckoned him over the day before. 'I saw a stranger in a dark coat down on the shore. Was he signalling the Germans do you think?'

The older ones, the ones who had fought the first time round, they knew. The way Uncle Donald nodded and patted his back. No need for words. He understood the tedium and the terror, ears strained for the threat of fire and death splattering from sea and sky. Days and nights, cracked with fear. When the attack came it was almost a relief.

Was it chance that he fell over the coil of rope when the boat suddenly bucked in a swell? They had just set off from Gibraltar, after three days ashore. Hit the turbulence of the Bay of Biscay on the way to meet another collection of ships. Atlantic or Mediterranean convoy? Who knew? Neither of them what you would choose. Last chance for a dram or two the night before. Then wham. Tripped and landed with his right foot bent underneath him. The captain was furious both about having to turn back and at being a man down.

'Lucky bugger,' his shipmates had said. He supposed he was lucky. No chance of being killed while he was laid up. He had smashed his spectacles as well as his ankle when he fell. 'Back to the old days. How many times did I have to mend them?' Pappa had laughed when he handed them over.

It had given John Norman a shock, though. Blundering around on a plunging deck and grovelling for the fallen spectacles. What if that had happened when all the fighting was going on? He would be no use to himself or anyone else. He shook his head to dislodge the troubling thoughts. The good news was that his unexpected leave had come at a time that his friends were home. The first time they had all been together since the war started. He hadn't seen them for so long and he wondered if they had changed, like he had. They were all going to meet that evening. Angus was giving him a lift down to the Royal in his father's butcher's van. He should be here any minute now.

The other surprise was crackling in his jacket pocket.

Dear John Norman,

I've good news. I've some surprise leave and I'm coming up to Skye for a couple of days. I should be there late on Tuesday. It's too much to expect that you might be at home too but I'm writing in case you are. If we're in luck we can meet on Wednesday.

Kind regards
Felicity

It was fortunate that he had been looking out of the window this morning and saw the postie before anyone else did. She was arriving in two days' time. He had rushed to reply. The note would be there, waiting for her.

Dear Felicity,

We are in luck i'm home too. i'll wait for you in the square at 11 o'clock on Wednesday morning.

Kind regards,
John Norman

He had bribed Lexie to post the letter. If Angus couldn't give him a lift that morning he would have to hobble down on his crutches.

Lexie heard the engine first. 'Come on, lean on me.'

'Hang on, you're not tall enough. Just hold the crutches till I'm on my feet. No fooling around now.'

'As if I would,' she said, round-eyed.

The worst part was making that first move. He could feel the broken ends of bone grinding together. Lexie held him until he could swing himself forward on the crutches and hobble out of the front door.

'Murdo and Donnie are in the back,' Angus said as he bundled him into the front seat.

'It's grand to see you, John Norman. The wounded warrior, eh?' Donnie called out, 'You're better in the front. It stinks to high heaven in the back here.'

'It's only carcasses. When did you get so fussy? You can walk if you like.'

'It's fine, Angus. I'll just hold my breath until we're there.'

'It'll stop you talking anyway.'

One thing hadn't changed then. Angus and Donnie goading each other but it seemed more out of habit than anger. They all looked different, grown men now, their faces pared down. They went into the bar of the Royal. Murdo waited for John Norman to catch up. They all sat down and John Norman propped himself up sideways so that he could stretch out his broken leg. Angus shouldered his way to the bar.

'Why the hell is he wearing his uniform?' Donnie asked the others.

'Showing off as usual,' Murdo said. 'I'm glad to get out of mine for a while.'

'What's it like in the posh Navy, then? Were you on convoy duty?' John Norman asked him.

'Aye, to the Arctic. Bloody freezing. Lots of stupid rules. And the officers making daft jokes. When we left Murmansk we found we still had the two Russian pilots aboard so the lieutenant said, "What a pity they're aren't four of them. They would have made another set for bridge." I didn't know what the hell he was talking about. We'd got enough bloody officers on the bridge already.'

'I was in the Atlantic and the Med but they say the Arctic run's the worst.'

Murdo shrugged. 'You get shot at the same wherever you are. We just got the cold to keep us on our toes.'

'What about you, Donnie? How's the army?' John Norman asked.

'You know – all drilling, spit and polish, sergeants yelling at you. I'm waiting for my posting. Here's Angus now with the drinks. Are you flying yet, lad?'

'No, it's just a matter of time.'

'What are you doing then? Aircraft maintenance? Sitting in an office?'

'Checking over the engines. Hey, look over at the door. Two girls coming in, would you believe? Must be strangers, showing their faces in here.'

They all turned. John Norman had to wipe his steamed-up spectacles. When he saw the two figures his mouth fell open. Surely not? But it was her and she had seen him. She strode over, smiling. A short, thickset girl bustled along beside her.

'Wha...what are you doing here?' John Norman asked.

Her smile faltered as she saw the gawping faces. 'You got my letter? We made better time than we expected so my friend Bertha said, "Let's go out, rather than stay in the cold house."'

John Norman had forgotten how shrill and English her voice sounded. Angus was the first to recover. 'Come and sit down with us. It's just odd seeing ladies in here.'

'Why's that? We're in the war too and my money's as good as yours,' Bertha said loudly. 'What's your names then?'

John Norman introduced his friends.

'What do you want to drink, ladies?' Angus asked.

He nudged John Norman to come with him to the bar to fetch Felicity's dry sherry and Bertha's beer. 'You're a dark horse, John Norman. Your one's not bad looking but her friend's a bit of a battle axe. Still, any port in a storm. We'll keep them topped up, eh? Get them on whisky if we can. It's a grand leg opener.'

John Norman was speechless. Angus grinned. 'You look like a minister who's gone into a brothel by mistake. You've not had... not with any girl? Still the wee virgin?'

The urge to hit Angus was so powerful that John Norman had to clench his fists in his pockets. When they returned Bertha was talking and banging the table with her fist. 'You're all lambs to the slaughter, then? Doing what the upper classes tell you? Just like the last war.'

'I believe it's called military discipline. Disobey and you're court martialled,' Donnie said.

'Well it's what you're used to, isn't it? You all kowtowed to the landowners before the war.'

'Did we? You're a wee bittie out of date. You've not heard about the Land Wars? Anyway, we're not crofters. My father's a joiner and so was I. Angus's father has a butcher's shop. Murdo and John Norman are fishermen.'

She snorted. 'But who governs the Highlands? Who's got all the money and power? The landowners, of course. We're just fighting to keep them in charge. When the war ends nothing will have changed. We'll be back at the bottom of the pile again.'

'You sound like that Lord Haw Haw. Well I would rather have Scottish or even English lords than German ones,' Angus said. 'Sup up girls and we'll get another round.'

'And where are the women, then?' Bertha said, looking around. 'Kept slaving at home? At least where I come from women can get out. My Granny was a chain maker. Had arms like a navvy. No one dared tell her what she could or couldn't do. Wouldn't stand any…'

Donnie interrupted, 'Sounds like my Granny, right enough, so what do you do, Bertha? Make chains too? You and Felicity together?'

Felicity giggled. 'We trained together but it's very hush-hush. We're forbidden to talk about it. We had to sign the Official Secrets Act.'

'Oh bugger that. We've been learning Morse Code so we can listen to German messages.'

'Shhs. Walls have ears,' Felicity whispered.

'Yeah and we're talking to German spies. Anyway, we've finished and we're to be given a new posting. Well, Felicity is anyway. I got into trouble and have to repeat the course.'

'Really?' Murdo asked open-eyed. 'What on earth could you have done to deserve that?'

She gave him a hard look. 'Stuck up for meself, of course. Unlike you soft lot.'

'Well, well what a surprise.' Murdo shook his head. 'I'll have to leave you to plan your revolution on your own, I'm afraid. I'm away home. Out early on the boat with my da tomorrow.'

'Me too,' said Donnie, getting up and slapping John Norman on the shoulder. 'I'll leave you to the pleasure of a ride home in the smelly old van.'

'I'm sorry your friends had to go so soon,' Felicity said to John Norman.

'You'll all have another dram?' Angus said. His face was slippery with sweat and he undid his uniform jacket.

'If you're paying.' Bertha thrust her empty glass at him and Angus strode off to the bar again.

'You look tired, John Norman,' Felicity said, reaching over to touch his hand. 'Is your leg troubling you?'

'A wee bit.'

'I would have given you a lift back home but I couldn't bring my motor. I couldn't get the petrol for the journey. I had to come on the train.'

'I was surprised you could get here at all. You need a special pass now to come to the Highlands.'

Felicity looked uncomfortable. Bertha tapped her nose with her mauled hand. John Norman forced himself not to flinch. 'Our Felicity's smart. She knows how to wangle things, don't you?'

'It's just knowing the right people,' Felicity said, with a shrug. 'Aren't you glad I managed to come?' Her eyes were pleading. John Norman replied, 'Of course I am.'

Her eyes shone. Angus came back with the drinks. 'I got us all a whisky to celebrate. *Slàinte Mhath.*' He clinked glasses with Bertha and grinned at John Norman who ignored him.

'Eh? "Bottoms up." I've not had one of these for a long time,' Bertha said, downing her glass.

John Norman sat nursing his drink and wishing that Felicity hadn't brought her coarse friend with the big mouth. Surely she was well beneath her? What on earth did she see in the woman? Felicity would never have come in here and shown him up if she had been on her own.

'I think we should get back now and let you rest your leg,' she said. She touched his arm and his heart sang. She was a lovely, kind lass, even though he couldn't fathom her.

Chapter 36

Later that evening

'Your carriage awaits, ladies.' Angus bowed as he pointed at the van. 'I'm sorry that you'll have to go in the back but the cripple needs to sit in the front.'

'We'll manage won't we, Bertha? We all have to make sacrifices in wartime,' Felicity said.

'Huh! What do you know about slumming it?' Bertha replied. She sounded jovial. The drink must have mellowed her.

'Just don't breathe and you'll be fine,' John Norman told them.

'I'll drop you two lovebirds at the end of the road so you can say goodnight. Bertha and I'll wait in the car. But don't spend too long canoodling or I'll sound the horn. Then I'll take you two lassies home,' Angus said, digging John Norman in the ribs. Once they were out of the car and walking slowly along, Felicity spoke.

'Bertha's a little forthright I'm afraid but I admire her boldness. She had a terrible childhood you know, living in a slum in Wolverhampton. I suppose it either kills you or makes you tough.'

He was jolted. Could she read his mind? 'You meet all sorts of different people I suppose with the war. Angus is full of himself too. I wonder how they'll get on together. She'll put him in his place if she needs to.'

Felicity looked puzzled for a minute. 'Oh, you mean he might try and take advantage of her? I can't imagine that happening.' She giggled. 'Her Granny made chains, remember? Yes, we do all have to muck in together. Not just with people like Bertha but the other extreme too. There were titled ladies, debutantes, where I used to work. They scared me a little. They were so elegant and confident. But then I lodged in Winnie's little house and she was so kind. She mothered me.'

'Well here we are.' He stopped several houses short of his own door. As he reached into his pocket for a cigarette, one of his crutches toppled over.

'It's alright I can manage.' But she had already picked it up and was holding it out to him. He leant against a gatepost and tried not to wince. They were standing very close, too close for him to manoeuvre his crutches out of her way.

'What a lovely surprise seeing you tonight. And I'm invited for lunch tomorrow.' She leant forward and her lips brushed his cheek. He could feel a strand of her hair under his nose. It made him sneeze and they both laughed. He turned his head and their mouths bumped together. The tip of her tongue was warm. He leant forward as she leapt back. 'I'll see you tomorrow, John Norman.'

What was this about being invited? Was the dreadful Bertha invited too? But before he could ask she was already running back to the car. He stood still, brushing his fingers against his lips in amazement. Had that kiss really happened? He glanced round. Had anyone seen them? It was still light enough to make them out. He walked up to his own house and saw that Lexie's curtains were gaping. He inched the back door open and there was his sister, grinning. 'This invitation. It's your doing isn't it?'

'Me?' she frowned in surprise but couldn't hide the glint in her eyes.

'Tell me.'

'It was Mamma who invited Felicity. Simon's coming tomorrow, isn't he? Well, Mamma and I were outside the baker's this afternoon and we saw Felicity so Mamma thought she could come too. The two *sasannachs* would be company for each other.'

'Wait a moment. Mamma's doesn't know Felicity. You arranged this, didn't you?'

'Well she recognised me and waved so I had to tell Mamma

who she was. You're not cross are you? You've not fallen out?'

He laughed out loud. 'Don't play the innocent. And you were peeping out of the window a moment ago.'

She giggled. 'Just call me Cupid. She's nice, I think, even though she's posh.'

'Aye, I think so too.' He felt the words ring out. 'But don't go shouting it from the rooftops.'

'If you say so. I'm planning to be a bridesmaid twice over, for Margaret's wedding and yours. Jeannie's no use at the moment while she's at the university.'

'What a little schemer you are. Wait a moment, though. Felicity's friend's not coming too, is she?'

'Her friend? No. I've not met her.'

'Thank Heavens for that. Bertha's like a tank. She doesn't talk to you. She tramples over you. You would remember her if you had met her.'

He climbed upstairs, humming as he swung his plastered leg up each step.

The next day Mamma was up early, preparing a *gigot* of lamb for roasting. 'Will it be big enough for seven of us, John?'

'I think those young folk who haven't eaten proper food since I don't know when will think they're in heaven when they taste it.' He put his arms round her waist.

'Away with you and get me the best potatoes you can find.'

'Look here's a car,' Lexie squawked. John Norman came to the window. Simon he expected to see, with Margaret who had left earlier to meet him in the Square but to his surprise Felicity emerged too. She and Simon walked up to the door together, talking as if they were old friends.

'What a stroke of luck,' Felicity said after greeting everyone. 'I had started to walk to Portree. It was either that or riding Mr Patterson's horse. Then Simon stopped to offer me a lift.'

'We've never met before but John Norman told me about

you,' Simon said. Felicity's face went pink. 'All good things,' he added.

John Norman noticed that Margaret's smile seemed tight. Then he received the full glow of Felicity's grin and he didn't care.

Mamma hustled them through to the kitchen. Everyone fell on the food. 'I've not tasted anything so good since ...years ago, before the war,' Simon said.

'It's delicious. I used to get rabbit pie at my digs but that wasn't a patch on this,' Felicity added.

Mamma smiled. 'We're lucky here. We don't have to worry so much about rationing.'

'Aye. It all depends on who you know,' John Norman said. Mamma flashed him a "not in front of strangers" look.

'It's a pity Jeannie's not here to enjoy it but she's in Glasgow, at the university,' she continued.

'Good for her. More than I ever managed,' Simon said. 'What about you Felicity? Did you have plans to go on to university?'

She shook her head. 'Nothing so clever, I'm afraid. I was packed off to a finishing school.'

John Norman saw how Margaret's jaw clenched tight. Simon smiled across the table at her before turning to Lexie. 'What about you, young lady? Are you going to follow in your sister's footsteps?'

Lexie made a face and jabbed the air with her fork. 'Stuck in a dusty library all day? No fear. I want to be an actress.'

Everyone laughed at her dramatic pose except for Mamma who frowned and asked if anyone wanted more. While the plates were being refilled Simon asked Felicity where she was working.

'Well, I've just finished a course and I'm waiting to hear about my new posting.' She took a deep breath. 'When I'm asked I'm supposed to say I work for the government but that's so boring and not true. I've done a crash course in Morse Code.'

Simon's face stiffened. 'It's never safe to talk about your

work, surely. Of course we'll all keep quiet. But the danger is that you get into the habit of talking about it. You never know who's listening. Someone might pass it on to the enemy.'

Felicity flushed. 'My friend Bertha says the government tries to rule us by fear, to stop us thinking for ourselves and to keep us in our place.'

John Norman grimaced and Lexie winked at him.

Simon put his knife and fork down. 'John Norman, when you went through the Straits I'm sure you saw all those Spanish fishing boats lit up like Christmas trees.'

'Aye. Our captain said they did it to show up the convoy and pass the information on to the Germans.'

'That's right. Spain, the so-called neutral country. That's why we can't afford to trust anyone. We're fighting on our own with our backs against the wall.'

'Will the Germans come and invade us?' There was a tremor in Lexie's voice.

Simon lightened his voice and touched her hand. 'No chance. I do believe the tide is turning. That last convoy getting through to Malta proves it. But we have to be watchful.'

Felicity looked down at her plate while Margaret smiled.

'Talking of those cheating Spaniards, did you hear about that tinker, Stewart?' Mamma turned to John Norman.

'No, last time I saw him he was in the queue with me, signing up for a boat.'

'Well, he slunk off to Ireland. Made sure he was out of danger.'

John Norman shivered, remembering how he had misread the premonition in his dream. He was relieved that Archie was alive but kept his thoughts to himself. A heavy silence fell over them all.

It was Margaret who broke it. 'Shall we tell them, Simon?'

He looked puzzled.

'About the stones, of course.'

'Oh, I thought we were going to…'

'Simon finally found some stones for my engagement ring but they're not ready yet. His mother is taking them to some London jeweller to be set so I have to wait.'

'Ma wanted to add a stone from one of her own rings to it. It should look really good when it's done.'

'I hope so. It's been a long wait.'

It was a relief to escape outside for a smoke. Simon took out a sheaf of fat cigars but John Norman declined and shook out a cigarette from its packet.

'I hope I wasn't too sharp with Felicity,' Simon said.

'She's a bit dazzled by her friend Bertha, I think. A fiery one that. All for revolution and class war.'

Simon groaned. 'She should leave all that to the Russians. Have you come across any Reds among your ship mates?'

'No. We haven't time to talk politics. We're just trying to keep our ship afloat.'

'Quite right too. All the argy bargy can wait until the war's over.'

Simon had to leave shortly afterwards. He offered Felicity a lift. She accepted at once and waited inside while Margaret went out with Simon to bid him goodbye. For a moment, he and Felicity were alone together in the parlour. She hurried up to him and took his hand. Surely she didn't expect him to kiss her here when Lexie or Mamma could appear at any moment? He dropped her hand as if he had reached into a net and picked up a conger eel. She flushed and he smiled in apology, hoping she would understand.

After they had all gone he went outside for another smoke. He was deep in thought and jumped when he felt arms around his waist.

'It's only me, I'm afraid. Not Felicity come back again.'

'And what do you want?'

He could hear the sharpness in his voice. His sister hesitated before taking something out of her pocket and handing it to him.

'I thought you might like it for writing to Felicity.'

He opened the narrow box and whistled. 'That's a very expensive pen. Handmade, I would think.'

'I like the pattern. It's a ballpoint pen,' she said. Very modern and used by pilots because you don't need ink.'

He could feel a lump in his throat. 'It's very kind of you, Lexie, but wouldn't you like to keep it yourself? You write much more than me.'

'But you've always given me your sweetie ration. And I like Felicity. You just make sure I get to be a bridesmaid when you marry her.'

They both laughed. 'You've not asked me how I got the magic pen,' Lexie said. 'Margaret gave it to me. She got given two, from different admirals or whatever. She kept one and said I could have the other. I said, "But wouldn't Jeannie like it? She's always writing at the university."'

'And what did Margaret say?'

'She sniffed and said, "She's got plenty of pens already."'

John Norman smiled at Lexie's perfect imitation of their older sister being superior.

'Well, I shall keep it safe – and even use it. But you better not tell Margaret that you've given it to me or she'll be offended.' She surprised him again by reaching up and kissing him on the cheek before skipping away.

Part 6

Felicity's Story

Chapter 37

Summer 1942

All too soon they were on the return journey. Bertha was in high spirits. 'I've enjoyed Scotland. All that open space. I can see why you like it, our kid. But the oppression! I'll have to tell my da about it. Them landowners were as bad as the industrialists. I suppose they were the same men, capitalists buying their way into the aristocracy.'

Felicity let the tide of words flow over her. She felt flat after all the anticipation of going to Skye. She had hated it when that Simon had showed her up, claiming she was giving away state secrets. What did he know about how clever she had been getting up there and she had said nothing about that strange weekend and what it might lead to. Bertha was making her see things in a different way, like looking through the other end of a telescope. All those men thought it was only their jobs that were vital for the war effort. They didn't like to imagine women doing anything important. They were supposed to pretend they were 'only doing filing in a government office'.

The other blow was that she and John Norman had so little time on their own after that sudden, wonderful kiss. She stroked her lips with her finger, reliving the excitement of it. Afterwards though, he had been reluctant to sit close or gaze at her when his family were there. She could understand it she supposed, with that nosey young sister and his rather proper mother always there. Still, she envied Margaret who was lovey dovey the whole time, at least when she wasn't glaring at Felicity. Why was that? Did she imagine she was making eyes at Simon? Not likely after how he had spoken to her. Of course, Margaret and Simon were engaged so that allowed them to be affectionate in front of other people. At least Felicity had managed to pull John Norman into a snatched hug before she left.

'Make sure you write. You've got Winnie's address? I almost gave up on you when you didn't write for so long.'

'I'm no good at writing. I hated school.'

'So did I. Do you think I care about spelling and full stops?' She squeezed his hand. 'I just want to know you're safe. I'm still hoping to be posted up to Scotland.'

He hadn't said anything but his eyes had shone. That was enough she had thought, smiling to herself.

By now the rhythm of the train had lulled Bertha to sleep. Her head was lolling sideways and she had started to snore. In repose her face had a soft-cheeked innocence. She would hate anyone to see her like that, Felicity thought. She sighed and gazed out at the muted greenish brown colours of the moors without seeing them. So much had happened during the last year or so.

It was true that she had almost given up with John Norman. She had written to him the winter before, soon after she had bumped into him so unexpectedly and he hadn't replied for so long, until this summer. When he finally did write it was guff about words from a song. She had a sense that he was hiding something. So, what had possessed her to rush up to Skye? Part of it was Bertha's influence. She was one for throwing caution to the winds. Not that Felicity regretted the adventure at all. She felt that she and John Norman were a proper couple now with a chance of a future together.

The Morse Code training had all ended in a rush with the girls packing ready for a short leave before going to their new postings. Felicity barely had time to say goodbye to them. She was envious that they all seemed to have destinations at various listening stations while she had been told to go back to London and await orders. She felt a pang that she hadn't got to know the others at all but she had been so caught up with Bertha. After the final interview with Captain Turner she had rushed back to their shared room to find her friend was cramming her belongings into her shabby holdall.

'What's happening?' Felicity asked her.

'What do you think? I'm being sent home,' she snapped.

'But you came top! What a waste. Won't they give you another chance?'

'Only if I grovel.'

'Apologise you mean? Why not just grit your teeth and do it? Otherwise you'll get something worse to do.'

Bertha yanked the straps tight on her bag. 'Why should I?' She glared at Felicity.

'Because you're cutting off your nose to spite your face, that's why.' Felicity put her hands on her hips and glowered back. She could feel her heart racing. She had never argued with Bertha before. Suddenly Bertha's broad shoulders slumped.

'Think about it,' Felicity said, 'I've been told to go back to London. It's not at all what I wanted. Look, I'm going to give you my address and I'll write down yours. I want to know what happens to you.'

Bertha nodded meekly. She looked deflated.

'I'll pack my things too. Then we can have a bite to eat and get the boat back together.'

Sailing back to the mainland they had both looked out glumly at the churning sea and the driving rain. Once she had returned home Felicity felt that her life was going backwards. She had been desperate to escape from the cheerless London house and here she was there again. Pa was still out most of the time. He tolerated her being there but there was no welcome, no fatted calf.

'I don't know why you're back here when you were supposed to be posted somewhere else.'

'Neither do I Pa, but it's not as if I've been expelled or anything. I did come top in the exams. I've just got to wait for further instructions.'

'Hmm,' he replied, looking over his glasses with a doubtful

expression on his face. Felicity had felt marooned and abandoned. There was still no word from John Norman. She knew that Winnie would have forwarded any letters that came, putting them in a new envelope so that Pa wouldn't be suspicious. He must surely be on some sort of leave before his next voyage? She hadn't felt lonely while she was on the course but now she was surrounded by a featureless expanse of time. She had felt so glad to bump into him and talk like old friends. Then he had seemed to hold himself back and she couldn't explain to him why she wouldn't invite him home. But surely he must have sensed that it would be difficult?

No news from Bertha either. All Felicity had was the grind of housekeeping. She had no cooking skills and found managing on rations very difficult. How could anyone exist on only one egg and one ounce of butter a week? She hadn't realised how lucky she had been living in the countryside with Winnie where there were plenty of rabbits, vegetables and preserves. Pa ate out most of the time at his club. At first she ate out too. There were still restaurants to go to if you had money but she got disheartened eating on her own. More and more she lived on bread and marge, with a spoonful of jam from some old jars she found in the larder. The waistbands of her skirts were getting loose and she seemed to have a permanent cold and no energy.

'You can't carry on moping around the house like this,' Pa said after several weeks had gone by. 'It looks as if the powers that be have forgotten about you. I'll find a job for you to do at the War Office. Not in my office. That would look like special treatment. It won't be anything responsible, just delivering mail or something like that and you'll get your meals there.'

She agreed. Working as a filing clerk and distributing internal mail kept her busy but she felt isolated. The other women kept their distance. She supposed it was because Pa had introduced her to everyone as his daughter. Maybe they thought she was there to spy on how hard they worked. The only instructions she received about her new role was that she had to see a French émigré for daily tuition in the language. So in the evenings she visited an elderly woman who frowned at her over her lorgnette. Felicity sensed she would like to rap her knuckles every time she made a mistake. No one told her what she was being prepared to do. So she probed Pa when she managed to catch him between his office and his club.

'Does the government need translators for talking to the Free French?'

'Hmm. They're slippery types. They'll be secretly recording them I suspect.' He peered at her. 'Why do you ask? They won't want a dizzy slip of a girl like you doing that work.' He was out of the front door without noticing her crushed expression.

The only consolation was that Madame Jules had smiled thinly and told her that her French was now *assez bien*. It was at that low point when she had stopped listening for the postman that the buff envelope plopped through the letter box. She took a ragged breath before opening it. Inside was a summons to attend a grand country house a week later. There were no more details. When she showed it to Pa he scrutinised it and handed it back.

'Well done. I wish your mother were here. She would be very proud of you.'

Felicity stared at him with her mouth gaping, not believing her ears. She couldn't remember when he had last spoken of her mother. She cleared her throat. 'Do you know what it's about, Pa? The letter doesn't explain at all.'

'Best wait and see.'

Chapter 38

Summer 1942

The mansion she had to report to wasn't a ramshackle affair like the Park but a classically proportioned Georgian building. She was shown to a sparsely furnished bedroom and then had to wait in a draughty corridor that reminded her of all her past interviews. A brisk army officer had soon appeared to interview her about her background. He switched constantly from English to French so that she struggled to keep up. A Morse test followed, both listening and transmitting. She was given a short time to practice beforehand and felt she had acquitted herself well.

After that she had been put in a room with fifteen other people, both men and women, some her age and others older. There had been no time to speak as question papers were handed out in silence. Her heart had sunk but it wasn't like a school exam, more like a moral debate. Was it ever acceptable to lie? Could she kill someone in cold blood? Would she describe herself as outgoing or reserved, impulsive or careful? What did a pattern of ink blots on the page suggest to her? All so peculiar that she hadn't felt nervous and answered honestly.

Next, they had been hustled into another room to listen to a lecture. Forbidden to take notes but told to memorise the details and answer questions afterwards. The officer had pinned up a map on a blackboard and was about to start talking when the door was flung open and two men ran in, shouting and pointing guns. No time to think. Some of the others had frozen, one woman started screaming and two of the men had tackled the intruders and tried to seize the guns. Acting on instinct, Felicity had run back out of the door but once through it she glanced back to see what was happening. To her amazement the two intruders had pushed away their attackers and made for the door. Felicity sprang back and pressed herself against the wall.

'Stand at ease everyone. The exercise is over,' the officer barked. 'Sit down and describe everything you saw.'

The stunned group sat down. Felicity closed her eyes and visualised the two men. Neither was remarkable in appearance but she could remember one of them looking at her as they rushed past her, a flash of intense blue eyes in an acne scarred face and a bent nose that looked as if it had been broken. All those years of being the wary outsider, the suspicious watcher, had made her observant. She decided to sketch a likeness to add to her description.

Afterwards came the physical tests. Some of the others were looking bewildered by this time but Felicity's time at boarding school had accustomed her to being herded around with no explanations given. She changed out of her pleated skirt and twinset to put on the pair of slacks they had been instructed to bring. They had to climb over, under and through obstacles as quickly as possible. All those holidays on Skye leaping over streams and sinking into peatbogs meant that the assault course held no fears for her. She had even offered a hand to a tearful girl who had got her hair caught crawling under barbed wire. It was only at the end that she was terrified. The last challenge was to climb a ladder propped against a tree and make their way on a rope across to another tree thirty feet away, with only a second rope at waist height to hold onto.

'You've a choice of two heights, five feet up or twenty feet,' the instructor told them.

'I'll go for the lower one. How about you?' the girl she had helped asked Felicity.

'I don't know.' Heights were Felicity's greatest fear. She had never been able to go near cliff edges and hated fairground rides. She sensed that she had done alright so far. Maybe she could risk doing the easier challenge? But a warning voice in her head told her that this test was the deciding one. Anyone who didn't tackle the higher rope crossing would fail.

She had no time to ponder because she was called to go first. She concentrated on climbing up the ladder to the higher platform. If John Norman could live through dangers he hadn't even spoken about, she could walk over this gap. She had felt her way over, looking ahead the whole time. And then it was over. She was clambering down, her thudding heartbeat mixing with the applause of the others.

'That will do. You're not at the theatre,' the instructor said, summoning the next person. The last ordeal was to be a cocktail party. What a rum do it all was, she had thought as she shook out a blue party frock she had bought before the war. It hung in loose folds about her body. Well it would have to do. She could pull the belt in more tightly. She followed the sound of lively conversations to see a tasty spread of proper food – dainty sandwiches with fillings of ham and cheese, sausage rolls, trifles and fruit pies. There was an end of term atmosphere as waitresses had plied them with drinks. Some of the others had fallen on the offerings, especially the alcohol, like starving beggars and were soon well-oiled. But this sudden affability from their inquisitors had made Felicity suspicious. She stayed watchful. Bertha's scepticism was contagious.

She had been right to be wary. After an hour they were taken away in turn and subjected to a quick-fire interview in French, then shooed off home with no more information except that they would receive another letter in two weeks' time.

Back to waiting again. And nothing further had come from John Norman. She didn't know how long his spells of duty at sea lasted. Had he given up writing to her or was he in such danger that he couldn't write? Since her time at Bletchley she had taken to reading the newspapers. She scanned Pa's *Times* every day for naval news. Thanks to Bertha she knew how the government censored everything. Although she had read that supplies were getting through she knew that the convoys were under constant attack. What if John Norman was injured or killed? How would she know? Would that cheeky young sister of his think to tell her?

Pa knew that he couldn't ask her about the course but he had surprised her by suggesting that she have a holiday while she waited for the letter.

Her heart leapt. 'There would be time to go up to Skye. I would love to see it again.'

His face had hardened. 'How on earth could you travel so far? You know that there's petrol rationing.'

'I could go by train.'

'That's impossible. There are restrictions on travelling to the Highlands. You need a special pass.'

'Couldn't you arrange that for me, Pa?'

'Certainly not, just for a holiday. Why don't you go to the south coast for a few days? I'll pay for a hotel. And you could go back and see your landlady. What's her name?'

'Winnie. Yes, I could. Thank you, Pa.' Felicity knew that it was no use arguing. Pa must suspect that she was hoping to see John Norman. And she was, of course, but even if he wasn't there she longed to go back to Skye. There must be a way to do it.

Two days later a letter had arrived, one with the address written in a neat, educated hand so Pa didn't question it.

Had to repeat part of the course, to teach me middle class manners. They know I'm bloody good at the codes. You'll be pleased to know I passed it this time. I was a model student, a credit to the aspiring (or bootlicking) working classes. I've got leave before my posting. What about meeting?

Felicity had laughed aloud. Bertha was nearly as terse a correspondent as John Norman. What would she do in this situation? Bertha charged at problems like a bull although maybe she was learning some diplomacy now. That night Felicity had lain in bed thinking how easy it had been to fool Commander Harrison. She smiled to herself as a plan began to form in her mind.

Chapter 39

Summer 1942

The next day Felicity had arrived earlier than usual at the office. 'I want to make sure I do as much work as possible before I have my holiday,' she told Pa at breakfast. He had glanced up from his newspaper. 'Very good,' he said and went back to reading.

She was able to move freely all over the building because of her role delivering letters. She had begun by slipping into Pa's office. His secretary hadn't arrived yet. A quick shuffle through a filing cabinet to find some official headed paper. Stuffing it into her bag she had peered through the glass on the doors of several offices until she found one that was empty apart from a young girl busy at her typewriter. Felicity flounced in and announced in her most queenly voice, 'I'm Miss MacDougall. My father the Commander needs me to travel up to the North of Scotland and I require a pass. Will you type it up now for me if I dictate the words?'

'Yes, Miss MacDougall, of course.'

Felicity had handed over a sheet of the headed paper. 'Here's what you write.'

To whom it may concern:
Miss Felicity MacDougall and Miss Bertha Wilkins are authorised to travel freely through the Highlands to the Isle of Skye in pursuance of official Government business.

'I don't know the other lady,' the girl said frowning. 'Does she work here too?'

'No, But the Commander knows her. Now type his official title at the bottom.'

'Should I take it to him to sign?'

'No need. I'll do that. Just give me an envelope.' Felicity had to fight the urge to snatch it from the girl. Next, she would have to forge Pa's signature on the paper and write to Bertha. Felicity could take the train to Birmingham, meet Bertha there and travel north with her. After Bertha had replied, agreeing to the plan, she scribbled a brief note to John Norman, saying she was coming. It would be good to have Bertha's company on the journey, especially if she had to face the disappointment of John Norman not being there. Money would be no trouble, thanks to Pa's generosity. Usually it saddened her that he gave her money instead of affection but this time it had worked out well.

Bertha had been waiting for her at New Street Station in Birmingham, a broad grin on her face.

'You look very cheerful,' Felicity said.

'Well, I'm going on me holidays. I've never been further than Skeggie before and that was only for a day.'

It was an adventure for them both, despite the crowded carriages, the slow trains and the delays. Once they reached Lancashire and Cumberland Bertha sat with her nose pressed to the window. 'I never knew there were all them fields and hills. Nothing but sheep and stone walls.'

'Just wait until we reach the Highlands.'

When they had arrived in Perth, Felicity bought first class tickets for the rest of the journey.

'I'm not sitting with a load of nobs going to their shooting estates.'

'You'll just have to swallow your principles, Bertha. And keep your mouth shut when we're asked to present our papers. It'll look much more convincing if we're travelling first class.'

Bertha pulled a face but she stopped protesting. Felicity had started to feel nervous once they boarded the Kyle train at Inverness. Luckily, she and Bertha had a carriage to themselves. She didn't know where the checkpoint would be and she couldn't be sure that her forgery would work. Her greatest fear was that the authorities would contact Pa. She quailed at the thought of how furious he would be with her. Bertha meanwhile was getting over her amazement at the countryside and was back to holding forth about politics.

'It's a wilderness out there. Why are there so few houses?'

'Well, it's hard to make a living from poor land.'

'But look. There's ruined houses over there. Why did the people leave? There's plenty of sheep about.'

'The sheep were more profitable so a lot of the crofters moved to the cities or emigrated.'

Bertha's eyes glinted. 'There's something you're not telling me, Felicity MacDougall. Did they choose to move or did the landowners force them out by any chance?'

Felicity sighed. 'You know I don't know much about history, not Scottish history anyway.'

'That's because your class came out on top. I bet it was the same here as it was in Ireland – folk being evicted.'

'You'll have to ask John Norman about it.'

When they had reached the tiny station of Achnasheen, Felicity's heart had started pounding. There were soldiers waiting on the platform and they started to fan out alongside the train as it slowed down. Felicity sat up very straight and looked the soldier in the eye as he asked for their papers. He was grey haired and wearing an ill-fitting uniform. He must be from the Home Guard. He read the note and frowned while she pressed her hands together to stop them shaking.

'It's not the usual pass.'

'Really?' She had smiled up at him, fluttering her eyelashes. 'Well it was all done in rather a rush. We're on a special sort of mission and I dare say that there wasn't time to arrange all the usual paperwork.'

She spoke in her clearest, most ringing tones. Bertha nodded but, thank goodness, kept her mouth shut. For what seemed like an eternity he had stood looking at them. Then he smiled and handed the letter back.

'There you are, Miss.'

'I understand that you have to be very thorough,' she had replied graciously, as she folded the letter with steady hands and put it back in her bag.

'You're a cool customer. I wouldn't want to play cards against you,' Bertha had said once they were on their way again.

'Don't underestimate the upper classes.' They had both laughed with the release of tension.

Chapter 40

Summer 1942

There was no checking of documents on the return journey. After they arrived in Inverness they travelled south on a succession of crowded, grubby trains. As they finally neared Birmingham, Felicity nudged Bertha awake.

'Come on, Sleeping Beauty. We're nearly there.'

'Sleeping maybe but no beauty. Me lungs can't cope with all this fresh air I've been breathing in. I'm worn out.'

'Did you enjoy our trip?' Felicity asked her friend as they parted.

'It was bostin'. All that scenery and lovely grub. Thank you, our kid.'

Felicity was touched by such unusual effusiveness and gave Bertha a hug. She looked surprised but grinned and patted Felicity's back.

'You take care. Don't let the buggers grind you down.' Then she was off, shouldering her way through the crowds, without a backward glance.

'How was Bletchley and Eastbourne?' Pa asked when she got home.

'Oh…' It took her a moment to orientate herself. 'Fine thank you. It was lovely walking in the countryside. I had a…'

'That's good. I've been as busy as ever.'

Her heart felt as if it was being squeezed by a frozen hand. It was so easy to lie to Pa because he didn't listen.

The official letter arrived as promised; a few curt words telling her that she had been successful in the initial stage and she was to travel to Arisaig. She was overjoyed. At last she was being posted to Scotland and to the Highlands, too. The what and the why didn't matter. If that first weekend had seemed tough this course at the rundown shooting lodge was ten times harder, physically and mentally. They were told that it was a form of military training but they were volunteers who could leave if they chose to. Nothing was said about what would happen afterwards. Remembering how Bertha had got into trouble asking questions, Felicity decided to keep quiet. She found to her surprise that she enjoyed the physical challenges, tramping through the rough countryside, often in the darkness, splashing through streams and crawling through tunnels. They moved onto fieldcraft skills, living off the land by trapping animals and learning how to hide and use cover to avoid capture. It all seemed like a game and she thought how much she would enjoy telling John Norman about it. She remembered how surprised he had been when she wasn't squeamish at all about killing the mackerel all those years ago.

She had never felt so exhausted yet so exhilarated. Her body, long an awkward burden, had become strong and sleek, like a leopard, whose hunting crawl they had been taught to imitate. Instruction in shooting and unarmed combat followed. It was hard to see what all this had to do with working with the Free French but Felicity didn't dare to ask any of the others. They had been warned that idle talk could lead to expulsion from the course. The numbers had whittled down from the original twenty as people left suddenly, with no explanation given.

The second stage involved working in two teams. One group was based on an island in a loch with wireless equipment that Felicity's team had to capture. One of their group would have to swim over to seize the wireless while the others created a diversion by rowing over on a raft.

'I can't be the one to swim over. I have to stay back because you need me to transmit the message to HQ,' she said. After they had completed the mission Felicity remembered John Norman telling her how he did a similar exercise with the Home Guard. How surprised he would be when she saw him again and told him how she had been on the winning side too and it wasn't just against a lot of old men either but fit young people. And she had been the technical expert. How she wished she could tell that superior Simon about how well she had done. That would give him something to chew over. She wasn't just doing clerical work like Margaret.

After that exercise they were all assessed individually.

'Come in MacDougall,' the instructor said, peering at her over his notes. 'You've shown competence at the physical and technical tests, especially as an operator in Morse Code.'

Felicity gave a silent thank you to Bertha, remembering how they had egged each other on to succeed.

'Only average at using firearms. I dare say that's because of your eyesight. But that's not too much of a problem.'

She nodded. She wore her spectacles all the time now because that was the price of succeeding and most of the time she forgot about them. But she still winced inside when anyone mentioned them

'However, you are deficient in one important respect.'

She held her breath, desperate in case she was going to be rejected.

'You lack leadership skills and seem to prefer working on your own initiative.'

That's how I've survived all my life, she thought, being on the outside, watching my back. She decided she had nothing to lose by defending herself.

'I can see, Sir, that could be a disadvantage in some situations. I don't know what role I might be asked to do but surely there is some value in being a lone wolf with a cool head?'

He raised his eyebrows. 'Let's see how you manage the final stage shall we?'

That evening the remaining twelve were told to pack. They went southwards on an army lorry to an airfield where they were taken to their quarters. As they clattered down the stairs for a briefing Felicity risked whispering to a woman beside her. 'I wonder what we'll be doing next.'

'What do you think? Learning to parachute of course.'

Felicity's face froze in horror. 'What?'

'You must have worked it out by now. We're going abroad.'

'Why?'

By now they were at the bottom of the stairs. The other woman stared at Felicity as if she were half witted.

'We'll be agents behind the lines, of course. Doing all we learnt but for real.'

Felicity hung back as the others surged ahead of her. She hadn't worked it out at all. She had been blind, much blinder than she was when she took her spectacles off. She hadn't thought beyond being back in the Highlands again. How could she have been so stupid? With a jolt she remembered Pa's response about being proud of her. He must have had a suspicion about what the course involved but he had let her stay ignorant.

She stumbled after the others in a daze. Her mind stayed numb throughout the brief lecture and the practice jumps in the enormous hangar where they learnt how to roll over on landing. Then they went outside for the final test. They were split into four groups of three and given parachutes. The numbness in her brain was being driven out by fear and her hands fumbled as she adjusted the straps. Everyone was too busy to notice. She was put in the first group and followed the others as they climbed aboard a hot air balloon. She knew that she would have to jump out once the balloon was high enough up. She closed her eyes, not daring to watch their ascent or her fear of heights would overwhelm her. If she opened her eyes at the last moment and jumped she could to it.

It felt eerie in the balloon, hanging in space and separated from the rest of the world. Suddenly, the memory of Charlotte Ponsonby exploded like a grenade in her head. She must have done this training too before being sent off to France to die there.

'Your turn now.'

Now the fear was tangled round her, tightening its grip. Every time she drew breath it crushed her harder. Her legs flinched away from the scratchy edge of the basket as she clambered onto it. Her brain was shouting 'No' but it was too late. She was falling, plummeting, as heavy as a rock and as fragile as china, her bones brittle as twigs. The ground loomed and the crashing pain was a relief.

Chapter 41

Late Summer/Early Autumn 1942

'The doctor says it's a bad sprain but not a break.'

'What happens now?'

The officer glared at her but she refused to look away. 'It's a real nuisance.' He flicked through her file. 'You did well up to this point. What a waste. I always had my doubts about allowing women to do the training. We'll have to see.'

She felt like saying that it wasn't her fault. She had been misled about the course but she pressed her lips together instead. Her thoughts were swirling like a shaken bottle of lemonade. When she loosened the top what came fizzing out was excitement. She would be able to hobble around on her injured ankle soon and she could go back to Skye. John Norman would probably be at sea but she would feel much closer to him there. Meanwhile she would have to endure going back to London but it wouldn't be for long. It was like the end of term but different this time. She used to dread the long summer holidays when she was at boarding school but this time she couldn't wait. In those days she had drifted through her life but now she was unfurling her sails and scanning the horizon. She wrote a quick note to John Norman.

Dear John Norman,

I hope this letter finds you at home. It was so good to see you but a shame it was all such a rush. I've just finished my course. You would have been surprised to see me. There was a lot of daring-do involved. Quite a shock to someone like me who hated games like lacrosse at school. I'll tell you about it when we meet. I was fine until near the end when I sprained my ankle badly. I must have caught that from you! If I strap it up I should be able to drive up

*soon. I know it would be a miracle if you're on leave but I shall keep
my fingers crossed.*

How to end it? *Kind Regards* seemed too cool after that wonderful
kiss. But she didn't want to be too revealing in case the letter
fell into the wrong hands. She suspected that Lexie was quite
capable of steaming open envelopes.

With all my love.
Felicity

That was true although she felt herself blush as she wrote it.
Then every day there was the same agonising ritual. Her ears
strained for the postman and she hobbled to the door, her heart
fluttering. Each time she tried not to hope too much, to protect
herself from crashing with disappointment. As time went on she
began to worry more about the practicalities, waking in the night
with questions swarming like midges in her head. She had been
lucky before, getting away with that suspect pass. Could she risk
using it again or would she need to get a new one? How could
she do that now that she wasn't working for Pa? Then with a
jolt she remembered that she had taken several sheets of headed
paper. Maybe she could somehow get hold of a typewriter?
Exhausted she would fall asleep, vowing that she would think
more about it the next day.

After a couple of weeks she noticed that she was walking
more easily although her ankle throbbed if she tried to do too
much. Pa insisted that she see the family doctor to check her
progress.

'You're healing well, young lady,' he told her. 'You've got a
strong constitution. You can manage without a stick now but
don't overdo it. No running up hills.'

She had smiled. If he only knew what she had been doing.
The next morning she tried to inoculate herself against

disappointment by lingering over her breakfast and not rushing to pick up the post. This time as she bent to pick up the letters her heart surged. There hiding among the correspondence addressed to Pa was an envelope covered in Winnie's immaculate copperplate writing. She ripped it open and as her eyes scanned the envelope inside she realised that something was different, in the way which John Norman had written Winnie's address. Puzzled she tore it open. That was it! The words weren't pressed into the paper by a pencil held in a heavy hand but written in ink. Surely John Norman wasn't using a fountain pen now? She would have to tease him about it.

> *Dear Felicity,*
> *I had a spot of illness after I last saw you and Mamma called the doctor against my wishes he said I had overstrained myself and was to stay at home for a while Lacrosse is a game I never heard of. I asked Lexie. She reads those books about boarding schools so she knew. It sounds nearly as dangerous as shinty to me. ive just heard that im to report to Glasgow in a few days for a new berth. can you get there? Find me at the seamens mission.*
> *Love,*
> *John Norman*

She had to sit down and wipe away her tears. What was making her well up so much? It was partly the relief of hearing from him. And they would meet again! But his scrappy note hid as much as it revealed. What did he mean by 'a spot of illness'? Why hadn't he written sooner? Was she deluding herself into imagining they were close? But then she remembered the warmth of that kiss and the way his eyes lit up when he looked at her. She blew her nose hard and smiled as she thought how he still couldn't punctuate properly, even though he was using a proper pen. And he had bothered to ask his minx of a sister about lacrosse. Maybe it was just how men were? She knew so few of them. Pa didn't really talk to her and she had got things wrong with Ted. She and John Norman would put things right between them when they met. She stood up quickly and felt a twinge in her ankle. Wincing, she rubbed it while she thought through her plan of action.

She found writing paper and sat down to reply.

Dear John Norman,

I was so relieved to hear from you and pleased that you are feeling better. I shall set out tomorrow because I don't know how long the journey might take with the trains being so uncertain. I'll find somewhere to stay and call for you at the Mission.
All my love,
Felicity

P.S. if I was coming up to Skye I'd bring my old lacrosse stick for Lexie.

Nothing about her turmoil of feelings. That would have to wait.

'You're off to Bletchley again? Are you sure that your ankle is up to it?'

'I think so Pa. I'll take it steady.'

'Very well. The change will probably do you good. Shall I drive you to the station?'

'No thank you. I know you're very busy. I'll get a taxi.'

He mustn't know that she was going to Euston for a train to the north west. She felt a pang at deceiving him yet again but she couldn't help noticing that he looked relieved. Was he as ill at ease in her company as she felt in his? It was too late to change that.

Her bandaged leg was throbbing by the time she reached Glasgow in the evening. She found a shabby but clean guest house not far from the docks. After unpacking she went outside and asked a passing middle-aged man for directions to the Seamen's Mission.

'Are you sure, hen? It's a bit rough round there.'

'I shall be quite alright, thank you. I'm meeting someone.' As she neared the docks she was aware of men turning to look at her but she held her head high and tried to stride out despite her limp. It was difficult picking her way in the dusk among the stone warehouses, wooden sheds and piled up sandbags. She spotted the Mission sign on a dingy, single storey building. A tough looking woman was standing smoking in the doorway. She opened a mouth empty of teeth when she saw Felicity.

'No lassies allowed inside.'

She stood her ground. 'I'm here to see John Norman MacPherson.'

And there he was! Coming through the doorway behind the toothless crone, his eyes lighting up as he saw her. Her heart spiralled but sank again when she saw the burly frame of Angus behind him. John Norman's smile was as wide as the ocean as he bounded towards her, arms stretched out. 'You came! Just in time. I've heard that I'm off tomorrow. But what's happened to you, you're limping?'

'Just a sprain but it meant I had leave and could come.'

'Fancy you both damaging an ankle in turn. It sounds like a plot to me.' Angus laughed and Felicity struggled not to scowl. 'Don't worry. I'll leave you two love birds alone soon.'

'Angus is on his way home to Skye. He's got compassionate leave. His father's seriously ill,' John Norman said.

'Oh, I'm sorry to hear that.' In her thoughts, though, she wished Angus far away.

'You've time for a quick drink, haven't you, before your train?' John Norman asked him.

Felicity suppressed a sigh but felt better as she took John Norman's arm. She leant on him more than she needed to, so that she could stay close. When they were settled in a nearby bar, John Norman said. 'There's more bad news, I'm afraid. About Murdo. We've just heard that he's missing.'

'Your friend with the nice smile who lives…lived next door? Oh dear, how sad. He was in the Navy, wasn't he?'

'Aye. He was. We tried to join up together. He was accepted. He memorised the sight chart for me before it was my turn to go in. But they kicked me out the door when they found I'd cheated. I can't take it in. I've not seen him for so long that I can't believe it that he's not out there somewhere.'

'Maybe he's still alive. They can't be sure.'

John Norman shook his head. 'That can happen in the army. You could get taken prisoner but there's not much hope when you're at sea.'

'It was odd, though, wasn't it – the letter his family got,' Angus said. "Died in home waters", they wrote.'

'What does that mean?' Felicity asked

Angus shrugged. 'That he wasn't killed in an enemy attack, I suppose.'

'I don't understand. Was it an accident of some sort? Did he drown? Was something wrong with the ship that made it sink suddenly? Have you heard of anything like that happening, John Norman?' Felicity asked.

'No, I haven't.'

'Why wouldn't they say? Did other sailors die? Have they found the bodies?'

'I don't know anything more,' John Norman said, his face shuttered.

'It sounds fishy to me. Bertha would say there's some sort of a cover up going on.'

'Who cares what she thinks? She's full to bursting with rubbish opinions.'

Felicity bridled at Angus's dismissive tone. 'You just don't want anyone else to have any opinions, especially women.'

'Leave it, the pair of you. It makes no difference. Murdo's dead.' John Norman's face was creased in distress.

Felicity knew she should drop the subject but her mouth kept blurting on. 'But it seems even worse when you don't know what happened. Do ships, ones on the same side, ever crash into each other by mistake?'

The other two looked at each other. She carried on. 'If that happened the government wouldn't want to say, would they? It would look bad.'

Angus stood up. 'I suppose you know all about it, with your huge experience of warfare?'

'I know more about it than you imagine. What about your experience? You're not in the Navy, are you? Air Force is it? Do you fly?' She peered at his uniform jacket. 'I don't see any wings.'

Angus banged his empty glass on the table. John Norman put a restraining hand on his arm.

'I'm off,' he said, shaking off the hand. 'Goodbye,' he said to John Norman, ignoring Felicity. He barged out of the door.

'I'm sorry,' she said reaching for John Norman's hand. He pulled it back into his pocket. 'I don't know what came over me. I was longing to see you and now I've made you cross. And your best friend dying. Please forgive me.'

'We're all on edge. Angus has always had a short fuse. He and Donnie were for ever having spats. Murdo and I were the ones who tried to keep the peace.'

He took a gulp of beer before looking hard at her. 'It's odd what you said, just then – about ships colliding.'

'How's that?'

'Well, just before I came down, I heard one or two rumours that something like that might have happened. How would you know?'

'I didn't. It was just a guess. But things go wrong, don't they? Things we don't get told about.'

'If it was an accident the bodies will come ashore somewhere in the end. I don't know if it's better or worse for the family to have something to bury.'

'Maybe it's better to know rather than live in false hope.' She could feel them being engulfed by the tides of war, splashing over them, separating them. She shuddered. 'It would be terrible to waste our last day together quarrelling with each other.'

He squeezed her hand. 'Angus and Bertha are two of a kind. They have to have the last word.'

She could see how hard he was trying to haul himself aboard the present moment. 'Have you heard from her, recently?'

'No. I'm worried. She's not replied to my letters at all. She'll be posted somewhere new but I don't know where.'

'Don't worry. I think Bertha can look after herself. She knew how to put Angus in his place. Maybe that's why he was short with you.'

'She told me she gave him a tongue lashing when he tried it on with her.'

'More than that. A kick where it hurts. He was hobbling around in agony.'

'I shouldn't laugh but I can't help it.'

'I know. It's funny though.'

She didn't quite like to ask where exactly it was that he had been kicked but she was glad it had hurt.

'That's enough about our daft friends. You haven't got that nice car of yours? It would be grand to go for a drive.'

'No. It's too hard to get petrol but I can walk if I can lean on you.'

'You don't mind walking around in the dark, then?' He took her hand and smiled.

Chapter 42

Later that evening

It was drizzling as they left the bar and turned down a narrow passageway beside it. After a few minutes they found some boxes piled up against a wall.

'You need to rest your leg but it's not much of a seat, I'm afraid.'

'Never mind. We can "Make do and Mend."'

She lowered herself carefully on the boxes and undid the top buttons of her coat.

'You're wearing something blue and shiny,' John Norman said.

'It's a party frock I had from before the war,' she replied, feeling her face glow. 'It's an old thing but I like the bright colour.'

'Did you wear it when you were being finished? Or maybe at the Skye Balls?'

'You're mocking me, John Norman,' she said, poking him in the chest.

He laughed. 'Do you remember that time when you picked me up at Sligachan? I thought you would be annoyed with me for soaking the seat.'

'That was a lifetime ago.'

'When I was the delivery boy and knew my place.' He laughed and kissed her.

'I'm glad you don't worry about that now.'

They kissed until she was breathless with an excitement she couldn't name. She was being swept out to sea, longing to lose her footing but fearing it too. 'We'd better get back before it's too late.'

'You're right. Whoops, you dropped your spectacles. I almost trod on them.'

'Poor old spectacles,' she said. 'But it was both of us wearing them that brought us together. If we both lost our spectacles we would have to stay here forever, hidden away.' She could hear the quiver in her voice as she stood up.

'Let's get some fish and chips.' She couldn't bear being inside a restaurant among strangers when they had such little time left together.

'I didn't think you had such common tastes,' John Norman said, grinning.

'Well, like everyone keeps saying, the war's changed everything. For instance, before the war Pa would never have let me have a proper job.'

'And I wouldn't be standing in the road with a posh young lady, one who's been finished, eating chips out of newspaper. Mamma would be horrified. She's very proper even though she's never been finished at all.'

'Is that all I am to you, "a posh young lady"?'

'No, of course not, just teasing. I suppose we're courting properly now? You know Lexie keeps saying she wants to be a bridesmaid?'

'Is that a proposal of marriage, John Norman?'

'Well, I suppose it is but we can't get married until the war's over.'

'I accept,' she said, her lips brushing his cheek. He looked so stunned that she laughed and said. 'I'll have you know that this is my second proposal.'

'Who was the first?' His voice was sharp.

'Don't worry. No one important.'

'Tell me or I'll tickle you to death.'

'No,' she shrieked. 'I'm very ticklish. He was an ugly, pompous fellow whose mother was a friend of Winnie's. I felt nothing for him at all. Well I did feel very angry that he thought he was doing me a huge favour in proposing.'

'The impudence of the fellow,' John Norman said, imitating an upper-class English voice.

She giggled and spluttered over her mouthful. When she had finished eating she screwed up the paper with a sigh. 'I thought I would be too miserable to eat but that fish was delicious. Will you walk me back to the guest house? I can't face that hatchet-faced woman at the Seamen's Mission again.'

'Before you go, I've something to give you. It's not a ring but I hope you like it.'

He reached into his jacket pocket and handed her a thin leather case. Intrigued she opened it.

'Oh, it's a beautiful pen!' She took it out and turned it over in her hand. Its surface was marbled in autumnal colours. She removed the top with its gold clip and turned it over in her hands.

'Do you notice anything odd about it?' John Norman asked, grinning.

'How do you fill it with ink?'

'It's special. One of those ballpoint pens that don't need ink. The Air Force use them but they're hard to get hold of.'

She smiled. 'This is what you used to write to me, isn't it?'

He nodded. 'Aye – but it didn't make me write better. It came from my sister Margaret. Some high up officer gave it to her. She had already been given one by another admiral so Lexie got this one and handed it to me when I left home this time.'

She hugged him. 'I shall keep it safe and think of you every time I write with it.'

'Won't you think of me at any other time?' he teased.

They linked arms to walk back, both falling silent. What could be said? she thought. The rain was heavier now. John Norman turned up his collar. Then he opened his jacket and squeezed her close so that she could share it. She tilted her head down onto his shoulder. She could feel his throat moving as he started to hum and then to sing softly, tunes she didn't know.

'I like that tune. What's the song about?'

'It's about a lassie, like most songs. "SÌne Bhàn" it's called – "Fair Jean". It's about a young soldier in the last war, going off to fight and longing to be back home.'

'What about a song we can sing together? Do you know, *It's a long way to Tipperary*?'

'Aye of course, the chorus anyway.'

They sang it together, hesitantly at first. Then their voices blended and soared together.

'I know some of the verses too,' she said, with a giggle.

'Go on then.'

She spluttered before finding her note:

Paddy wrote a letter
To his Irish Molly O
Saying, 'Should you not receive it
Write and let me know
If I make mistakes in spelling
Molly dear,' said he,
'Remember that it's the pen that's bad
Don't lay the blame on me.'

'Are you getting your own back, then?' John Norman said, pretending to frown while hugging her tight.

'Who me? Never!'

When they had both stopped laughing they sauntered on and he sang *The Skye Boat Song*.

'You've a lovely tenor voice. I never knew.' This time she had to swallow the sob that rose in her throat.

'Well, there's a lot we don't know yet about each other,' he said, squeezing her waist and making her body melt. They stopped outside the gaunt, peeling guest house.

'You keep yourself safe, my love,' she whispered, hugging him so hard that he stumbled. Then he was sprinting away, huddled against the driving rain.

Chapter 43

Later still

Felicity felt bereft once she closed the door of her bedroom. Now she was alone she was besieged by all her fears about the future. Once her ankle was better she would have to go back and finish the special training. But she knew now that she couldn't endure being any sort of a special agent. She would have to admit it. But how? By becoming hysterical, pretending she was insane? Wouldn't they reject her if they thought she would break under pressure? Or would she have to repeat the course and make sure that she failed it?

Exhausted, she slipped under the stiff, cold sheet and pulled the blankets up. She felt she would never be able to sleep but she must have done because she was woken by something. There it was again, like hailstones on the window. She lay rigid, listening. Another sound. Singing! Must be drunks in the street outside. But it was too tuneful.

'*Speed bonny boat, like a bird on the wing,*'

John Norman! She rushed to the window and wrenched back the heavy blackout curtains. She was on the first floor and as she opened the window she could see a figure crouching on the roof of an outbuilding beneath her. The figure stood up and wobbled as he reached for the window ledge. She gasped and stretched her arms out through the gap, holding his hand as he reached up.

'What are you doing here?' she demanded as he catapulted into the room.

'I couldn't keep away. I went out for a drink and my feet led me here – quite against my will.'

'You're soaking. Take those wet things off,' she said. 'Come into bed and get warm.'

They lay side by side, their legs entwined, nuzzling and stroking each other. His kisses became more frantic until he pulled himself away. She pulled him back and kissed him hard.

'Are you sure?' he asked.

'Yes, of everything,' she replied. Although she didn't quite know what would happen she knew that she wanted it to happen. Pressure, stretching, a jolt that was nearly pain but then a flooding of pleasure. They fell asleep in a tangle of limbs but woke again. No pressure this time just an overflowing completeness followed by sliding into deep sleep.

Part 7

John Norman's Story

Chapter 44

The same night

He watched Felicity as she slept. With a tender hand he brushed back the red tangles from her forehead. She was snuffling in her sleep, like a puppy. He could not believe that they had done anything wrong, not when their actions sprang from love. The sailors who sought out prostitutes, used them and despised them – that was wrong. He must stay awake. He would have to climb out of the window again and collect his kit from the Mission. He would tease her about her snoring when she woke up. His first love and his last love too – the one who would endure for his whole life. Their hearts beat together now.

He must have fallen asleep because he was suddenly wide awake again, his heart thumping.

'I can't do it! What if I'm caught?' Felicity was sitting up, her eyes staring.

'You're having a nightmare,' he said, holding her. 'Wake up.' He shook her lightly.

She stared at him unseeing until his shaking made her blink.

'What is it you're scared of? You were talking about being caught.'

She looked away. 'I don't know. It was just a bad dream.'

'Something's on your mind. Is it to do with your new posting?'

'I can't talk about it. I'm sworn to secrecy.'

'But you could tell me. Is there something wrong?'

She shook her head.

'Is it something to do with that Bertha? Has she asked you to do something wrong? She supports that Blackshirt man, what's his name, Mosely?'

'Don't be ridiculous. He's a Fascist, not a Socialist. What do you imagine I'm doing – spying?'

The doubt had wriggled into his mind and she must have seen it on his face.

'You do think that. How could you? If you only knew. You've got the wrong end of the stick completely.' She pushed him hard in the chest, leapt out of the bed and started to put on her clothes.

'I'm sorry. Of course, I believe you. I just wondered how you knew about accidents at sea when we talked before.'

'I didn't. I just guessed. I do have a brain in my head, you know.'

She looked frantic, torn between pain and anger. He reached out to her but she moved away. How he wished that he hadn't blurted those words out.

'Look, I don't trust your friend. She's so violent in how she talks and....'

'And you thought I was a giddy girl – one who could be so easily taken in that I would betray my country? Even if Bertha was a spy – and she's not.'

He got up too and dragged on his clothes. He didn't know what more he could say to calm her down. 'I'll have to go but we can't part as enemies. Not now, we're together.'

He could hear the catch in his voice as he spoke. She looked at him, unshed tears brimming from her eyes. He grabbed her clenched hand and held it until her fingers uncurled. Her shoulders slumped and he pulled her close to kiss her forehead. 'This is the beginning of our lives together.'

But her hand stayed cold and limp. He could feel the tide rushing between them, creating an ocean of separation.

Chapter 45

The next day

Exhausted, he stumbled back to the Mission and threw himself on the bed without undressing. He fell asleep but was tormented by nightmares. He was on a stormy sea, hauling in nets but when he released the catch the silvery fish turned to slime, the slime of drowned bodies with blind fingers and eye sockets picked clean. The sea had spewed out its dead – Iain, Sam and Murdo. They clutched at his ankles and although he ran away they groped and crawled after him. He woke, clammy and shivering. This was the same dream he kept having night after night when he had come back from the Med. Mamma had nagged him until he went to the doctor.

'He'll give you a sleeping draught to help,' she had said.

He did go in the end. The doctor heard him out, gave him a sleeping draught and then signed him off work.

'You must rest or you'll get pneumonia again,' he had said, not meeting John Norman's gaze.

That's when he knew that the doctor was sparing his feelings by not naming the madness that was attacking him but pretending it was the problem with his lungs again. The medicine dampened down the nightmares and he learnt to control his shaking hands in the daytime. After a month the doctor declared him better but now the nightmare had exploded in his head again. Feeling too queasy for breakfast he set off early for the docks instead. As he walked along he told himself that he must stow away all doubts about Felicity until they could talk again. Why would he doubt her? After all, she must love him to have risked giving herself to him as she had. He would find his ship and go to sea but the dread of facing danger was stronger now that he had more to live for. But he was lucky. He had survived the last convoy. It couldn't be worse this time.

'You're on the Atlantic run,' the man with the list told him.

'What sort of boat?'

'A tanker, I think. You have to board this evening.'

He reeled back on his heels, his mouth filling with bile. The worst berth of all. He couldn't face it. What should he do? Should he go back and find Felicity? But she would be gone already. Should he just melt away into the city, even escape to Ireland, like Stewart did? But if he did how would he live with himself, knowing he was a coward? Live with shaming his family? He had to sit down and think. He went inside the nearest bar. A dram would settle his nerves. Only it didn't. His thoughts rolled and pitched. He had another whisky while he tried to banish the stories he had heard about tankers. The thought of drowning was hard but not as bad as the idea of lighting up like a torch and dying in terrible pain. He'd heard the stories of burnt men being pulled out of the sea, writhing and gasping in the bottom of the rescue boat, lungs scalded and blistered flesh red raw. Begging to be put out of their misery and trying to throw themselves over the side.

He downed his glass and went up for another. After a while he decided to walk around the docks and find his boat. He was surprised to see that dusk was falling. His ankle started throbbing. He must have jarred the old injury when he climbed up onto that shed roof behind Felicity's guest house. Best to get aboard and hope that the old routines of being at sea would calm him. There she was, the *Dundee*. His heart clenched as he saw the flat contours of the tanker.

There was no one else about as he swung his aching leg up first onto the gangplank, set at a steep angle because of the low tide. Slipping on the oily surface he reached out for an overhanging rope. Stretching too far he was caught off balance. He keeled over the edge of the gangplank and slid into the oily water between the ship and the quay. He lunged at the hull, groping for something to cling to but the ship's side was a sheer cliff. Lines wound themselves around his legs. He was a trapped fish, thrashing in the net. But Pappa would see him, drag in the net and cut him free. He only had to shout. And he did. He roared, groaned and sobbed. Until the sea swamped his voice and silenced him.

Part 8

Felicity's Story

Chapter 46

Winter 1942

'You'll have to be a war widow, my dear.' Winnie reached for her hands. 'No ring? No matter. I've still got my mother's wedding ring. She had slender fingers like you. Now sit down and I'll bring you some tea.' She shuffled off to the scullery.

Felicity slumped in the chair, her head in her hands. Why had she spilt it all out before she was even inside the house? She looked up as Winnie returned. 'You'll think badly of me for... you know, when I wasn't married.'

Winnie shook her head. 'I know what war does to folk. "Let he who is without sin cast the first stone."'

Felicity smiled and blew her nose. 'I can't regret it. Maybe we both knew it was our only chance. "Died in home waters." Like his friend. I was back in town when his mother wrote to me. His young sister found my address among his belongings but she didn't say how it happened. I don't know if she knows.'

'Here's your tea, dear. Did you go back up there?'

'No, I didn't get the letter until after the funeral. I thought about going but then I had to go for my medical – to see if my ankle had healed.'

She took a slurp of tea, her hands shaking. 'It's like the old days, isn't it Winnie, sitting by your fire? I didn't know where else to come or if you'd have a new lodger.'

'I don't take lodgers anymore, now.'

'Oh? Lucky for me then. Anyway, my ankle was fine but I told the doctor I wasn't feeling too well. Light-headed, being sick. The more I said, the more he frowned. Made me lie down on the couch. Looked up from prodding my stomach with such disgust on his face. "Surely you must realise you're expecting, *Miss* MacDougall?"

"Expecting what?"

"A child of course. You must have had sexual intercourse. You're experiencing the consequences."'

'Poor lamb. You didn't have a mother to explain these things to you.'

'John Norman said. "You'll be alright, won't you? We'll be careful next time." But I didn't know what he meant. I was stunned by what the doctor said. In disgrace and all that,' she sobbed. 'But, the funny thing – I can't tell anyone else this but you. Half of me is so glad. This kernel inside me is part of him. He lives on and that can't be bad. And it means I don't have to do the final training. The thought of it terrified me to death.' She blew her nose hard. 'But I'm still in a terrible pickle.'

'Who else knows about the baby?'

Her teeth rattled against the cup. 'When I told Pa about the... the...baby he was livid. And when I admitted John Norman was the father he went so red that I thought he would have a seizure. "You can't keep it," he shouted.

"It! Your own grandchild!" I cried out.

"Illegitimate, a mongrel. Get it adopted. You're young. You can still marry and have others. No one need know. I'll pay for you to lodge somewhere out of town. And for the nursing home."

I couldn't believe it. "I have to pretend the child doesn't exist, like I had to pretend that Mamma never existed." When I said that I thought he would hit me.

"You've disgraced your poor mother," he said. That finished it for me.'

She rocked backwards and forwards, groaning until Winnie lowered herself down on her knees and held her close.

'He won't change his mind. I know him. I can stay here Winnie, can't I? I can pay rent.'

'Yes, of course you can. We must get our thinking caps on, though. It's a small place and people tittle tattle. We'll stick to saying you're widowed but what about your ration book? It's in your own name. No, don't cry, dear, we'll take it a step at a time. You can think about telling John Norman's family later.'

At first Felicity just wanted to hide inside the house. She was tormented by remembering their last meeting. Sometimes she was angry with John Norman for abandoning her, sometimes overcome by losing him when they had only just found each other and other times tortured by guilt that she had been so distant with him when he wondered if she was some sort of spy. If he had only known, he was near the truth in a way. Both of them were prisoners of their own pain and doubts but unable to share them. Locked in separate cells, shouting in the dark for help that didn't come.

Winnie tried to persuade her to occupy herself. 'I'll teach you to knit. It doesn't take long to make baby clothes.' But Felicity shook her head. It was all too much effort.

'What about learning to cook? That will come in useful. Rabbit stew, apple pie, an omelette. It's not much use learning to bake though. It's so hard to get the ingredients now. If someone wants to make a wedding cake they have to get everyone else's coupons for the sugar and butter. To say nothing of the fruit.'

Felicity stared at her and felt tears flowing down her face as if they would never stop.

'Oh dear, I was just prattling on. That was a silly thing to say. I'm sorry, my dear. The last thing I want to do is to upset you.'

'It's just that it reminded me of the first time I ever saw John Norman. I was making a cake with Mrs Patterson and there he was in the doorway, holding a basket of groceries. He was frowning, with his spectacles slipping down his nose. He looked as if he wanted the earth to swallow him up.' She sobbed. 'It feels as if that happened to someone else in another life.'

'You have a good cry. Let the grieving out.'

Afterwards she felt hollowed out but the growing baby began to fill the emptiness in her mind and body. She was a chrysalis, suspended between her old life and what would come.

'Have you felt the baby quicken yet?' Winnie asked her one day.

'I don't know how to tell. Is it different from tummy rumbles?'

Then one day she felt a fluttering, a stretching of wings. The horrible sickness ended and she felt ready to venture out with Winnie. If people talked about her behind her back they were pleasant to her face, accepted her story of sudden widowhood. Winnie would walk with her to the shops but didn't want to venture any further. She seemed to fall asleep in her chair more often than Felicity remembered from before. The cooking lessons became useful. She found that she enjoyed pummelling dough and rolling out pastry. She smiled as she remembered how back at the finishing school it had all been about planning menus, arranging flowers and telling domestic staff what to do.

She found the old bicycle, propped up in the lean-to shed. It was neglected but serviceable. She followed Winnie's advice and rode it sedately. No more hurtling down hills until her feet became unstuck from the pedals. One day she heard a voice behind her.

'Coo-ee! It's Felicity, isn't it? Fancy seeing you again!'

It was bound to happen. She squeezed the brakes and dismounted, checking that her coat was done up. 'I know it's hot but you have to cover yourself up now you're starting to show,' Winnie had tutted.

'Hello Susan. Yes, it's me. Large as life.' She saw Susan's glance slide downwards to her belly before shifting back to her face. Deep breath. Brave smile. Get it over with. 'Larger, as you can see. I was sent on another course but then I got married, to a merchant seaman but he was lost at sea.'

'How sad. Please accept my condolences. But the baby will be a comfort, I'm sure.'

Felicity nodded and squeezed out a few tears. Not difficult these days. Her eyes were always on the verge of leaking.

Susan hurtled on, 'You won't know but I've got engaged since you left the Park.' She halted, seeming to fear that she was being insensitive.

'Congratulations! Is it one of the Scottish country dancers? The ones who looked as if they weren't wearing anything underneath their coats?' Felicity found herself giggling.

Susan joined in. 'It is as it happens. And I've improved at the dancing with all the practising we do.'

So, it ended well enough but neither of them suggested meeting again. It would be like shouting to someone on the other bank of a wide river, Felicity thought. She refused to look back. To fret at all the might have beens.

She observed her body changing with a sort of detachment. Did that alien mound of a belly really belong to her? When she found herself jammed in the doorway of the outside toilet she bellowed with frustration. When an agitated Winnie appeared they both burst out laughing at the silliness of it all.

Chapter 47

Summer 1943

As the weather became warmer and her belly expanded Felicity began to droop.

'You'll have to decide where you want to have the baby,' Winnie said.

'Plenty of time yet.'

'No, only a month before your time, I think. And sometimes they can come early. Wouldn't you be better in a London hospital? They'd look after you there.'

'Why can't I have it here at home?'

'It can be very tiring, you know. That's why it's called labour.'

'Well, you can help me, along with the midwife. That's settled.'

Winnie's comments were getting irritating, rubbing her like burrs. A sigh and back to the book, waiting for Winnie to shuffle off to the kitchen. She stretched out on the old, lumpy sofa and picked up *Gone with the Wind*. Escaping into the American south, more humid, more dangerous and more trying for women but somewhere else. Had she really been the girl who had gone to the pictures with the ghastly Ted? That episode had put her off ever reading the book. Was it then that she had started to admit that she cared about John Norman? She squeezed her eyes shut as grief ambushed her again. The words blurred. She put the marker carefully in place and closed the book, remembering Winnie's earlier admonishment, 'That's a library book. You can't just dog ear it.'

Maybe it was time for a nap.

A knock on the door roused her. She heard Winnie's slippers slide over the hall floor. The rumble of a man's voice followed and then the solid tread of what sounded like two pairs of shoes.

'These gentlemen have come to see you, Felicity.' Winnie's face looked strained as she led them into the parlour. They were wearing dark suits and carrying briefcases. Still bewildered from her sleep, she swung her feet down on the floor and prepared to stand up. The older man motioned that she should stay. Silently they settled themselves in the armchairs. The older one crossed his legs, straightening out the crease in his trousers as he did so. He nodded to the other man who unclipped his briefcase to extract a notebook and pencil. What was going on? The silence weighed her down. She licked her dry lips and swallowed. Winnie stood, poised half in and half out of the room, her hand tight on the door handle.

'Miss MacDougall, we've come to ask you some questions. My colleague will take notes.'

She gasped, looking from one to the other. 'Why?' Her voice came out as a squeak.

Winnie slid towards her. She sat down beside Felicity and grasped her hand. Her voice was quiet but clear as she turned to look at the men. 'As you can see, gentlemen, my young friend is in a delicate state. So, I'm staying with her.'

The older man, the one in charge, stared at Winnie. She stared back, chin up, a mother defending her cub.

'Very well. You're Winifred Boulton, Miss MacDougall's landlady?'

'Much more than that,' Felicity said, squeezing Winnie's clenched hand.

'Hmm. We'll make a start, Miss MacDougall. Tell me about how you met Miss Wilkins.'

'Miss Wilkins?' She frowned. 'Oh, you mean Bertha? My p...' She could feel Winnie pressing hard with her fingers. She took a deep breath. 'We trained together.'

His lips stretched wide but his eyes stayed cold, reptilian. 'We know all about your training together.' He turned to Winnie. 'You're staying under sufferance and must keep everything you hear to yourself.' She nodded, her lips pressed together.

'And how did Miss Wilkins conduct herself?'

'Conduct herself? She was one of the best operators. Top of the class.' He waited but Winnie squeezed her hand again and Felicity knew that she must not fill the empty space with a flood of words.

'So how come this model student was obliged to repeat part of the course?'

'She had strong opinions.'

'A troublemaker, you mean. A barrack room lawyer? Unpatriotic too. A follower of Lord Haw Haw?'

His voice slithered and hissed. He leant towards her and she felt herself retreat. Her bladder was straining and she feared the shame of losing control.

'She talked about politics but she hated the Nazis.'

'Really?' He raised his eyebrows and she could hear the sneer in his voice. A spark of anger struck in her mind, lighting up the stockpile of insults she had felt in these last weeks. She couldn't defend herself. She knew she had broken society's rules but she could still be angry on Bertha's behalf.

'She stood up for the Communists, not the Germans. And the Russians are our allies.'

She clung to Winnie's hand. They wanted her to lose her temper. She took a deep breath. 'You haven't said who you are and why you're asking these questions.'

Again the raised eyebrow and the silence. She refused to look away.

'And you've seen her since?'

'No. I wrote to her at her last address but there was no reply. I suppose you've got my letter.'

Winnie pressed her hand hard again but she added. 'What's happened to her? Is she in some sort of trouble?'

'Don't upset yourself, especially in your condition.' He nodded to his companion who snapped his notebook shut.

'That's all for now. You haven't any plans to travel, I hope. We may need to speak to you again.'

They stood up and Winnie was instantly on her feet, hovering at their heels, worrying them out of the front door. She came back and sat down, white faced beside the shaking Felicity.

'As if I could be travelling anywhere. My life's finished.' Felicity looked down at the alien mound of her stomach. Winnie put her arm around her and in between sobs Felicity looked closely at her friend. She seemed to have shrunk. Her lips had fallen in and her cheeks were crazed with wrinkles. It must have happened all at once or she would surely have noticed? She was so thin, her ribs frail as chicken bones. But sort of bloated too, her ankles spilling over her slippers.

But her smile was the same. 'I don't think they'll trouble you again. They could tell you're innocent.'

'But they suspected Bertha of...what? Not spying surely? It's a load of nonsense. She's my friend and I won't abandon her.'

'How can you be sure of what she was up to? You've not seen her for ages.'

Felicity frowned. 'John Norman was suspicious of her. So were his friends. It made me cross. But that was just because she spoke her mind, wasn't it?' She felt dizzy as if her whole world was tilting and listing.

Winnie's grip on her wrist was so hard that she winced. 'Whether it's something or nothing, you keep out of it. You've another life to think about as well as your own. From what you've said about Bertha she can look after herself. Now what about a nice boiled egg for your tea?'

Chapter 48

Summer 1943

Winnie never referred again to the visit of the two officials. Felicity supposed it was because she didn't want her to be upset so near the birth. It felt as if she had conjured up the whole event from some jumbled memories of a play she had once seen. It became part of her strange, detached state. Her body was no longer under her control. It had been taken over. Perhaps her mind was invaded too? She didn't dare think about it anymore for fear of going crazy.

By late June when the blossom in the lanes had fallen and small fruits had begun to ripen on the hawthorn Felicity woke with agonising cramps in her stomach. Crawling out of bed she doubled up as the next spasm wrenched her. It felt as if her innards were breaking out. Horror of horrors! She cried out as she saw she had wet herself. Then Winnie was there beside her, tying up the belt of her faded candlewick dressing gown and breathing hard.

'It's the baby deciding to come. Your waters have broken. How often are the pains coming?'

'How am I supposed to know? I don't wear my watch in be...' The pain savaged her again, cutting off her words in a groan. It was a noise a wounded animal would make. She couldn't believe it had come from her own throat.

'I'll get Tommy next door to fetch the doctor.' Felicity had been worn down by Winnie's barrage of nagging and agreed that she should book Dr Thompson, rather than just the midwife. By the time he arrived she was circling endlessly round her bedroom, supported by Winnie.

'Back to bed, now, so that I can examine you.' She did as she was told although lying down made her feel terrified and helpless.

'Not long to go. You're lucky not to be having a long labour.'

'Lucky! How long now? Ten minutes?'

He shook his head and tutted. 'Don't be silly. Babies don't pop out like peas, you know, especially first ones. A few hours.'

'A few hours! I can't survive a few minutes of this agony!'

'Of course, you can. You're young and strong. It's nature's way.'

'That's easy for you to say.' A howl tore out of her throat.

'Very well. If you can't manage I'll give you some morphine for the pain.'

Felicity didn't care about his disapproval. An injured soldier wouldn't be expected to suffer unbearable pain, nor someone having their teeth pulled.

She sank weightless, a floating feather, until later when both the doctor and Winnie shouted at her to push. It felt as if she was straining on the toilet to pass something enormous, as hard as metal or stone. Something that would rip her insides apart.

'It's a boy! Small but healthy.' She heard it shriek and glanced at the squashed face. What have you got to cry about? she thought. I'm the one who's suffered. Then blessed sleep lapped around her.

Chapter 49

Summer 1943

She didn't know what to make of this strange little creature, this scrunched up animal that had human features but didn't look like anyone. Certainly not like John Norman as she had imagined he would. It was still so hard to say his name, even to herself, without sobbing. Even the colour of his eyes seemed to waver and they were closed most of the time.

'When do babies open their eyes?'

'From the start. He's not a puppy. He just needs to sleep. Be thankful he's contented,' Winnie told her, an edge of exasperation in her voice.

'How do you know so much about babies?'

'I wasn't blessed with my own but I was the eldest in my family so I learnt fast.'

Felicity had insisted on a bottle. She couldn't bear the thought of being suckled and nuzzled. She found it hard not to resent this noisy, demanding creature, leaving him to cry, jamming her hands over her ears. Then when he fell silent she would rush to him, stunned by remorse and fearing he had died.

'He just wants to be held,' Winnie told her. Felicity was both relieved and riven with jealousy when Winnie soothed him so readily. She decided to name him Kenneth, to honour his Scottish ancestry.

'Maybe Norman as his second name?' Winnie suggested. Felicity flinched. It would be like prodding a wound.

Winnie hesitated and then asked,' But you'll have him christened?'

'How can I when I don't know what's happening to him?' Her sharp reply turned into a wail.

But Winnie stayed firm. 'You want to keep him, of course. If you take him to show your father maybe his heart will soften.'

'See him after everything he's said to me? How I've ruined my life and the family name? And how horrified my mother would be if she hadn't died giving birth to me? '

'Don't worry for now. We'll have to see what happens. It's amazing how people can change their tune once the baby's arrived,' Winnie said, with a sigh.

Felicity felt herself sinking into a marsh, every step a struggle as despair sucked at her. And Winnie wasn't much help, staring into space or falling asleep in her chair, with her reading glasses still on her nose. One afternoon Felicity bent down to pick up the scattered pages of the newspaper that had slid from her lap as she sat snoring.

She had given up following the news. She couldn't bring herself to care any more about the progress of the war but as she smoothed out the pages a column snagged her eye. She sat back on her heels on the floor to look more closely.

GOVERNMENT CLERK SENTENCED TO SEVEN YEARS
Bertha Wilkins, a burly young woman, stood impassively in the dock while she was sentenced. She was found guilty of illegally making wireless equipment. She will be sent down to Holloway Prison.

Felicity rocked backwards and stifled the cry in her throat. She mustn't wake Winnie. Could it be true that Bertha was a spy? Bertha who she admired so much for her courage? When everything else in her life was being sucked down into a whirlpool, Bertha was never sunk. She was indestructible, a warning buoy anchored to the seabed. No one could dislodge her.

But doubts, like storm-tossed boats, began to butt and bump against the buoy. She remembered how John Norman and his friends had distrusted her. Felicity had thought it was because

Bertha was outspoken and unladylike. She needed to think. Maybe a walk would help. She bundled a sleeping Kenneth into his pram. She could go to the bank and pick up Pa's cheque. Her thumping heart slowed with the rhythm of pushing the pram along.

'Ah, Miss MacDougall. Here's your cheque. And a letter too.' How she hated the bank clerk who managed to sneer and fawn on her at the same time. Pa's writing on the envelope. Dread clutched her as she hurried outside. Kenneth snuffled as if he was about to waken. She jiggled the pram while she tore the envelope open.

Felicity,
I can only assume that the child is born although you've not had the courtesy to inform me. I trust that you are well. I shall not make any further payment until I hear from you that you have completed your side of our agreement.'
Your sorrowing father.

Hot tears leaked down her cheeks. She crumpled the letter and ran, thrusting the pram like a battering ram in front of her. Past the knots of women outside the grocer's, the queue at the baker's, the policeman talking to the butcher wiping his bloodied hands on his striped apron. Heads turned, of course. Let them talk. She had to escape.

Kenneth woke up and grizzled as she lifted him out of the pram and hurried through the back door.

'I wondered where you were. I must have dozed off,' Winnie said.

'I decided to go to the bank.'

'Yes, dear. Now, does my little man want his bottle? Shall I take him?'

Felicity scrutinised Winnie as if she was a suspect. Her face looked as open as usual but a little flushed. Was that from her sleep or because she was feeling guilty? Had she read the piece about Bertha? She usually pored over everything in the paper – obituaries, advertisements, lost pets, holding the page up to her nose and complaining about the small print. Had she fallen asleep before reaching the article about Bertha? There was no sign of the newspaper on the table. While Winnie went to warm up the baby's milk she flicked through the papers in the kindling basket by the fire.

'What are you after?' Winnie came back in, Kenneth tucked under one arm and the bottle in the other hand.

'Oh, I was looking for today's paper.'

Winnie hesitated for a minute before saying. 'It must have slipped down the side of the armchair. Here you take Kenneth and I'll put the kettle on for us.'

She handed the damp, smelly bundle over and Felicity tried not to wince. The moment had passed. She wouldn't ask. She feared that Winnie would condemn Bertha and she couldn't bear to hear that. She would have to make her own mind up about what to do.

Chapter 50

Summer 1943

'Could you look after the baby for me today while I go up to town? I've had a letter from Pa,' Felicity asked as she stretched the butter thinly to the edges of her piece of toast.

'You're going to talk to him? I'm so glad. Perhaps it's better to go up on your own the first time. At least you've got photographs to show him.'

Felicity swallowed both toast and guilt as she nodded at Winnie's beaming face.

Would they let her in? she wondered as she approached the prison's fortress entrance. She hadn't thought to check about visiting times. There was a bedraggled looking group near the doorway. She squared her shoulders as their eyes slid over her. A grille in the door rattled open and a woman glared through it before wrenching open the heavy door. Felicity hung behind the other visitors as they followed the clatter of the warder's iron-tipped shoes. The corridor stank of old cabbage, sweat and desperation. Like her school, she thought, as she felt vomit crawl up her throat. The warder unlocked a series of clanging doors until they reached a fusty room with scuffed chairs. Everyone shuffled onto the seats and the warder asked each in turn who they had come to visit. Felicity squeezed her clammy hands together. She had got inside but what if she needed some sort of paperwork? When the warder approached her she lifted her chin, looked down her nose and announced,

'I'm here to see Miss Bertha Wilkins. Prisoners' Welfare Committee.'

She held the warder's gaze while the woman ran her finger down her list and frowned.

'Surely the secretary wrote to say I was expected?' she said in the tone Pa used when he spoke to servants or shop girls.

The warder shrugged and moved onto the next visitor. Felicity smiled in triumph once the woman's back was turned. After the warder had spoken to all the visitors she directed them into a larger room, set out with a row of booths with a grille across the front, like bird cages. She gulped as she saw Bertha sitting in the end one, flightless in dingy grey plumage. She smiled and sat down on the bench in front of the barrier. She mustn't show pity. Bertha would despise it.

'What are you doing here? Are you a bloody Lady Visitor?' As Bertha opened her mouth Felicity gasped. Her front teeth were missing. 'What happened? Have you been hurt?'

'I tripped and lost me teeth. Not me own ones of course. I got a nice false set when I started work in the factory.'

Tears welled up in Felicity's eyes but she blew her nose to clear them. 'I wanted to see how you are.'

'Well, take a look. Alive if not kicking. What's up with you. You look different – older.'

'A lot's happened since I saw you last. John Norman died at sea.'

'The quiet one? Nicer than his friend with the big mouth. It wouldn't have worked out, though. You and him. Like marries like.'

'We never had a chance to try.' Felicity's voice was tight with anger. 'I've got a baby, though.'

'Phew. You daft cow.'

'I'll go if that's all you can say.' But as she started to stand up Bertha stared at her and tapped softly with her fingers on the ledge in front of her, short and long. She spelt out 'innocent' in Morse Code.

Felicity settled down again.

'I got bored. Made a wireless for a laugh,' she tapped out.

Felicity nodded to show she understood. How could she reply? It would look suspicious if they both tapped away. She closed her eyes and hunched forward, groaning. The nearest warder bustled over. Close too, she looked young and anxious.

'I'm so sorry to trouble you but I feel faint. I've recently given birth, you know.' She lifted her head and made retching noises. 'Would you be good enough to bring me a glass of water?'

The warder jumped back and nodded. Off she scampered.

Bertha grinned and spoke fast. 'You've always known how to put on a good act. I was at a listening station on the coast. Understaffed it was and lots of mistakes made in the transmissions. Not by me. I dared to complain to the officer in charge so the snotty little Wrens wouldn't talk to me. I made a radio just for something to do. Got accused of sending stuff to the enemy. Load of rubbish.'

'Is that all? So why did two men come to question me. Interrogated me as if I was a spy.'

Bertha shrugged. 'It's what they do.' She blinked and lifted her eyebrows to warn Felicity of the warder's return.

'Oh, thank you so much, you're very kind.' Felicity sipped the tepid water from the proffered glass with her best smile.

A bell clanged. 'Time up,' Bertha said, standing up. Felicity looked over her shoulder as she followed the warder but Bertha had already turned away.

She plodded away from the prison, shaky and tearful. She had no one left. John Norman dead, Pa heartless, Bertha a prisoner. A liar too? She must have done something wrong to be arrested. Worst of all she was a hopeless mother, frightened of her own child, disgusted by him. She didn't know how to treat a baby. Unlike Winnie who could understand him, comfort him, love him.

As the train rumbled along she decided she would tell Winnie about her deception today. Thank goodness for Winnie. What would she do without her?

Chapter 51

Later that day

The trains were delayed so it was well into the evening before she struggled back home. She was parched and longing for Winnie's welcoming cup of tea. Maybe they could celebrate with the scrapings from the cocoa tin. She broke into a run as she reached the end of the road.

The back door swung open into a dark and silent house. The curtains hadn't been drawn or the ashes cleared from the night before. Felicity clattered through the downstairs rooms. All empty. No note on the kitchen table or behind the mantelpiece clock. She thudded up the stairs, two at a time. Where was Winnie? She never went visiting, not these days anyway. Felicity hung back outside Winnie's bedroom. She had never been inside it, had always considered it private. Feeling foolish, she tapped on the door and peeped round it. A spartan cell, like Van Gogh's painting, the bedcovers smooth, undented by a resting body. She examined the bedside table. A magnifying glass and a chemical smelling glass for her teeth stood on a crocheted mat along with an array of brown medicine bottles.

She jumped backwards as she suddenly thought about the backyard. Had Winnie fallen over and hurt herself? And what about Kenneth? He must be with her. Guilt gnawed her heart as she realised she hadn't thought about him until that moment. She hurtled down the stairs and out the back but there was no one there. There was nothing for it. She would have to go next door and ask. She licked her fingers and damped down her hair. It kept springing out in all directions now that she cut it shorter. No time to look for a comb. It was Tom who opened the door. His eyes crawled down her body. He always made her flinch.

'I'll get Ma.'

Mrs Armstrong appeared, her brawny arms folded across her large bosom. She spoke while looking over Felicity's shoulder. 'She's been taken to hospital. This afternoon. Poor soul needs taking proper care of.'

'And Kenneth?'

'The baby's with me. Sound asleep, the poor mite. She was worried sick about leaving him. Even though she was so poorly · herself.' Her lips crimped together.

'Please keep him a little longer while I go and see Winnie.'

'They won't let you in if it's not visiting...'

But Felicity had run to fetch her bicycle.

'I must see her,' she told the nurse when she arrived.

'Are you a relation?'

'Of course. I'm her niece. I've just come from London.'

'Very well. Just a few minutes.'

Felicity didn't recognise Winnie at first. She had shrivelled into an anonymous old woman, a shrunken husk of herself, eyes shut, breathing shallow and rasping. Felicity stroked the back of her hand, not holding the twigs of her fingers for fear of them snapping.

Then her eyes slid open and Winnie returned. She tried to smile but her dry lips wouldn't open properly.

'Would you like a drink of water? I've been so worried about you.'

'I'm sorry. Kenneth – I had to leave him with Ma Armstrong. I couldn't think who else. Did you see your dad?'

Felicity busied herself pouring water into a glass so that she didn't have to respond, then eased Winnie into a sitting position. She sipped and coughed. 'You must have been worried about Kenneth.'

'And about you. What happened?' Felicity could hardly get the words out. She wanted to know but at the same time couldn't bear hearing.

'I just had a funny turn. Must have blacked out and fallen

over.'

Winnie's matter of fact tone only stoked up Felicity's fears.

'But why did you have a turn?'

A nurse at the end of the ward turned round and frowned. Felicity, realising that she was almost shouting, took a deep breath and forced herself to whisper.

'But there must be a reason. What does the doctor say?'

'It's my ticker. It's not been so good for a while.'

'But I didn't know. Why didn't I know?' But as the words tumbled out she realised that she did know. She knew but had not let herself admit her knowledge. All the signs of Winnie's illness had been there – the slowness, the falling asleep, the swollen legs. Right from the start when she said she didn't take lodgers anymore. Everyone had someone billeted on them unless there was a pressing reason not to. Her own neediness had blinded her and Winnie was too kind to explain. She put her hand over her mouth and chewed her fingers to hold in the howl of anguish.

'I didn't want to upset you,' Winnie gasped. 'You had enough on your plate already.'

'Now I know, I'll make sure I look after you. You can sit down like a grand lady and I'll do all the work around the house.'

Winnie smiled. 'You'll wait on me hand, foot and finger?' but her eyes were sad. She pointed at the bedside cupboard.

'Shall I open it? What is it you want? Oh, there's an envelope with my name on it.'

'Take it, my dear.'

Felicity heard a starched rustling sound behind her. 'You must go now. You're tiring the patient.'

'Yes, nurse. I'll be back tomorrow.'

Felicity bent over to kiss Winnie's cheek, a dry, withered leaf. 'I'll be back soon.'

She couldn't remember cycling back, collecting Kenneth and tucking him into his cot but she must have done all these things before she found herself sitting in front of the cold hearth and opening the letter. She noticed it was dated two months earlier and that the writing writhed across the page.

My dearest Felicity,
The last few months have been one of the happiest times of my life. I feel as if you are my daughter and Kenneth my grandson. I wish these days could last for ever but I know they can't. My old heart is failing and I must plan for the future before it's too late. I wish I had something to leave you but I don't own this house and my pension dies with me. There is enough money in my Post Office account to bury me. I have put aside some more for you in an envelope under my mattress. Please take it and anything else of mine that you might want.

Make peace with your father so that you can keep Kenneth. He needs you. I'm so blessed to have a chance to love a child. No one still alive knows this but I found that I was expecting when Alf and I were courting but I miscarried the child. We never had a chance again to create a new life. Then you came and gave me the gift of being a Grandma.

God bless you both.
With all my heart,
Winnie.

Chapter 52

The next few days

Felicity found Winnie's emergency bottle of brandy at the back of the larder. Three glasses gave her a few hours of stupefied sleep before the early morning when she awoke to memories of the day before bursting in. She sat up in bed, her hand pressed to her chest. Her heart was a trapped bird beating its wings against her ribs. Had something else terrible happened? Had the baby woken her? She peered into his cot but he was quiet and still. So still that she bent closer to make sure he was alive. It was no use tossing in bed. Better to get up and occupy her hands. She cleaned out the grate and laid a fire. She couldn't arrange the kindling in a neat criss-cross pattern like Winnie did but it would be ready to light when she returned from hospital.

She delivered Kenneth next door, too preoccupied to care about Mrs Armstrong's stiff, disapproving face or Tom's greedy leer. She raced along the road, jumped off her bicycle and threw it down on the grass outside the hospital entrance. The mudguard ground down on a stone as the pedals kept spinning. Suddenly she saw John Norman's bicycle when he dropped it with a resigned sigh that first time they met. Shaking her head, she tried to tear that page from her memory.

There was a nurse waiting, a different one this time. Middle-aged and round faced. She stepped in front of Felicity at the entrance of the ward. 'Mrs Boulton passed away in the night.'

'When?'

'When?' She looked puzzled. 'In the small hours. About 4 o'clock, I believe.'

Felicity sagged at the knees and moaned.

'Come on now. Buck up and I'll let you see her.'

Did that mean she was still alive? She must have misheard

the nurse. She tottered after her and held her breath while the nurse drew back the curtains from round the bed. It was Winnie there, tucked in with her scanty white hair brushed into a soft wisp around her face. But as Felicity looked more closely she saw that it wasn't really her, at least not a version of Winnie that she recognised. It was a younger, smoothed out version, as if the dried-out leaf had been plumped up and softened. A sleeping, younger Winnie. She put a fingertip to her cheek but snatched it away as she felt the chill. No warmth, no life.

'How can I carry on without you?'

Did she say the words out loud or only in her head? She looked behind her but the nurse had moved away. Felicity stood up and walked to the entrance of the ward. One last glance backward. Could it be a mistake? Maybe Winnie would open her eyes again? She had to wheel the bicycle home as her legs were shaking. What should she do first?

'Find the money. You'll need it.'

Was that John Norman's voice in her head? He was calm and sensible, like Winnie. She lifted the mattress and found the envelope holding a wad of notes secured with a rubber band and a small bag weighted down with coins. She crammed them all into her purse without counting them. She saw a photograph on the bedside table of Winnie holding Kenneth. She was gazing at him with such tenderness that Felicity wanted to howl. She stuffed it into her bag, along with a locket containing a picture of a grinning man in army uniform. Winnie's husband, Alf, deserved to be remembered too. As she closed the bag, she grew hot with panic. She had no picture of John Norman. How was that? They had so few hours of time, no chance to record their life together.

'Coo-ee?' It was Mrs Armstrong shouting up the stairs. 'I saw you come back. What's going on?' Felicity's face told her. To Felicity's surprise she didn't criticise her for not coming to tell her straight away. Instead with a rough sort of kindness she took charge, talking to the vicar and undertaker and arranging the funeral tea. All Felicity had to do was take care of Kenneth. She fed him, changed him and bathed him but couldn't look at him. When he was asleep she sat on the floor of Winnie's bedroom, rocking backwards and forwards. Plates of food appeared in the kitchen but she left them to go cold and then scraped the congealed offerings into the bin, retching as she did so.

The chapel was bursting with people for Winnie's funeral. Felicity squeezed into a back pew with Kenneth in her arms. The minister's words were as muffled to her as a bad train announcement and she couldn't moisten her lips enough to join in the hymns. At the funeral tea people greeted her politely but didn't linger in conversation, looking past her to find someone else to speak to. Then what she most dreaded happened. While she was balancing a plate and a cup of tea she saw Ted coming towards her. She could only stand her ground. His mouth twisted, more of a sneer than a smile before he turned away. Even worse his mother was bustling along behind him. The pinkness of her cheeks was the only sign she had seen Felicity as she stared straight ahead and hurried after her son. Being ignored as if she didn't exist affected her even more than the reluctant courtesy or the eyes that slid away. The sight of the paste sandwiches and the glistening slice of pie on her plate made her stomach heave. She had to escape. The cup rattled as she put it down on a side table. The treacle coloured tea slopped into the saucer and dripped on the floor but she was out through the door. Kenneth was starting to grumble as he woke up. As she released the brake on the pram her hearing came back. She could hear tutting and muttering behind her. Or was it the wind hissing through the trees?

Back in Winnie's house she paced the faded mat in the parlour. What was she to do? She was alone in the world. Worse than alone. She had the weight and worry of Kenneth. Could she bear to face Pa? Try to make peace with him? He wouldn't relent and agree to her keeping her child. She was sure of that. It was only Winnie's sweet nature that made her believe the best in people. But she couldn't support the baby on her own with no money and no job. And even if she had an income she couldn't love him properly. Not in the way Winnie had. That was her dreadful secret. She was an unnatural mother.

Give him up for adoption? Her heart shrank at the idea. He wasn't a stray puppy or an unwanted Christmas present to be handed to a stranger. His past wiped clean, he would never know who he was, a seed blown by the wind. Not like his father, John Norman, whose roots spread deep and wide. She stopped pacing and fetched her bag to count out the money. Winnie's last gift. £80 altogether. How has she managed to save so much? There was enough there to keep her and Kenneth going for a while if she was careful. Enough to move away from here, to reject the threadbare charity of the neighbours. She knew what she must do. She climbed on a chair to reach the battered suitcases on top of Winnie's wardrobe. In a frenzy she raced into her bedroom, pulled open drawers and wrenched clothes off hangers. She had made up her mind.

Chapter 53

Autumn 1943

How strange it felt to be on a train again. The last time she had come by rail was with Bertha, her friend jiggling in her seat like an excited child, in between the usual speechifying. Felicity had never seen Bertha's lighter side before. It had made her smile but now her mind skidded away from remembering any more. She was too afraid of crashing and burning. It was better to think about the present even though it was grim sitting in grubby carriages with people piled up in the corridors. People squeezed a space for her when they saw she had Kenneth in her arms. They settled her into a corner seat and an older woman burbled at him in that silly high-pitched voice that adults used with a baby. What a relief that he had taken to the bottle. She could never have managed to breast feed him here. Winnie had been saying that she would need to wean him soon. She pressed her eyelids closed to stop the tears spilling out. She couldn't bear it if the kind-looking old couple squashed next to her tried to offer comfort. There was no comfort. She and Kenneth were both orphaned.

She had to stay overnight in Perth before she could continue her journey. She stopped at a hotel near the station because she was too tired and uncertain to look for something cheaper. It was hard to speak to the receptionist as she felt her throat closing down and she stumbled over her words. The next day she continued to Inverness and finally sank down in the train that would take her to Kyle. As it trundled out from the town and over the moors she was blind to the beauty of the landscape. The nearer she got to Skye the more doubtful her plan seemed. How would she ask John Norman's parents to adopt Kenneth? She hadn't even let them know that Kenneth existed. She remembered when she last saw John Norman and how he had been so insistent she take care of herself. But wasn't that just the usual wartime fears? She shivered as she wondered if he had some premonition of his approaching death and his son's conception. Winnie, dear wise Winnie, had suggested once or twice that Felicity should write to them.

'Wouldn't they be pleased to know that part of their son survived?' she had said. Each time Felicity had shouted that she couldn't do that. It was her way of refusing to believe what had happened to her. She couldn't accept the reality that banged on the door and rattled the letterbox while she put her hands over her ears.

What would his parents make of her arrival now? They had welcomed her into their home and been kind to her. His mother had seemed flustered, nervous even. It had made Felicity uncertain too because she didn't know the source of Mrs MacPherson's disquiet. The truth was that she didn't know his parents. There had not been enough time to get to know them. Would they be horrified and angry like Pa? Send her and Kenneth away in disgust? Or, just as bad, invite her in but be unable to hide their disapproval. She knew that his mother was a staunch church goer. Would that make her forgiving or fill her with shame? The truth was that she couldn't face them.

The train rattled along. As a child she had always tried to fit a rhyme to the sounds. 'We're going away to the seaside' or 'I hate horrible school'. The words that banged in her head now were, 'I can't face them.' The nearer they got to the island the more insistent the drumming in her head became. Suddenly she gasped aloud, making Kenneth whimper in his sleep. It was fortunate that there was no one else in her carriage to see her. She had forgotten about Achnasheen, the station where everyone's papers were checked. And she had none. How could she begin to explain? It was impossible. The train was juddering to a halt. What station was this? The name was whitewashed out. She put

Kenneth down on the seat and opened the door. There was a man getting out of the next carriage.

'Excuse me, please? What station is this?'

'Lochluichart.'

'I want to get off at Achnasheen. Is it soon?'

'The next stops's Achanalt. Achnasheen is the one after.'

'Thank you so much.'

As the train gathered speed she leant her head back, feeling the sweat trickling down her spine. She closed her eyes as she tried to work out what to do. Her eyes snapped open as she realised that the answer had been there looming in front of her all along. With a new calmness she put Kenneth down, lifted her case from the overhead rack, opened it and rummaged inside for her writing pad. She tore out a page and scrawled some words down in capital letters with a pencil. Kenneth shuddered as if he sensed that he was not being held any longer. She picked him up, pressing him so close to her body that he squirmed and woke up. His blue eyes looked startled. Then he gurgled and seemed to smile as she watched him.

Was she doing the right thing? But what choice did she have? There was no time to change direction. She rifled through her jacket pocket and took out a nappy pin, attaching it to the piece of paper. Kenneth snuffled and waved a podgy hand as she secured the pin to his blanket. She wedged him into the back of the seat with the bag containing his bottles and nappies. Clenching her teeth to stop herself crying out, she looked through the window. The train seemed to be slowing down. As it juddered to a halt she wrenched open the door and looked around. No one else was getting out at the small halt of Achanalt. What a relief. The last thing she wanted was someone to offer to help her with her suitcase. As she leapt out her momentum made her stumble and fall forward onto to her knees. She scrambled up and grabbed her fallen suitcase. Resisting the urge to run, she strode out of the tiny station without a backward glance. She heard the guard blow his whistle as the train lumbered away. She wasn't religious at all so she was surprised to find herself murmuring a prayer.

'Please, dear God, let the guard find him and deliver him safely to his grandparents.'

Tears were coursing down her cheeks. She stopped to brush them away with the back of her hand and slowed down to a walk. She mustn't look odd or conspicuous. Her task now was to find somewhere to stay for the night. She had plenty of money to dull the suspicions of any householder who wondered what she was doing. Then onto the southward bound train tomorrow. She had done the right thing she kept telling herself. It was for the best but she had to bite her lip until it bled to stop herself from weeping.

Chapter 54

Late Autumn 1943

'Thank you, Nurse Blake.' Dr Jones sighed as he took the folder. He opened it and started to read, alternately screwing up his eyes and holding it at arm's length. Another sigh as he patted the pockets of his white coat.

'Shall I go and ask the nurses if they've seen your spectacles anywhere?'

'That's a good idea. No, wait a moment.' He hauled a grubby handkerchief out of a trouser pocket and unwrapped it to reveal a pair of spectacles. Dr Anne Pritchard looked away to hide her grimace.

'What are we going to do with this young woman? Still unresponsive, catatonic even after all this time?'

'Do we know anything more about the patient?'

He snorted. 'Her father finally deigned to send a note. Confirmed she had given birth recently but no more details. Illegitimate baby and the family disgraced, no doubt.'

'There are so many casualties in this war. Will he come to see her?'

'Unlikely, but at least he thanked us and made a £200 donation to the hospital funds.' He tapped the sheaf of notes. 'Time to try some convulsive treatment and see if that jolts her to life.'

Anne winced. 'I suspect she would be very resistant to that. She's been furious when we've tried to press her in any way.'

'But patients don't remember anything about it afterwards and it might well do the trick.'

She took a deep breath. 'I've read some of the papers about convulsive treatment and I know it's worked with patients who have entrenched symptoms but...' she noticed his frown and pressed on. 'She's young and capable of change. I wonder if she would fare better if we could gain her trust?'

'You're allowing personal feelings to cloud your clinical judgment. Too much identification with the patient. Our role is to decide what's best, not to bend to the patient's whims.'

She forced a smile to her lips. 'You're right, I'm sure. She's probably from a family similar to mine, has had an education and formed her own opinions. Then found the war brought her the chance of a different sort of life, at least until things went wrong for her.'

Dr Jones was shuffling through the papers without looking at his colleague. Anne released her held breath while he removed his spectacles and swung them by one of their arms. 'What do you suggest, then?' He leant back in his chair, arms behind his neck and the hint of a smirk on his lips.

'I've given this case a great deal of thought. During my training we were given some lectures about therapy through art. A new discipline, as is convulsive therapy, but effective with suitable patients, in particular young ones.'

'And you believe this patient is suitable?'

'She could be. She's lost the will to communicate with the world. Art would give her another means of expression, a new language.'

He grunted. 'Sounds like the basket weaving for soldiers during the last war, a way of keeping them docile.'

She held his gaze but stayed silent. He sighed heavily. 'Very well. You can give it a trial. I suppose her father's donation entitles her to something extra.'

'Thank you. I'll make a start straight away.' Anne stood up and padded down the corridor, willing her legs not to skip.

Chapter 55

Summer 1944

Felicity put her easel down and looked around her. There were so many trees to choose from. She wandered towards a copse of beech. The trees were marshalled together in full dress foliage, drilled into shape by a long-gone gardener. Behind them brambles straggled towards the sunlight. She elbowed her way inside the copse and high stepped over the tangles. She found a few trailing branches of wild raspberries. She tumbled them into her mouth, her tongue recoiling at their tartness. Peering ahead in the gloom, she stubbed her foot against a fallen tree furred with moss. One of the beeches had crashed to earth. Its higher branches, still sprouting, leant against two of the other trees while the thick lower limbs lay on the ground, covered by ivy netting. A felled green giant, its companions arching overhead to form a hammer beam roof. Was it waiting for some magic spell that would make it stand upright again? How was it still alive? She looked down at its roots. Most of them were bare and shrivelled but a few of them had scrabbled and tunnelled their way into the leaf mould. She stood still, letting her tears spill down. She had found her subject.

Several hours later she strode back inside, clutching her picture. She was heading for the storeroom that Anne Pritchard had turned into a studio. She gasped as she opened the door. For an instant she felt the old sickening lurching as the world flickered and swirled. Stalking forests, growing like bamboo, sliding and slithering towards her in a sinister game of Grandmother's Footsteps. She could never turn around fast enough to catch the snaking branches catching at her heels. She gulped and clung on to the door frame. The doctor looked up from where she was mounting a painting on the wall.

'Just take your time, Felicity. Then look around.'

The walls were covered in her work, all her paintings of trees, the history of her stay here. She settled her canvas on a table and began a slow circuit of the exhibition. The first ones were lathered and layered with blackened branches. Some were slashed, wounds seething among the flaking, scorched bark. There were spectral silver birches, naked except for a leprous lichen that muffled their limbs. An ornamental monkey puzzle tree lashed itself in frozen contortions, straining to escape.

She was aware of Anne watching her, an attentive robin poised for a juicy worm from Felicity's lips. She couldn't respond, only shake her head and recoil from the monstrous trees. The next wall showed pruned garden specimens. Felicity was pleased with them at the time. They were normal, symmetrical as trees should be. How angry she had felt when Anne had said, 'Where are their roots, their berries?'

She had replied with a new forest, studies of storm-damaged firs. Spindly trunks leant over, staggering together like sailors returning to port. But their intertwined branches hid splinters and gouges where they had collided together.

'I thought it was time to see all your paintings displayed together.' Anne looked at her, waiting for an answer but Felicity wasn't ready yet. She fetched her new painting and held it out.

'That's an interesting tree. Tell me about it.'

Felicity smiled to herself. That's what Anne always did. Tapped the earth and tweaked out the worm. Tugged at it while it wriggled away. Tried to look unconcerned but couldn't hide the gleam in her eye. Felicity had let her pull out so much, about Pa, about Winnie and Kenneth. Anne would know that the tree represented Felicity herself, uprooted and struggling to survive. But she wouldn't know that the tree also stood for John Norman, drowning and gasping for air. Maybe she would tell her but not yet.

'It's half dead but it's not given in,' she said.

Anne bobbed her head.

'But it won't ever get back on its feet, will it?'

'The other trees are supporting it.'

'That's not enough.'

'What do you suggest?'

'I think it's time I left here. See if I can get on outside,' Felicity gasped in surprise. She hadn't meant to be so bold.

'Hmm. That's a big step all at once. I agree that you're much better but I think you should take things gradually. You've never been outside the grounds. Maybe a walk down into the town, with one of the nurses, first. Then try on your own.'

'Like a dog on a lead?'

Anne sighed. 'No. Like a convalescent. If you've been in bed for weeks you wouldn't leap out and run a race, would you? You would be uncertain on your feet. Take it gently.'

'Alright. Can I hand you this picture? My arms are going numb.'

'Of course. Where would you like it to hang?'

'On its own, on the far wall.'

'How about here? We'll have to let it dry first, of course, before it goes up.'

Chapter 56

Summer 1944

The first trip out was terrifying. She wanted to crouch down and hide behind Nurse Brown's heavy worsted cape. Instead she forced herself upright and clenched her fists deep into her pockets.

'Do you remember arriving in Warwick? You came on the train and sat in the waiting room for so long that the station master became worried.'

'No, not a thing.' She refused to think about that time. She had blundered from one train to another until she froze, an overwound clockwork toy.

'Well, we'll just have a little walk, shall we? You can see the castle, look at the shops – not that there's much in them of course. Perhaps have a cup of tea?'

Nurse Brown's chirpy tone irritated her but she knew she would have to co-operate if she was to be allowed out on her own so she agreed to being steered along past the half-timbered buildings. They looked not just old but neglected, the wooden framework splitting underneath the flaking black paintwork. The Georgian buildings, like their counterparts in London, were dowdy and careworn. The looming, turreted walls of the castle made her shudder. They reminded her of that grim visit to Holloway Prison. The whole town depressed her.

'Yes, very picturesque, isn't it? And what a tall spire on the church,' she chirruped, like the docile child she once was, scampering along behind her grumbling aunts in the school holidays. Always having to be grateful. 'Hurry up. We're only doing this for your sake.'

'St Mary's is beautiful inside. Shall we take a look? You could come to a service here.' Jolted back to the present she nodded and smiled. So much of her early life had been spent playing a part she had been given. Then she had gone her own way and ended up at the Park. It was after that when everything unravelled but she wouldn't think about it. She had done the best she could for the baby, what she needed to do.

'Are you alright, dear? You've stopped dead.'

Felicity shook herself. 'Yes, thank you. It just feels a bit strange being out in the world again.' She smiled. 'Shall we go and have that cup of tea? Maybe even a bun, if they have one?'

Nurse Brown's round face cracked into a smile. 'That's the ticket. Come this way.' She squeezed Felicity's arm and she braced herself not to flinch.

Over the next few weeks Felicity was allowed out on her own, always with a task to complete. She had to buy a newspaper or a loaf of bread, post a letter. Against all her inclinations she had written a letter to her father.

Dear Pa,

I've been ill as you know but I'm on the mend and getting out and about. The doctor is pleased with my progress but won't tell me when I will be ready to leave the hospital for good. I would like to find some useful work but I don't know what yet.

I hope you are keeping well.

Your loving daughter,

Felicity

She had kept the sheet of paper by her bed, hoping that she could add to it but after a few days she had dragged her pen to form the lie in the last line and posted the stunted words to him. It was the best she could do.

By return, she had her father's response.

My dear Felicity,

Thank you for your letter. You still only write the bare minimum,

as you did when you were at school. I would have hoped you would
have learnt by now to express yourself in a more flowing style.

The hospital seems to be well run. I received an appreciative
letter of thanks after I made my donation. I'm pleased that there
are people who can formulate their thoughts clearly and pen an
elegant turn of phrase. You must follow Dr Jones's advice about
when you should leave the hospital. I think it would be best for you
to stay in Warwick where the pace of life is slower than in London.
The hospital almoner could no doubt help you settle in some sort of
hostel for young women.

Despite everything that has happened I've not forgotten my
promise to resume your allowance once you fulfilled your side of
the bargain. I shall arrange an account for you at a local bank and
forward the details when that is completed.

I am well. My time is filled with business at the Ministry and I
have little leisure for anything else.

Your loving father.

The letter was a splinter of ice. At first it froze her fingers but
the throbbing pain as the blood thawed was worse. She kept it
to herself. What use was it to share it with Anne? The warmth
of her sympathy would only make the pain more unbearable.
Better to bury that ice deep inside her. She would relish taking
his money. His stiff sense of duty, of honouring a promise, gave
her the freedom to launch her life again. All she had to do was
convince Dr Jones that she was well enough to leave.

Chapter 57

Autumn 1944

Felicity found that she could convince Dr Jones with her show of cheery competence. He was happy to see what he wanted and take the credit for her recovery. But as always at the hospital, everything took a long time to happen. A nip of autumn was in the air by the time that lodgings were found for her with a doctor's widow in the town. It was much more luxurious accommodation than Winnie's house. She had her own sitting room, bathroom and tiny kitchen but she doubted if she would ever feel at home there.

Doctor Anne was not so easily deceived, of course. Felicity caught her watching her carefully, her head tilted. She felt a quiver of remorse about tricking Anne, letting her believe she was cured. Felicity had never let her peer down into the chasm of despair and loss she felt over John Norman and Kenneth. If she let all that pour out it would be like the magic porridge pot in her childhood book. Her grief would spurt out until it engulfed the whole world. Neither of the doctors knew the magic words to stop it, any more than she did herself. It was better for everyone to hold to the straightforward story that her breakdown was caused by the shame of giving birth to an illegitimate child. A temporary madness that had now been banished.

It took all her strength to sustain the pretence that she was better. Inside she was a husk, a Christmas walnut kept too long, the shell intact but withered and bitter tasting inside. What would she do with her new life? No family, no friends, no occupation. She sat in the shabby café, stirring her anaemic coffee, stranded between the high and low tide, a place that didn't exist. What was that sad song they had bellowed out at school, something about 'between the saltwater and the sea strand?'

Someone was blotting out the light. She looked up in irritation. Why was the waitress hovering there? No, it was the bluish blur of a uniform. Surely not someone wanting to chat her up?

'We've met before,' he said, 'I recognise your face.'

That was a feeble trick. She glowered but he stayed put, half smiling.

'You don't remember? Me, I never forget a face.'

Hint of an accent. He still stood in the way, like a pestering dog.

'No, I don't recollect you.'

She looked down at the tablecloth, staring at a spilt blob of milk.

'Well, it's not surprising. You only had eyes for one man.'

Despite herself, she was curious. Her head jerked up.

'Getting warmer, now?' He put his hand on the back of the empty chair.

'I really don't know you. Please leave.'

'Come on, I can't have changed that much. I'm Angus, John Norman's friend.'

She gasped while he pulled out the chair and sat down. He did look different. His face was thinner, his thick hair scythed short and his expression more sombre.

'We met in Portree that time. You were there with a friend. And then again in Glasgow with John Norman.'

He stopped, looking uncomfortable. Her eyes narrowed as she remembered what Bertha had said about him trying it on with her.

He seemed to read Felicity's mind as he said,' Your friend put me in my place, though.'

'So I heard.'

'Oh dear.'

His downcast face made a laugh well up in her throat, a laugh that turned into choking.

'Are you alright? Can I get you a glass of water?'

Red-faced she shook her head.

'What a war, eh?' Angus took a deep breath. 'It was terrible John Norman's dying like that.'

She could only nod, her eyes swimming.

'I'll go. I'm upsetting you.'

She reached over and brushed his sleeve. 'No. Stay. Get a coffee.'

The elderly waitress shuffled over and he ordered a cup of tea. 'And a biscuit or piece of bread. Whatever you've got.'

They were silent until his order came. Then both started to speak at once. He waved at her to speak first. 'What are you doing?'

'Aircraft maintenance, at an airfield near here. I used to long to fly.'

She looked down, focusing on a razor nick on his chin. She remembered how she had mocked him, last time they had met.

'Now, I'm relieved to stay alive.'

'That's what matters.'

They both fell silent. She felt they had made peace with each other. She peered into his hazel eyes. 'I have to ask you.' Suddenly she felt brave. 'Do you know what happened to John Norman? His mother wrote that he died in home waters.' Her hands kneaded the edge of the tablecloth.

He wriggled his shoulders and looked away. 'I don't know more than that. He drowned on active service.' He fumbled in his breast pocket for a cigarette and offered her one.

She thrust the packet aside. 'But in home waters? Did he fall overboard in a storm?'

'I don't know,' he mumbled as he lit up. 'I suppose so. There's a lot of things we don't get told. And I've not been back home much. His parents have adopted a wee boy, a war orphan.' He shrugged. 'Helps them get over what happened to John Norman, I suppose.'

'Really?' she squeaked. Her hand shook and coffee spurted

over the tablecloth. Mopping it up with her napkin gave her a chance to hide her face.

'You hadn't heard? Look, I have to go back to camp now. Let's meet here again next week at the same time.'

He stood up and straightened his tunic. A quick grin and he was off before she could gather herself to say anything. Felicity stayed sitting for some time after he left, swirling the spilt coffee in the saucer. No wonder she hadn't recognised Angus at first. She remembered him as being brash and coarse. War changed people, of course, made them grow up. She had never imagined that she would be pleased to see him again but meeting him in this alien town he seemed like an old friend, someone she could talk to about John Norman.

She had been shocked to hear Kenneth referred to as a 'war orphan', as if he was some anonymous baby, not John Norman's flesh and blood. But how could John Norman's parents admit publicly to people that their grandchild had arrived on the train, with a label pinned to him? Handed over like a parcel by his mother. People would be scandalised. At least they knew who he really was. She wished him well but in her heart of hearts did she truly miss him? There was something lacking in her, she knew. She wasn't fit to be a mother. She could worry about him, try to protect him from harm but she couldn't love him. Her hands clawed at the edge of the tablecloth. The old panic was smothering her, squeezing its tentacles round her neck. She stumbled to her feet and tipped out the contents of her purse onto the table before hurrying out into the street. She ran down a sideroad that became a country lane. When she found an abandoned cowshed she propped herself up against the wall, pressing the rough stones into her back. She closed her eyes and dug her fingernails into her palms. After a while she could stop herself gasping for breath. Someone was watching her. She was back again in the old nightmare world of hallucinations. She eased her eyes open and saw a row of placid dark eyes, whiskery chins and moist noses. She laughed at the cows peering over the fence and set off back to her lodgings.

Chapter 58

Autumn and Winter 1944

Felicity was fidgeting and looking at her watch. She had decided that he was not going to come when the door opened and he was there, handsome and smiling in his blue uniform.

'You didn't think I would stand you up, did you?'

'I didn't know what to think. It was such a surprise to see you last week.'

'You didn't look very pleased to see me.'

'Well, I didn't recognise you.'

'You must get bothered by a lot of strange men.'

'Who me? You must be joking!'

'I'm not. You're the sort of girl who turns heads.'

'What nonsense!' She could feel herself blushing.

'Let's change the subject then. Tell me what you've been doing this last year.'

She had prepared herself for likely questions and invented a story not too far removed from the truth. Simple lies were best. Maybe she could have been a spy after all. She explained that she had gone back to her job for the government until she became ill.

'All the night shifts were too much of a strain in the end. Now I'm better I'll look for another position.'

'Back in London? That's where your family live isn't it?'

'There's only my Pa. He works for the War Office. I don't want to go back there. We had a few words, something of a falling out. We write to each other but we get on better at a distance. What about your family? Your father was seriously ill, wasn't he?'

'Aye. He was at death's door with pneumonia but he picked up again. Had to stop working though and sell the shop.'

'Didn't you want to carry it on?'

'No, I never wanted to be a butcher.'

Over the next weeks they met as often as Angus' work allowed. They were courting she supposed. It was more like courting than what she had experienced before, with either Ted or John Norman. More like what she supposed happened in romances. Country walks, visits to the pictures, lunch outings. Sometimes she didn't see him for several weeks when he was especially busy at the airfield. She was relieved that he didn't expect more than a few kisses. Her body and mind weren't ready for anything more. She got used to his company and enjoyed it. He was clever at asking the right sort of questions so that she told him about her early life in India, her schooldays and her prickly relationship with Pa, more than she had ever told anyone else, even John Norman. But her uneasiness at what she was hiding became more difficult to bear. She hadn't told Angus outright lies. What was it that fierce vicar used to say in his sermons when she was at school? There were lies of omission and half-truths as well as outright lies and all of them were sinful. Her deception hobbled her, like a pebble trapped inside her shoe but how could she ever tell him the truth after keeping secrets for so long?

The rest of the time she involved herself with war work, helping the old chaps with their digging on the allotments, serving meals at a canteen for workers at nearby anti-aircraft batteries and knitting socks for the troops. Doing those practical, useful tasks made her feel close to Winnie and left her too tired to have time to brood.

She didn't know how long she would be allowed to continue like this before she was called up for official war work but in the end it wasn't the government but Angus who forced her out into the open. They were walking along the river one evening when he grabbed her hand and pressed it into his tunic pocket. 'There's something for you there.'

Her fingers closed on a small box. She lifted it out and snapped it open. An engagement ring with two small diamonds and a sapphire between them. Her hands shook as she held it.

'I can't marry you. You don't know who I really am.'

'Yes, I do.' He led her to a bench and they sat down. 'I know more than you think. I know what's eating away at you.'

She stared at him open mouthed.

'Surely you know that you can't keep anything secret on Skye? I heard the rumours about the MacPhersons when I was home on leave, about their mysterious adopted baby. Just one glance at the wee boy gave the game away. Flame red hair like yours and a face that's the spit of his father's.' He laughed. 'Even his nose is like John Norman's.'

She stared at him. 'You don't mind about me having a child out of wedlock?'

'No. The war has turned everything upside down, changed the old rules.'

'I'm sorry I couldn't tell you. I thought you would despise me.'

'If we get married you can get him back again. He won't be a bastard if I adopt him.'

She winced at the harsh word. 'It's all too much to take in.' Her thoughts were scattering in panic, like rooks at the sound of gun fire.

He put an arm round her shoulders. 'Wouldn't it make you happy if we married? We would be a proper family with Kenny. And your father would be pleased too, wouldn't he? He would have a grandson he could be proud of. And other grandchildren too – when we have our own.'

Felicity supposed she should be happy. She wouldn't be alone anymore. She would have a husband who cared for her, not just anyone but a friend of John Norman's. She had to seize this chance of a normal life, with a husband and child. They would have to get Kenneth back. If she told Angus about finding it hard to love the baby he would think her unnatural, mad even. If she was married she would be able to make her peace with Pa. Angus was smart and respectable. She was certain Pa would approve of him. She was amazed at how much Angus had changed since she first met him. How thoughtful of him to consider Pa's happiness as well as her own. She was very lucky to have found him again.

Postscript: Portree 1972

Summer 1972

Lisa trudged along the narrow coastal path as it zigzagged uphill. She was leaning forward against the wind and frowning, oblivious to her surroundings – the wide bay opening out to the sea, the spring light flickering over the waves or the yellow iris pushing up through the boggy soil. She didn't notice the figure coming towards her until a cough made her look up and see the stranger standing on a rock, waiting for her to pass him on the narrow path.

She nodded her thanks at the youngish man who half smiled and pushed his glasses back up his nose.

'It's a lovely day, isn't it?' he said. A hesitant voice with an English accent but a flavour of something local there too.

Lisa forced her lips into a reluctant smile. She really wasn't in the mood for chitchat with a tourist but found herself replying, 'Not bad at all.'

He kept looking at her, making her feel uncomfortable but curious too. There was something about him, something almost familiar in his long face, slight build and sharp cheek bones. Maybe he was yet another second or third cousin she didn't know about. She had come across so many distant relatives since coming back. At first it had been exciting until she realised that the connection was as frail as the filaments of a spider's web. Their lives, experiences and opinions too different from hers to make any sort of bond. She started to move forward.

'Do you live here on Skye?' he asked.

She supressed a sigh. 'I do.'

'I feel that I should know you. Are your family from here?'

Was this a chat up line? she wondered. He looked so earnest that it seemed churlish not to answer.

'Yes, my mother was born here but I was brought up in England.'

'Just like me, except in my case it was my father who was born here, in Portree. Maybe we're related to each other?'

I really can't be bothered with this, Lisa thought.

'John Norman MacPherson my father was called.'

Lisa was startled. No, it couldn't be. Plenty of people here had the same names. She opened her mouth to speak but her lips were suddenly dry. 'Really?' she croaked.

'Yes. He was a fisherman who joined the Merchant Navy in the last war. Died at sea.'

Lisa put her hands into her jacket pockets to stop them trembling. It must be another coincidence.

'I've found out from the census that he had three sisters but they all moved away a long time ago.'

'Really? You've not met any close relatives, then?'

Her brain was whirring and fizzing like a Catherine Wheel. The coincidences were building up. But how could they be related? She knew about John Norman and had even seen a few photos but he was never spoken about in the family. The one time she had asked her granny she got into terrible trouble from her mother: "How dare you upset her like that. She was sunk in a depression for years after John Norman died."

She rifled through what little she knew about her long dead uncle. She remembered he was only about twenty when he died and he certainly hadn't been married. Not that he couldn't have fathered a child. She took a deep breath

'And what were the names of his sisters?'

He counted them on his fingers. 'Margaret, Jeannie and Lexie. You look a bit stunned. Do you know them?'

'Margaret's my mother.'

'No! Really? Then we're cousins! I've found my family at last!'

He leapt forward and hugged her tight, almost lifting her off her feet. She held herself rigid until he let go and she could stand back.

'My name's Kenneth and you're…?'

'Lisa.'

'Let's go and have a coffee, cousin Lisa, and I can explain everything to you. I can't believe that I've finally found someone from my family.'

Lisa stepped back. All her instincts were telling her to run away from this intense young man.

'I can't just now. I need time to take this all in.'

His face fell, making him look like a lost small boy. To her annoyance she felt guilty at upsetting him.

'Listen. Are you here for a while?'

He nodded.

'I'll give you my phone number and address. Get in touch in a few days and we can speak again.'

She found a piece of paper in her pocket and wrote down the information. His crushed expression disappeared in a grin.

'I can't wait!'

Then he was bounding down the path, leaving Lisa watching him.

* * *

The next morning was a Saturday. Lisa was finishing her breakfast when she heard a knock on the front door. She half rose but then froze, holding the piece of toast in her hand. Who was it? Not anyone she knew. They would come round the back. Was it him, Kenneth, back again? She wasn't ready to see him yet. He was just too pushy. She waited, heart thumping to see if he knocked on the back door. No, she could hear some rustling, the sound of something being shoved through the letterbox and the flop as it landed on the floor. Nothing more, and after a few deep breaths she tiptoed to the front door and picked up an envelope from the mat. It felt thick. She saw it was addressed to 'My newly discovered cousin, Lisa.' She felt relieved that she hadn't answered the door. A bit over the top, she thought, as she sat down on the battered sofa, sighed and opened it with reluctant fingers, unfolding the typed sheets inside. There was a handwritten note.

Dear Lisa,

I'm sorry I missed you. I was so excited to meet you yesterday. It was a dream coming true. Here's the stuff I wrote down about my memories when I was having counselling last year. I think it will help you understand me better. I'll call round again.

Love,

Kenneth

Lisa felt a flash of irritation. Why couldn't he phone to ask her when would suit her? But she was curious and settled down to read what he had sent.

My Early Memories

I can't remember being a baby. Who can? But when I came back to Skye I recognised the smell of the place – the moisture and salt in the air.

I had nightmares when I was small – all the time. Waves sucking me down as I clambered up a ladder. And a booming sound. Being lifted up over a ledge and being dragged down steps to another monster, rearing up from the toilet. Gobbling me down. I think that nightmare must have come from when I was taken away from the island on the steamer. Every morning I woke up chilled and wet with tears and wee.

'It's about bloody time you stopped wetting the bed.'

That was him. The man Mummy married. 'Call me Daddy.' I wouldn't, not even when he shook me or cuffed me round the ears. I didn't call him anything, wouldn't even look at him.

I remember going to the shops with Mummy. We stood in a queue at the greengrocer's. There were heaps of dirty potatoes and carrots piled up and spotty apples. I put my hand out to stroke the funny grass underneath them. It was hard and spiky. Suddenly there was a crash. Mummy had fallen over.

'Oh dear, poor thing. She's passed out,' someone said.

Mr Jenkins, the greengrocer, brought a chair for her. 'Here you are young man,' he said as he pushed a long, yellow squashy thing into my hand.

I dropped it in disgust. 'What an ungrateful child,' he said, 'A banana's a real treat.'

Everyone fussed over her. 'Are you expecting, my dear?'

'Come on, we're going home,' Mummy sprang up and tugged my arm.

A while after that I heard them arguing when I was in bed. He came back late, stamped around, made the whole house shake. He threw things round the kitchen. He did that all the time so every pan was buckled, every plate chipped. I slid under the blankets and flattened myself against the mattress.

'Lost another one? What's wrong with you? You, who got caught with the brat the very first time – so you say.' I didn't understand what he meant of course, until I was older.

Who else can I remember in the family?

Grandad, Mummy's father. He lived in a big, gloomy house in London. I was terrified of him.

'Do you know your letters yet? Tell me the Ten Commandments. Speak up boy, I can't hear you when you mumble.'

We always had slippery cold ox tongue for tea there. I was usually sick on the way home.

Photos? I don't remember any. There weren't any of me with my Skye grandparents. The only one was of Mummy's wedding on the mantelpiece. I longed to trample on it, smash the glass and rip up the photo. But one day I found another photo. I was looking for my toy car when I found it – tiny and creased. An edge of it poked out between the floorboards under the sofa. It was a picture of an old lady, holding a baby.

'Is that me and my Granny?' I asked Mummy when he was out.

'Of course not. Your Granny died long ago.'

'I know your Mummy died but I've two Grannies.'

'No, she's not your other Granny. She's a lady I used to stay with when I was working during the War.'

'Is that me with her?'

She nodded.

'Can we go and see her? She looks nice.'

'She was nice but she's dead. She died a long time ago.'

Mummy looked sad but I knew she would get cross if I asked her anything else.

* * *

How old was I when that man left? I can't remember exactly but I had started school. Mummy and I moved away, to a smaller house. It was in a cul de sac and I played with the other children who lived there but I don't remember anyone coming to tea. It was quiet at home but I liked that.

One day Mummy said we were going up to London.

'Can we go to the Tower of London? Or the zoo?'

'I'll see. We have to go somewhere else first.'

We went to a place that looked like a dark castle. 'Does an ogre live here?'

'Don't be silly. We're meeting someone outside.'

There she was. 'Say "Hello" nicely to Bertha,' Mummy said. She was a big, frowning woman.

'You mustn't tell a soul that Bertha was in prison. She didn't kill or hurt anyone.'

More secrets. I didn't dare to ask any more questions.

Bertha came to live with us after that. What was she like? Not as bad as that man. She didn't hit me or bully me. But I was pushed out again. Bertha always came first with Mummy. One good thing Bertha did, when I was a teenager, was to tell me who I am. It was a shock to hear that Mummy had made me live a lie, pretending that

*man was my Dad. I couldn't forgive her for that, still can't. Bertha
and Mummy had a huge row about Bertha telling me. But that's
another instalment. I'll write it later.*

After reading the sheet of paper, Lisa sat gnawing her biro. There
were some more sheets but she couldn't face reading them. She
chewed off the black plastic end and spat it into the wastepaper
bin. What on earth was she going to write in reply?

I'm returning this because it's too much for me.

She crossed it out. That was true but a bit blunt. What could she
say? Admit that she was a bit shaky herself? Having a drowning
man clinging to her was the last thing she wanted. She tore out a
new sheet and started again.

*I can tell that you've had a hard time. I hope writing it down has
helped. Maybe it would be a good idea to go back and talk to the
counsellor again.*

She started biting at the side of the pen. A transparent shard
broke off and she threw it towards the bin. She sighed when
it missed. She would never dream of talking to some stranger,
someone who sat there and nodded like one of those silly little
dogs people put in the back window of their cars. It would be
like stripping yourself naked, while the other person sat, fully
clothed, watching you. She shuddered. No. It was better to work
things out in your own head, especially when you hadn't been
invited to spill it all out. She sighed and picked up the pen again.

*Like you, I came here, to Skye, to find answers about who I was. I
fell apart when my marriage ended.*

She thought how he had never bothered to ask her about herself, only vomited his own distress over her. Barging into her life. Rescue me. Love me. As what? A long-lost cousin – or something more? The crushing hug, the gaze that kept plucking at her, that sucking kiss on her cheek when they met for the first time! As if he was just managing to hold back his jabbing tongue. All too much. She crossed out the sentence about her marriage ending and screwed up the second piece of paper, put down the mutilated pen and wandered through to the kitchen to put the kettle on.

Bumping into Kenneth was like facing one of those 3D laser pictures that made you jump back in alarm. He seemed to spring out from the old photograph of the young John Norman in the fisherman's jersey, the one tucked into the back of her mother's album. Thinking about their meeting now she realised how much Kenneth looked like John Norman with his narrow shoulders, bony face and neat beard. He was like all the family. There was a glint in the grey-green eyes that reminded her of Auntie Lexie, a turning down of the mouth, like her mother's. Only the blaze of red hair was his own.

If only he hadn't ambushed her. All her instincts screamed that he would cling and wrap himself round her. That was the last thing she needed. She had to push him away before that happened. If only he had kept a distance, let her orbit him. Instead she had to fight against being pulled into the black hole of his neediness. Somehow she had to put that thought into writing.

I can see that you felt you had come home – found somewhere you belonged. That's all very exciting but the sad truth is that you can't go back in time and change your story into a happy ending. That's what I found anyway. You can't relive a parent's life. You can't even understand it properly. You were born somewhere else and you have to make your own future, without looking back over your shoulder.

She re-read her words. They sounded OK. Not harsh – a little bleak but honest. She was trying to help, by pricking the bubble of illusion. She found herself remembering a biology field trip when she was at school. It was back when she went through that phase of wanting to be a marine biologist. A full moon had caused the tide to recede further than usual and exposed the hidden world, stranded between sea and shore. It was the home of strange matted creatures, sprawling across rocks. 'Are those plants or animals?' Mr Watson had asked. He showed them a blenny, hiding motionless on the sand. 'Now, fish can only survive in water. Right? This little fellow is one of the exceptions. If you live on the margins you can get caught out when the tide suddenly turns. The blenny has evolved to walk on its fins. It's developed a coating of slime so that it can manage for a while out of water.'

That's what Kenneth was like. Trying to live in a space between his own life and his father's life. A place that didn't properly exist. He would have to decide if he belonged to the sea or the land.

I came here to find myself nearly a year ago but it didn't work out. I'm not a complete outsider – family roots help you to connect with people. But I'm not a local either and can never be accepted as one. I shall keep coming back but only for holidays. I know now that I was running away but you can't run away from yourself. I had already decided to go back south before I met you and I'm packing my stuff up now. I'm ready to go in a few days.

He hadn't even given her the chance to explain that she was leaving. He was too full of his own dream.

Should she add that she would be interested to hear about how he got on? No. She didn't want to encourage endless letters. Keep it cool.

All the best for the future,
Lisa.

That would do. Not a brush off. Just giving herself room to breathe. She would make scrambled eggs for her tea, to be quick. Do some more tidying up and packing. Then get to the Post Office tomorrow and send the package to Kenneth.

* * *

Lisa hauled her luggage to the front door. Her taxi would be arriving in a minute. How she hated all this business about packing. If only there was a magic carpet to spirit her to her destination. There was Alec's horn sounding. She propped the door open with her hip while she lifted her bulging case. Something was jamming the door. Two envelopes. The post must have come while she was upstairs. She grabbed them. She recognised the writing on the first one, Mother's looping hand, spreading across all the space. How like her to forget the date Lisa was leaving. She folded it into her jacket pocket. The writing on the second package was written in an unfamiliar hand. She crammed it into the space beside the first one.

Journeys always made her anxious. She kept checking her tickets and belongings while she was on the bus and then waiting for the ferry in Kyleakin. All the paraphernalia of boats scared her – the rattling metal flooring, ladder-like stairs and weighted doors. It went back to trips on the old steamer when she was small. In those days, she had a miniature leather suitcase, scuffed and scratched. It contained a picture book, an apple, woolly hat and most important – Teddy. He was only a small bear, wearing navy dungarees and a stripy red and white jumper Mummy had knitted. But he was a special bear. Daddy had scoured all of London to buy her a soft toy when she was a baby. It was almost impossible to get new toys with rationing still on but he wanted her to have her own bear. Her dolls were left jumbled on a shelf in her bedroom but Teddy went everywhere with her. One year she was running ahead of Mummy after they left the steamer when she suddenly stopped dead.

'I've left Teddy on the steamer.'

'How silly of you. Go back and find it.'

'But what if the boat goes?'

'Hurry up then.'

Sobbing, her socks sliding down her wobbly legs, she stuttered up the gangplank and tripped off the end.

'Up you get, *isean*. What's the matter?' The kind sailor took her hand and helped her search for the case. It had fallen off the seat and spilled open. Teddy was lying on his back.

'Ah, here's your friend. Safe and sound.'

Once ashore again, she turned back to wave to him.

'Get a move on now,' Mummy had snapped. 'I'm tired and I don't want any more bother.'

What had happened to Teddy? She couldn't remember when she had thrown him out. She had never been sentimental about possessions. So why was she being ambushed now by old memories? She must be feeling more unsettled than she had realised. Once Lisa boarded the Inverness train at Kyle she felt she could relax. She was properly on her way. The train clattered along, its wheels hemming the edge of the shore to the sea. She remembered how as a child she had tried to count all the tiny islands scattered like Smarties. She used to imagine rowing from one to the other until she found the best one to live on, one that had trees to protect her and a beach to play on. Everything had seemed possible then. And it did now. She could leave teaching for good.

'It's the best job for you. Fits in well when we have a family,' Peter had said. Well, it didn't matter now what he thought. She could go back to her dream of marine research. Maybe write about it too, go back to university.

She felt tired. She would just doze for a little while and gather her strength before getting down to London and Gill's spare bedroom. Something made her remember her old Welsh RE teacher from her school days, Mr Thomas, surely well past retirement age. He would set them to reading on a Friday afternoon lesson. His head would slump forward onto his tweedy waistcoat, dusted with ash. Snuffling like some woodland rodent, his nose started to twitch when the noise in the classroom got too loud. Jerked awake, he would say, 'Just resting my eyes, children.'

* * *

She jarred awake, neck stiff and tongue parched. How long . had she been asleep? Was she snoring like old Mr Thomas? Her eyes skittered around the carriage. It had been empty at Kyle but now there was a group of three middle-aged women sitting opposite her, engrossed in their conversation. They must have got on at Plockton. Lisa glanced out of the window. Moorland had replaced the sea and shoreline. They would soon arrive at Achnasheen. She seemed to remember that it recorded one of the lowest temperatures in Britain.

Lisa's eyes felt prickly. She half closed them again and let the women's conversation lap against her ears.

'I'm glad Morag's feeling better. It's a shame her daughter isn't staying longer to get her back on her feet properly.' The woman shook her head while her newly permed hair stood to attention.

Her friend beside her was wearing a headscarf of splashy autumnal colours. 'Well she couldn't leave her husband and children down in Glasgow for too long on their own.'

'Children? They're big lassies now. They could fend for themselves.'

'Did you hear about that poor young man?' The third member

of the group spoke, a small woman with sparse white hair.

'What young man, Kirsty?' the first speaker leant forward.

'The one on the ferry to the Outer Isles, Dolly.' She paused. 'I heard from Sandy MacLean whose son was there. He tried to kill himself by jumping overboard.'

'How terrible. What happened?' Mrs Headscarf shook her head.

'They pulled him back as he was climbing over the rail. It took three of them.'

'Who was he?' Dolly asked.

'A stranger, a visitor. Kenneth Ross I think was his name.'

'It's a relief that it was a stranger. Thank the Lord it's not someone we know.'

'It's a good Highland name though,' Mrs Headscarf added.

'Well, looking at the sky, I think we might have good weather for our trip. What shops do you want to go to in Inverness?' Kirsty asked the others.

Lisa was fully alert now. She perched on the edge of her seat, fists clenched. She had that plunging sensation that kicks you when you're almost asleep and your heart forgets to beat. She told herself that she was over-reacting. The surname was wrong. She had no reason to think…

She shuffled in her seat and felt a crackling in her pocket. Perhaps she should open her post. But did she feel ready to read Mother's complaints? No. What about the other one? It could be more interesting. Her fingers reached in and hesitated. She told herself she was being ridiculous, superstitious. The dread, flapping in her heart, was down to stress, not some ridiculous second sight.

The best thing would be to open it and put the matter to rest. She fished out the package and tore it open. Just one sheet of writing and a narrow box, faded so it must be quite old. She prised it open to discover a pen, a handsome one, with a marbled pattern. Where on earth had it come from? The writing on the package was small. Was it a man's or a woman's hand? Impossible to tell. Who could it be? It wasn't as if she got many letters. She wasn't the world's greatest correspondent, unlike Granny who had used up books of stamps each week, writing to relatives scattered far and wide. Lisa peered at the postmark. Smudged but she could make out 'Port'. Still she waited, holding the package by one corner, as if it would scorch her.

Taking a deep breath she unfolded the flimsy sheet. It was creased and hard to read, like airmail paper or the tissue fine sheets of Granny's Bible. She smoothed it out. No date.

Dear Lisa,

I'm sorry to send this to you but I don't know who else I could write to. I can't bear the disappointment of coming back. I'm using the pen that my father gave to my mother the last time they met. Mother gave it to me after she and Bertha had that row about Bertha spilling the family secrets. It's the only thing of my fathers' that I own and I wanted you to have it. It's an early ballpoint pen and was very new and unusual at the time.

It's not your fault but I can't go on. I'm crossing the sea for the last time.

Your cousin, Kenny MacPherson

That's the name I want on my stone. Not the name of that bastard, Ross.

She must have cried aloud. 'Are you alright, dear?' Kirsty was leaning over her, patting her arm.

'That young man you were talking about – what happened to him?'

'You're white as a shroud. Did you know him?'

'Slightly.'

'He wasn't injured but he was in a state. They took him to Craig Dunain.'

'Craig Dunain?'

'Aye. The asylum, in Inverness. He was a danger to himself.'
Lisa nodded.

'You've had a nasty shock.' She gestured to the others. 'We've
a flask of tea. I'll get you a cup. You just sit there quietly.'

Dolly waddled over, cradling a thermos cup and looking a
little uncomfortable. 'We had no idea...when we were talking. Is
he a relative of yours?'

'Shush, Dolly. Don't make the lassie talk when she's had a
shock.'

Lisa, like an obedient child, sipped the hot drink. 'Thank you.
You're very kind.'

'Not at all. You get your breath back, now. It's good that he
was saved, isn't it? You could go and see him.'

Lisa nodded. 'Thank you. I'm better now. What a relief to
know that he didn't kill himself.'

The women settled down again but Lisa could sense that they
were watching her. She willed herself to sit still and after a few
minutes they began talking quietly together. Her mind shied
away from thinking about Kenneth's suicide attempt and settled
on the pen instead. She had never seen it before but she knew
the story behind it. Her mother had another old ballpoint pen, a
shiny black one with a gold trim. She never used it but kept it in
a drawer of her bedside table.

Lisa remembered a time when her mother was cross with
Dad – something that happened often: 'I could have done so
much better if I'd married that commander who was sweet on
me, instead of marrying your father. He gave me that valuable
pen. I was given another one too by another officer but it wasn't
quite as nice.'

'What happened to it?' Lisa had asked. She didn't really care
about the pen but she didn't want to hear Dad's name being
blackened any more.

'I gave it to your Auntie Lexie,' her mother frowned. 'But then
I never saw her use it. In the end I asked her, 'Where's that good

pen I gave you?'

'I gave it away.'

'What do you mean? You had no right to do that.'

'Yes, I did, Margaret. You gave it to me as a present. If you must know, I gave it to John Norman so that he would have something nice to take with him to sea.'

'Then Lexie burst into tears. It wasn't long after we had heard that John Norman was dead.'

Her mother suddenly looked stricken and Lisa had known that was the end of the subject. Now she thrust the pen back in her pocket. Somehow it had survived but it was tainted, its ink composed of pain and loss. Lisa shook her head. She had to decide what to do about Kenneth. Would she go to see him, the war orphan? All her generation were prisoners from the war. She was one, too.

She opened her handbag and tore a page from her notepad. She picked up the old pen.

Dear Kenneth,

I was shocked to hear about you feeling so low but relieved to know that you're safe in hospital. There has been so much misery in our family, so many arguments and secrets. You and I got off on the wrong foot. I should have paid more attention to what you were saying. Can we start again? We can both choose not to be trapped in the coils of the past.

I'm writing this on the train to Inverness, with your pen. I know the story behind it. My mother gave it to our Auntie Lexie and she passed it on to your Dad as a reminder of home. You must take it back and treasure it.

I shall see you soon,

Lisa

She sighed and folded the sheet. She would get an envelope in Inverness and take the letter up to the hospital.

Kirsty caught her eye from across the aisle and Lisa smiled.

'Your colour's back again, my dear,' she said. 'You had gone as white as a sheet.'

'Yes, I shall be alright now, thank you.'

Note to reader

Thank you for buying *Had We Never Loved So Blindly*. I hope that you enjoyed reading it as much as I enjoyed writing it. If you have a few moments, please feel free to add your review of the book at your favourite online site for feedback. Also if you would like to know about other books that I have coming in the near future, please visit my website www.lizmacraeshaw.com or email me at lizmacraeshaw@outlook.com for news on upcoming works.

Sincerely
Liz MacRae Shaw

Glossary

Bodach: old man

Cailleach: old woman

Caman: stick for playing shinty

Camus Bàn: lit. light-coloured beach, a sandy cove opposite Portree harbour

Cèilidh: informal gathering

Isean: chick

Paravane: apparatus on warships for cutting the moorings of submerged mines

Sasannach: lit. Saxon, English person

Slàinte Mhath: Good health

Strupag: snack

The Rural: Scottish Women's Institute

Also by Liz MacRae Shaw

Love and Music Will Endure

Great Mary of the Songs was a poet and political campaigner
born on the Isle of Skye. Through force of character she
overcame the barriers of background, class and gender to
become the champion of her fellow Highlanders who were
being driven from their homes.
Published by The Islands Book Trust, 2013,
ISBN: 978-1-907443-58-9

No Safe Anchorage

Tom Masters, a nineteenth-century naval officer, has a
tantalising glimpse of a stranger. This leads him to jump ship
on a quest to find her. His adventures take him from the Isle of
Skye to Canada. When danger and exposure threaten him once
more he has to go on his travels again...
Published by Top Hat Books, 2017,
ISBN: 978-1-78279-706-7

Top Hat Books

Historical fiction that lives

We publish fiction that captures the contrasts, the achievements, the optimism and the radicalism of ordinary and extraordinary times across the world.

We're open to all time periods and we strive to go beyond the narrow, foggy slums of Victorian London. Where are the tales of the people of fifteenth century Australasia? The stories of eighth century India? The voices from Africa, Arabia, cities and forests, deserts and towns? Our books thrill, excite, delight and inspire. The genres will be broad but clear. Whether we're publishing romance, thrillers, crime, or something else entirely, the unifying themes are timescale and enthusiasm. These books will be a celebration of the chaotic power of the human spirit in difficult times. The reader, when they finish, will snap the book closed with a satisfied smile.

If you have enjoyed this book, why not tell other readers by posting a review on your preferred book site.

Recent bestsellers from Tops Hat Books are:

Grendel's Mother
The Saga of the Wyrd-Wife
Susan Signe Morrison
Grendel's mother, a queen from Beowulf, threatens the fragile political stability on this windswept land.
Paperback: 978-1-78535-009-2 ebook: 978-1-78535-010-8

Queen of Sparta

A Novel of Ancient Greece

T.S. Chaudhry

History has relegated her to the role of bystander, what if Gorgo, Queen of Sparta, had played a central role in the Greek resistance to the Persian invasion?

Paperback: 978-1-78279-750-0 ebook: 978-1-78279-749-4

Mercenary

R.J. Connor

Richard Longsword is a mercenary, but this time it's not for money, this time it's for revenge…

Paperback: 978-1-78279-236-9 ebook: 978-1-78279-198-0

Black Tom

Terror on the Hudson

Ron Semple

A tale of sabotage, subterfuge and political shenanigans in Jersey City in 1916; America is on the cusp of war and the fate of the nation hinges on the decision of one young policeman.

Paperback: 978-1-78535-110-5 ebook: 978-1-78535-111-2

Readers of ebooks can buy or view any of these bestsellers by clicking on the live link in the title. Most titles are published in paperback and as an ebook. Paperbacks are available in traditional bookshops. Both print and ebook formats are available online.

Find more titles and sign up to our readers' newsletter at http://www.johnhuntpublishing.com/fiction

Follow us on Facebook at https://www.facebook.com/JHPfiction and Twitter at https://twitter.com/JHPFiction